A TIME FOR TRUTH

Rory was not going to make it easy. Gillian had supposed, or at least hoped, he would overwhelm her with passion. He would take the decision out of her hands, so that afterward she could claim it was he who forced her to this fateful step.

Instead he looked down at her, his gaze cool and calm, as if mocking her trembling heart. "I will ask you once only. Are you sure this is what you want? You've a lamentable habit of playing with fire without any real intention of getting burned. And I must assure you now that if we continue, this time, you will not get off so easily, Miss Gillian Thorn-cliff."

He would force her to say it, then. She lifted her chin and said distinctly, "Yes, this is what I want. You are right. This is what I came for."

And now there was no turning back, even if she wanted to, as his lips came down on hers.

But turning back was the last thing she wanted now. . . .

SIGNET REGENCY ROMANCE
COMING IN MARCH 1994

Marcy Rothman
The Kinder Heart

Emily Hendrickson
Miss Cheney's Charade

Patricia Oliver
Miss Drayton's Downfall

An
Independent
Woman

by

Dawn Lindsey

A SIGNET BOOK

SIGNET
Published by the Penguin Group
Penguin Books USA Inc., 375 Hudson Street,
New York, New York 10014, U.S.A.
Penguin Books Ltd, 27 Wrights Lane,
London W8 5TZ, England
Penguin Books Australia Ltd, Ringwood,
Victoria, Australia
Penguin Books Canada Ltd, 10 Alcorn Avenue,
Toronto, Ontario, Canada M4V 3B2
Penguin Books (N.Z.) Ltd, 182–190 Wairau Road,
Auckland 10, New Zealand

Penguin Books Ltd, Registered Offices:
Harmondsworth, Middlesex, England

First published by Signet, an imprint of Dutton Signet,
a division of Penguin Books USA Inc.

First Printing, February, 1994
10 9 8 7 6 5 4 3 2 1

Chapter 1

UNTIL their coach was held up by highwaymen, Miss Gillian Thorncliff had all but decided, with faint but undeniable disappointment, that the wilds of Scotland were proving to be just as tame as civilized England.

It was not that she wished to be held up, of course. After all she was a sensible woman of six-and-twenty who had long since come to the reluctant conclusion that such things only happened to someone else. She had dragged her grandfather on this trip into Western Scotland against his will with no more than the practical intention of discovering for herself whether, on closer acquaintance, she should accept an offer of marriage from the Earl of Kintyre, a Scots landowner. She had not really expected any adventure.

And except for experiencing a broken wheel the day before to the coach carrying the valet and maid and the bulk of their luggage, making it necessary that they leave it behind in Glasgow that morning, the journey had so far been notable only for the bad roads they had encountered and the even worse inns. Add to that the fact that it had rained steadily since they had crossed the border into Scotland five days before, limiting their view of the countryside to what could be seen through streaming carriage windows, and that Sir Giles, always a bad traveler, had woken that morning with a ticklish throat, which invariably presaged a cold in the head. In short, it was as well that she had not expected much excitement.

When the first shot rang out she was wholly unprepared for it. Sir Giles was frankly snoring in one corner and

Gillian herself was half-asleep, with nothing more on her mind than a concern for her grandfather and a wish to be out of the jolting carriage. It did not even occur to her that they might be in any danger. They were driving along a loch, visible only now and then through the thick mist, with no habitations in sight, and her first thought was that the shot must have been fired by some hunter dangerously near the road.

It was only when the second shot sounded, even more alarmingly close to the window where she sat, that she was startled upright, thoughts of a warm fire and mustard plasters scattering. It was her first inkling that Scotland might not be quite so civilized as she had come to fear after all.

Not until it was far too late did she realize it should have been a warning to be careful what she wished for, for fear she might get it.

But at the moment everything happened too quickly for either thought or reaction. In fact, she was afterward to be annoyed at how little use she had proved to be in an emergency. There was a shout, whether from their own coachman or their attackers Gillian couldn't tell, but it at last succeeded in waking Sir Giles with a snort. Before Gillian had time to warn him, the heavy coach had half-slewed across the muddy road and come to so abrupt a halt that they were both thrown completely out of their seats.

She found herself almost on top of her grandfather, who thus rudely awakened, swore lamentably and thrust her off, making a belated grab for the pistols kept hanging on either side of the seat for just such an emergency. She was annoyed to realize the pistols hadn't occurred to her, and had time to wonder what had become of the groom sitting up beside the coachman with a heavy blunderbuss, whose duty it was to protect them.

But before Sir Giles could reach the pistol, the door nearest Gillian was violently pulled open, and a very large and wet figure appeared in the opening, heavily cloaked and muffled to the eyes. The only thing about him that appeared dry was the silver-chased pistol pointing steadily in at Gillian and her grandfather.

She had at least managed to regain her seat by then. She was breathing a little fast, as if she had been running, and her heartbeat had accelerated; but it did not seem to be from fear. Surely even Scots highwaymen would do no more than relieve them of their purses and what few trinkets they had with them and let them go on their way. There could be no motive to do them personal harm.

She merely found herself thinking, incongruously, first that it was a surprisingly elegant pistol for a highwayman to possess; and second, that if she had been longing for an adventure, she would seem to have gotten her wish.

Her grandfather seemed far from taking the situation so philosophically, however. His color had risen alarmingly and he was looking furious, but under that steady aim he had no choice but to sit back again in frustration, his own pistol just out of reach. For all his eighty-three years, his was a still-powerful figure, and his brain was as sharp as ever. Gillian knew it galled him unbearably to be obliged to sit there helplessly.

"Aye, that's it, Sir," said the highwayman in the doorway, in the broadest of Scots accents. "Sit back doucely with yer hands up, and no one'll be hurt. In the meantime, I'll relieve ye o' the temptation to do something foolish."

He reached in and removed both pistols, to Sir Giles' seething resentment. Gillian was surprised that at such a moment she could notice that the highwayman brought the smell of rain in with him, and something else, sharp and rather pleasant, that she couldn't quite identify, but afterward came to be forever associated with Scotland in her mind. The man was so heavily cloaked and muffled that it was impossible to guess what he looked like, but she had an impression that he was unexpectedly young, and he had a deep voice, oddly appealing for all its almost impenetrable accent, in which a faint amusement seemed, incongruously, to be discernible.

"I've no wish to inconvenience ye any more than I must," he said cheerfully, once he had pocketed the pistols, "so if ye'll gi' me your word ye'll no' try anything, Sir, I'll spare ye and the lass the necessity o' descending into the rain. The coach is surrounded and your servant at the moment trussed up like a chicken at the side o' the road, so it will do ye little good to resist."

Gillian had to bite back an untimely impulse to laugh. She could indeed see that the groom who, armed with the blunderbuss, had sat up on the box beside the coachman, was indeed lying trussed up on the side of the road, his weapon thrown down in the mud without a shot being fired; and that a second highwayman, armed and muffled as the first, sat holding a pistol on the coachman, whose hands were full anyway in keeping his team from bolting and offered very little threat.

Both of the servants looked extremely sheepish, as well they might. She suspected they had more to fear from her grandfather's blistering tongue than the highwaymen, for she would not like to be in their shoes and have to explain how they had managed to be taken so completely off guard.

"Give you my word?" barked Sir Giles furiously, a hectic flush in his gaunt old cheeks. "You'll get no word from me, you damned scoundrel! The only thing I'll give you is my solemn promise to see you hanged from the highest gibbet for this afternoon's piece of work."

This time the amusement in the highwayman's voice was unmistakable. "I'm loath to deprive ye of that pleasure, Grandfather, but ye'll find that this is no' England, and the law has less force in these parts than you might expect. Now I must trouble you to empty your pockets. You too, Mistress. It will save time in the end—and your own dignity—if ye'll cooperate. I've no wish to be obliged to search you, but I will if necessary."

Under that steady pistol, Sir Giles while still seething had, perforce, to hand over his purse, watch and chain, and a valuable gold snuff box. In the meantime, a third cloaked and muffled figure, slighter than the other two, could be seen pulling down the baggage from the boot. Gillian found herself wondering if it was he who had managed to truss up the servant so efficiently. In fact, it had all been done so neatly that she had to acknowledge a certain admiration for the speed and daring of the plan.

The tall highwayman in the open door seemed in some indefinable way to be the leader. He accepted Sir Giles' grimly proffered items and said now in his rough voice, still with that faint hint of amusement, "I'm obliged to ye, sir. If it's any comfort to ye, they'll afford me a good deal more pleasure than they ever did you. And now, Mistress." He turned to Gillian, his pistol gleaming dully. "I dislike being obliged to be so ungallant, especially to so young and charming a lady, but I'll ha' those pearls at yer throat, and then yer jewel box, if ye don't mind."

Gillian reached up and calmly unclasped her pearls. "I do mind," she said steadily, "but I seem to have little choice in the matter. But I regret that my jewel box is with my maid, who was detained in Glasgow with a broken axle to the coach. I fear you will have to make do with what little I have on my person at the moment."

She spoke with a certain sarcasm, but of course it had little effect on the highwayman. He accepted the pearls and hefted them appreciatively, something in his manner still communicating his unexpected amusement with the whole. The next moment they had disappeared into the capacious pocket of his heavy greatcoat along with her grandfather's trinkets.

She swallowed, for despite her brave words she was aware of a certain pang. The pearls had belonged to her mother, and she hated to part with them. The thing was of a sudden less amusing than it had been, but she would not stoop to pleading or tears, and so, to hide her hurt, added composedly, "And now that you have what you wanted, pray let us proceed unmolested. You are letting the wind and rain in and my grandfather is suffering from a cold in the head already."

"Ha! Much he cares for that!" interposed Sir Giles furiously. "Damned blackguard! But then it's no more than I deserve for venturing into such a damned uncivilized country."

The tall highwayman bowed ironically. "We will endeavor not to keep you overlong, Mistress," he acknowledged, tongue very definitely in cheek.

"Good. While we're on the subject, the trunks your man has just thrown down are locked. There is little of value in them, but since I doubt you will accept my word for it, I would prefer you not to break the locks. Here are the keys. Be so good to request to refrain your man from tossing their contents into the mud. Until our baggage can catch up with us they are all the clothes we have with us, and on top of everything else I have no intention of sitting down to dinner in a wet gown."

The highwayman laughed out loud, a startling sound in that damp gray afternoon, and accepted the keys. "Ye've a ready tongue, Mistress," he said, and issued a short command in some strange language. The slender figure with the baggage, in the very act of forcing one of the locks with a wicked-looking dirk, looked astonished, but caught the keys that were deftly tossed to him and afterward displayed almost exaggerated care in searching the bags.

Sir Giles had in the meanwhile remained silent, his grim old face rigid and his pale eyes fierce. At any other time Gillian might have suspected that apparent docility, but at the moment she was preoccupied with other matters, and merely relieved that her grandfather was behaving himself so well. There was clearly nothing they could do, and the sooner it was over and they were free to go on their way, the better.

But she should have known him better. The tall highwayman, no doubt thinking an old man and a woman posed little threat to him, had turned away slightly to answer something the one at the horses' heads had said to him, still in that incomprehensible language, and had, for an instant, taken his eyes off Gillian and her grandfather. Gillian had only an instant's warning of what her grandfather intended to do. She caught a slight movement out of the corner of her eye, and the next moment he had triumphantly loosed off a pistol he'd kept secreted in his pocket.

The report sounded even more deafening in the confines of the coach, and the smell of the burning powder was acrid and choking. Gillian had jumped at the sound, and now watched in horror as the tall highwayman in the door turned back sharply, only to clap a hand to his left shoulder a second later.

If Gillian had not been afraid before, she had to acknowledge that she was desperately afraid now. It had been a dangerously foolhardy thing for her grandfather to do, but it was clearly useless to remonstrate with him. Instead, she waited, heart pounding and mouth dry, for repercussions. If they were all murdered in cold blood on the spot it would be little more than she expected.

The outcome seemed to hang in the balance an interminable moment. But somewhat to her astonishment, the highwayman showed far more restraint than her grandfather had, though both of his companions had swung their weapons menacingly around and were now aiming unswervingly at Gillian and her grandfather. The highwayman swayed a little where he stood, his hand still clapped tightly to his shoulder, which was now showing alarmingly red, but he made no move to retaliate, and instead said something short and sharp to his companions.

Then the robber said, still sounding merely amused, "I make you my compliments, Grandfather. You're a braw old fool, and I've no wish to have your death upon my hands. But if you've any other weapons concealed up your sleeve, you'd best hand it over now."

"And you can go to the devil! Grandfather indeed!" roared Sir Giles, in no whit chastened by the narrow escape he had just had. "Damn you, even with my years I'll teach you not to prey on your betters! You're all alike, you craven thatchgallows, hiding behind a mask and a brace of pistols. But you'll sing a different tune when the rope's 'round your neck, I'll warrant."

"I've little doubt of it. I'll admit I came closer just now to meeting a far more impartial justice than I'd anticipated. It's a good thing your aim was shakier than your courage."

When her grandfather would have answered, Gillian intervened sharply. "Grandfather, behave yourself!" Her racing pulse had begun to steady a little, so that she felt almost faint with the release of tension, but she discovered she had had enough. "I will stand surety for my grandfather's good behavior," she told the other coldly. "Now, unless you mean to murder us both, take what you must and get on with it. No, Grandfather, be quiet! This has taken too long already, and I am cold and tired and have endured more than enough. They warned me that Scotland was far less civilized than England, but I must confess until now I had begun to doubt it."

She had an impression, gone in an instant, of a pair of laughing gray eyes between the deep brim and upturned muffler, but all the man said, in his rough, unpolished voice, was, "Then perhaps ye should pay more attention to such warnings in future, Mistress. It might have saved ye a most alarming experience."

"I am not in the least alarmed," she countered. "Merely impatient to be on my way."

He laughed again and swept her a surprisingly creditable bow, despite the hand still held to his shoulder. "In that case, pray accept my apologies for inconveniencing you. It's seldom we meet with so accommodating a victim—or one so charming if it comes to that."

"Spare me compliments I am unlikely to find in the least flattering."

"Then we'll no' burden you with our unwelcome presence any longer. Enjoy your stay in Scotland, Mistress. Grandfather."

He bowed again, and the next moment had stepped back from the coach and shut the door. Before Gillian quite realized it, he had remounted quickly despite his wound, and the three of them were gone as unexpectedly as they had come, leaving only the trunks in the mud and the chaos they had left behind them as proof that they had been there at all.

Gillian should have felt relieved; but in fact, once they were gone, she was aware of a faint stab of disappointment. For all its frightening elements, she had felt sharply alive, as she had not done during all the rest of that interminable journey. Nor had she any real hope that her stay at Kintyre's house, even though located in Scotland, would provide her any further opportunity for excitement.

Chapter 2

E VEN after the highwaymen had gone, it took ridiculously long to get back on the road again. The groom
had to be untied and the trunks loaded back on the boot, all
in the pouring rain, and both the groom and the coachman
wasted a good deal of valuable time trying to explain to an
irate Sir Giles why they had allowed themselves to be taken
unawares.

In the end Gillian tired of the delay, and got out into the
wet road herself to call a halt. "For heavens sake, what does
it matter? It happened and now it's over. Pray let us not
stand here endlessly wrangling. Grandfather, get back inside before you catch your death. Besides, Lord Kintyre
will be wondering what has happened to us, and will
scarcely be pleased to have us arrive in the middle of the
night."

At this broad hint the quarrel was finally abandoned. The
servants went with alacrity back to their posts, grateful to
abandon a defense even they could see was extremely feeble, and Sir Giles, though by no means mollified, climbed
stiffly back into the coach. He had by then added being wet
to his catalog of general complaints, along with the loss of
his watch and pocketbook, and spent some moments, while
the baggage was reloaded and they got back on the road, in
relieving his feelings.

"As for you, my girl," he finished, abruptly bringing his
diatribe back to a more personal note, "all I can say is that
I hope you're satisfied! This is all your fault. I warned you
what would happen if you insisted upon gallivanting off on
such a harebrained journey. Damned barbaric country!"

"Grandfather, you have never been fair a day in your life," Gillian responded, used to his temper. "Besides, it is no thanks to you we weren't all murdered where we stood. How could you be so foolish? Good God, it's a miracle he didn't kill you!"

"Pooh! Nonsense!" Sir Giles brushed that off easily. "Such fellows are brave enough as long as they're hiding behind a mask and a pistol, but they're all cowards underneath, the lot of 'em. Fool should have checked my pockets," he added, not without a certain enjoyment. "'Grandfather,' indeed! I'll teach him to respect his elders and betters. I'm only sorry my aim was off and I merely succeeded in winging the villain. Might have done the world a service and saved them the expense of hanging him."

"Well, I'd not like to see any man hung for no more than a few trinkets," she admitted truthfully. "Though I'll confess I'm sorry enough to have lost my pearls. But then I daresay it's my fault for having worn them."

She spoke lightly, but her grandfather was not deceived. "Aye, they were your mother's, and I'm sorry for that," he said gruffly. "But as for being glad I didn't succeed in killing the leader, it's like a woman to romanticize what is, after all, no more than a common thief."

"I'm not romanticizing—!" Then Gillian caught herself up, realizing the futility of trying to argue with him while he was in that mood. "I swear, Grandfather, sometimes you would try the patience of a saint. Pray let us talk of something else. In fact, I am tired of the whole subject."

Sir Giles snorted. "Well, if it's not romanticizing to trek all this way to a damned barbaric country to wed a man you scarcely know, and who's a half-civilized Scot to boot, when you might have had any one of the fools at home forever dangling after you and making a nuisance of themselves, I don't know what is."

She held on to her temper with an effort, knowing he was only trying to get a rise out of her. "You know perfectly well I have not yet consented to wed Lord Kintyre. And since he was reared and educated in England, you can scarcely, in all conscience, call him that—or at least you couldn't if you possessed a shred of conscience, which frankly I'm beginning to doubt! In fact, as near as I can tell the only thing you have against Kintyre is that it wasn't your idea."

"Hmmph! He has a damned smooth tongue in his head, and I never trust anyone so much in control of his emotions. Not that it makes much odds, for one man's much like another anyway. You might as well have stayed at home and been comfortable."

She had to laugh. "Yes, if I wished to find myself married to a man who is far more interested in his dinner than me and only achieves anything approaching animation on the hunting field. Be fair, Grandfather! I might have married Cousin Joshua, who has not had one thought unconnected with his estates in the last twenty years, and bores even you so much you cannot spend twenty minutes in his company without discovering urgent business elsewhere; or Sir Morton Quillers, who is kindly enough, I grant you. But I have known him all my life and, even more important I dislike his mother."

"You ain't marrying his mother! Good God, girl, it ain't like you to be missish!" he snapped. "Marry one or t'other of 'em and have done with it, and maybe I can have a little peace."

"You don't desire peace and you know it. It is one of the reasons I am so determined to be sure of my choice. Much as I love you, I have no desire to wake up one day to find myself married to a domestic tyrant, as you have been all your life. I am no saint, as Grandmother was, and I fear I lack the patience to put up with it."

"Bah! The truth is I'm a martyr to women, and have been all my life!" But Sir Giles was more pleased than otherwise by this accusation. "Anyway, you'll learn soon enough that all of life's a gamble. Besides, it all sounds devilish cold-blooded if you ask me. Just proves my point. You can't be in love with the fellow."

"No, I'm not in love with him—or at least I don't think I am. I like him very well, but I'm sorry to admit I'm not sure I know what love is. And having made that humiliating admission at the ripe age of six-and-twenty, all I can say is that I mean to choose a husband with at least as much care as I would choose a hat. In that light, you must admit Kintyre represents a rather exotic hat compared to those in our local shop windows. Whether or not I will buy it in the end remains to be seen, but I at least want to try it on once, to see how it fits me."

Sir Giles gave a bark of laughter. "Only a woman would make such a fuss over a perfectly normal part of life. Hats indeed! Well, I've humored you this far, though how you can consider coming to live in an infernal country where it rains all the time and the roads are unsafe for honest travellers, is more than I can understand."

She saw it was no use to say anything more, and wisely held her tongue. She could not say herself exactly why she had come or why she had been so restless the last year or two. She might, as her grandfather had said, have had her pick of several respectable suitors and have had a brood of children around her knee by now. But she had held off, wanting something more, though she herself scarcely knew what.

Love? She was not even sure it existed. Companionship? She might have had that with one or two men whom she had liked well enough. But companionship seemed, in her experience, to dwindle all too quickly into boredom, if the marriages of her friends were anything to go by.

Adventure, then? That seemed the most absurd of the lot and almost merited her grandfather's contempt. And yet, if she were honest, it was what had brought her so many miles from home to a strange country. The sense had been growing in her for some time that she knew exactly what each day was going to bring, and each successive year had grown more and more indistinguishable from the last. It had seemed unpleasantly as if life was passing her by and she would be dead before she had ever really lived.

It was then that the Earl of Kintyre had come to stay with friends in the neighborhood. She liked him well enough, but he had not swept her off her feet. At her age she doubted if it was possible, and had always supposed it to be a very uncomfortable feeling anyway. And yet when he had unexpectedly proposed, it had occurred to her that with his Scots birth and estates, it might be the very thing she'd been unconsciously waiting for. At the very least he could offer her something different that none of her local suitors could. Not merely the same old neighborhood and people she'd known all her life.

She might find, of course, on closer acquaintance, that he was as boring as all the rest. Or her grandfather might be right that the discomforts of such a foreign life outweighed its advantages. But she was stubborn enough to want to discover it for herself.

Besides, she had never traveled farther from home than London, and at the very least she would have had this trip, and one adventure.

And so far it had proven even more adventurous than she had expected. She began to hope faintly that she would find Scotland even more to her taste than she had dared believe.

As she had feared, because of the delay it was well after dark before they arrived at their destination. She had been expecting an ancient castle, along the lines of those she had seen dotted throughout the country, but she was a little disappointed to see that Kintyre House was a solid building no more than two hundred years old, if that.

But it was obvious Kintyre had been worried by their delay. He himself came out into the rainy night to hand her down from the coach, saying warmly, "Thank goodness you are come at last. I hope there was no mishap?"

Sir Giles, emerging stiff and weary from the depths of the coach, snorted. Gillian said quickly to forestall him, "Nothing of moment. We were held up some ten miles from here, which is what delayed us, but luckily we lost no more than a few trinkets."

The Earl of Kintyre, in the fitful light cast by the lantern held by his butler, looked reliably solid and civilized. "Held up?" he repeated as if thunderstruck. "Are you serious?"

"Of course she is!" snapped Sir Giles irritably. "Do you imagine it a subject for jesting? Nor do I wish to stand about in the rain discussing it."

Thus recalled to a sense of his duties, Kintyre took in Gillian's weary appearance, and pressed the hand he still held, saying quickly and warmly, "Of course! Of course. You are tired and half-frozen. Come in and get out of your wet things. Mrs. MacDonald has a hot meal waiting for you. I fear we expected you some hours ago."

He hurried them inside, a fair, pleasant-looking man of medium height, with an intelligent forehead and slightly receding hairline. Despite Sir Giles' prejudice, Kintyre looked exactly what he was: a man of restraint and polish. To Gillian at least, he had always seemed wholly English in education and thinking, despite his Scottish birth and title.

Inside, he bustled around them solicitously, insisting on helping them both out of their wet things and urging them nearer the fire. "Mrs. MacDonald will be here shortly to take you upstairs to your rooms. You may, of course, choose to have supper there on a tray, but I am hoping that when you are warm enough you will return to tell me all about your misadventure. I hope I need not say that I would not for the world have had such a thing happen! In fact, I can only hope it has not given you a distaste of the place before you have properly seen it."

He gave his particularly warm smile, and Gillian could not help but return it. "I believe I am not so weak-willed, my lord. In fact, I rather enjoyed it, for you must know that until then the journey was woefully tedious. As for myself, I will confess a hot meal sounds wonderful, for I have been thinking of little but my dinner for the last hour. But I fear Grandfather is coming down with a cold and would be the better for an early night."

Kintyre laughed. "Well, I can think of better ways to relieve the tedium. But at least it does not sound as if you were overly terrified. Ah, here is Mrs. MacDonald! She will be happy to bring up some hot soup to Sir Giles, or whatever he fancies. Good, then I will look forward to seeing you in—half an hour?"

He bade her grandfather a formal good night, then bowed and kissed her hand. The house seemed larger and more comfortable than Gillian had expected, and in his own setting Kintyre was more at ease, a solid and respectable citizen. She was suddenly glad that she had come. She had always thought it helpful to see someone in his own home.

The housekeeper, a discreet woman in black, bobbed a respectful curtsy but offered no smile in greeting, and turned quietly to lead them upstairs.

As they followed, Gillian found it more and more difficult to reconcile the curious incident of the holdup with this normal and pleasant world of hot soup and warm fires and respectable housekeepers. Perhaps she was making too much of it. One might be held up anywhere, of course. Sir Giles had been help up not ten miles from home only last year, and had continued to rail about the modern state of lawlessness for weeks afterward.

Gillian kissed her grandfather fondly at his door, regarding his spare, upright figure a little anxiously as she did so. For all his stamina he was growing increasingly frail, and she had feared dragging him on such a journey. But to her relief his carriage seemed as upright as ever, and he returned her salute with his usual vigor.

After the door had closed upon him, Mrs. MacDonald said calmly, in the broad Scots Gillian was becoming used to, "Dinna fret, Mistress. I will send Angus up wi' his supper in a bit. They tell me his man and your maid were left behind, so Angus will help him make ready for bed the while."

Gillian thanked her, aware they were the first words the housekeeper had uttered. She was herself shown into a large, comfortable room where a fire burned brightly, dispelling the gloom, and where her few things had already been unpacked and laid out.

It all looked comfortable and a thousand miles from Sir Giles' cynical predictions of ancient stone floors and draughty rooms. Gillian found herself smiling at her own absurd disappointment and declined the housekeeper's offer of help in absence of her maid. If she had herself envisioned something far more romantic, based on the lending library and her own inadequate knowledge of the country and its history, she should no doubt be grateful to find herself mistaken. Adventure was all very well, in its way, as her grandfather would say, but it was no exchange for comfort.

Oddly enough, though, it was not of that she was thinking as she changed out of her creased traveling gown and tidied her hair. In fact, she scarcely saw the warm fire or the comfortable room or her own image in the glass. The housekeeper's voice had reminded her sharply of the tall highwayman, and for the first time it had occurred to her that the rough accent he had used at the beginning had suffered an unaccountable lapse toward the end.

She could not help wondering, in fact, if he knew just how much he had given himself away, and what on earth an obviously educated man was doing holding up coaches in broad daylight.

Chapter 3

THEN Gillian shook her head and deliberately dragged her attention back to her own reflection in the mirror. After all, it made little difference how or why the man had come to be a highwayman. And if one thing was more certain than any other, it was that she would never see him—or her pearls, for that matter—again.

She wasted little time after that, so that it was no more than twenty minutes later when she went back downstairs again, very aware that her stomach was growling most ungenteelly. She was a most unlikely heroine indeed, for she was astonishingly hungry.

Kintyre was waiting for her at the foot of the stairs. "I was afraid you would not find the way on your own. If you don't mind, Mrs. MacDonald has laid supper out in the morning room. It's cozier and a fire is already lit there. Are you sure you're not too tired and would rather go to bed?"

She wondered if he thought it unfeminine of her to be so unaffected by such an ordeal, but he seemed genuinely relieved when she again declined, and escorted her to a room at the back of the house. "I will show you over it all properly in the morning," he said, "but you will recall that I warned you it is nothing out of the ordinary. My late uncle was not one who concerned himself much with his comfort, and when I took the place over less than a year ago, it was in pretty bad shape. I have made it more comfortable, I hope, but it still lacks the touch of a mistress." Again he gave her his warm smile. "You might say it is a house, and not a home, yet. I will look to my wife to turn it into that."

Gillian smiled, but had no desire to venture into such

deep waters so quickly, and so answered calmly, "It seems more than comfortable to me. You are fortunate in your housekeeper—or perhaps I should say that she is fortunate in her master. I should know, for my grandfather has driven away three housekeepers in the last year. He can never get along with any of them for more than a few months."

Kintyre smiled again, but it was somewhat perfunctory. He looked, indeed, as if he was on the point of saying something, but they reached the morning room then, where a maid was waiting to serve them, and instead he pulled out a chair for her. Throughout the pleasant meal that followed he was flatteringly attentive, making sure she was warm enough, and insisting upon adjusting both the candles and the firescreen to suit her.

It was gratifying to be waited on and fussed over, especially after the long and tiring journey, and Gillian was aware of a sleepy contentment. After the many nights in less-than-comfortable inns, it was nice to look forward to the warm bed she had seen upstairs, and she was again very glad she had come despite the day's adventures and her uncertainty about what the future might hold for her here.

As they ate she regarded Kintyre from between her lashes whenever she got the chance, reflecting that it had been some weeks since she had seen him. She was encouraged to find him as pleasant as ever. She had feared there would be some natural awkwardness between them, and was grateful to him for dispelling it.

Once Kintyre was sure she had everything she wanted, he dismissed the maid. But if she had feared he might take advantage of the intimacy of the situation, she was amused to see she need not have worried. There was no hint of the impatient lover in him, for his talk was all of the holdup. "Now, if you don't mind, I would like to hear more of this holdup," he said quietly. "I need not tell you I am shocked and appalled, and in fact blame myself for not having escorted you here. You may rest assured I will get to the bottom of it as soon as possible and see the perpetrators brought to justice."

He sounded unusually grim, and for some reason she

again had a mental picture of the tall highwayman as he bowed absurdly to her, his eyes amused. Kintyre's words made her shiver a little, despite herself.

He was instantly concerned. "You are still cold!" he accused her. "Come nearer to the fire. Would you like something stronger to drink than tea? I won't offer you any of the Scots usquebaugh, which even I find quite undrinkable. But I am sure there is something milder in the house. Let me ring for Mrs. MacDonald."

She made herself banish the lingering image with an almost physical act of will, and said truthfully, "No, indeed I am not cold after that delicious meal. Nor will I hear of you disturbing your housekeeper. But my dear sir—"

"James," he said quickly, giving her one of his warm looks.

"James," she repeated obediently. "I wish you would forget the incident. I already have. In truth it was nothing—no more than a passing nuisance."

He gave her another warm look, but still seemed oddly preoccupied. "It is like you to say so, my dear. But to have you held up—and so close to my own land—passes all bounds! My God, it is no wonder we have the reputation of being little more than barbarians still. Can you describe them? How many were there? Was there anything out of the ordinary about any of them you might have noticed?"

She took a moment to sip her tea, stalling for time. She knew it was absurd, but despite her stolen pearls she had no particular desire to see the men arrested. "I believe there were three of them," she said truthfully. "But honestly, they were so muffled and heavily cloaked that it was impossible to tell anything about them. Anyway, I daresay they are long gone by now."

He looked rueful. "The one thing you will learn about the west of Scotland is that it is a remarkably small place. They will not have gone far. And everyone knows everyone else, so it should not be too hard to trace them. Of course, I am still considered an outsider, and they all stick up for one another to a ridiculous degree. But I shall find them out, never fear. What exactly was stolen?"

"Really, you are making far too much of it. A few trinkets, nothing more. Luckily my jewel case was with my maid, or I would be less forgiving, I promise you. But as it is, I would prefer it be forgotten." She did not know why she neglected to mention her pearls, whose loss could have made her weep. "But I am curious. I realize you only came into the title some eighteen months ago, but surely you are scarcely an outsider? I thought I understood you were born here?"

He grimaced and seemed to hesitate. "It must seem strange to you. It does to me, I'll admit. Yes, I was born here. But these are people with very long memories. No one's forgotten—or forgiven—my father for leaving Scotland for good shortly after that, or that I was brought up in England. It is a notoriously poor country, as you know, and there are few enough opportunities for a second son, so that you'd think they'd understand it. I certainly don't think my father ever regretted leaving. Nor was there any thought, then, that I would one day inherit the title. But none of that seems to matter. I fear I am . . . not universally accepted here yet."

"Give it time. It is scarcely your fault your father chose to leave. But had your uncle no heirs?"

Again he grimaced. "Yes, my uncle had a son—my cousin Alex. It was his birth, as a matter of fact, that convinced my father that there was no future for him here, and led to the move to England."

He seemed to have fallen into a brown study, and she asked curiously after a moment, "And what became of him? You must have been much of an age."

He looked up, as if he had forgotten her existence. "What? Oh, yes. There was no more than two years between us. I was the elder, for my uncle had married late in life, and had been slow in producing an heir. I think my father had become almost convinced he would never do so, for even then my uncle's way of life was fairly notorious. But then my cousin Alex was born and it became clear that Father would have to make his way on his own. Perhaps I should explain that the brothers were not close, and my uncle had made it clear he would not continue to support my father and his family once he himself had married. But lest that should sound harsh, in fairness to him I believe he could scarcely have done so. The estates are poor—I have only just begun to realize how poor—and my uncle was always extravagant. I don't think my father ever held it against him. He was, in any event, soon able to buy a small, neat estate that suited him perfectly, and that will, I confess, always seem more like home to me."

"Your father sounds a most rational and sensible man. But pray go on."

He shrugged. "I fear it is scarcely a pleasant story. But you will come to hear of it soon enough. And it may in some small way have a bearing on your own decision, so I may as well tell you now as later."

She was naturally intrigued, but said nothing. After a moment he went on, as if unwillingly. "Although we were near in age, my cousin and I naturally came into little contact with each other. My father did not come back often, and I can only positively remember seeing Alex once or twice in my life, when we were both quite small. He was, naturally, educated in Scotland, and I in England. In short, our paths did not cross, and it seems that even had we grown up together we would have had very little in common where temperaments are concerned. In fact, from all I have ever heard, my cousin grew up as wild as my uncle had always been—and even more expensive. I know that when he went away to university in Edinburgh he was involved in more than one scandal involving women that cost my uncle a fortune to hush up, for my father and uncle did correspond infrequently. After my father died, I rather lost touch, but I came to hear the story later, of course. It seems that my cousin finally went too far, and was involved in the murder of a man in Edinburgh. Yes, I know," he said at her exclamation. "Scarcely an elevating story. I should perhaps have told you earlier, but you will understand why I dislike speaking of it. Anyway, no one seems to know exactly what happened, but my cousin was forced to flee to the continent to escape arrest. There, far from being chastened by his near-escape and the disgrace he had brought on his father, by all reports he continued his ruinous behavior. He finally topped it all off by being killed in a drunken brawl in a low tavern. The news was what killed my uncle as well," he concluded evenly.

It was scarcely an elevating story, and she was a little shocked. But she said calmly, "A sad history, to be sure. But it has little to do with you, surely?"

"You would think so, but you do not yet know the Scots, my dear. I am one of them, if only by birth, and I confess I understand them little better. It would seem my cousin Alex has taken on something of the color of a romantic hero in these parts, and I am naturally resented as the outsider and interloper."

She was not, perhaps, as surprised as he seemed to be. A wild young man—the son of their own local laird—no, it had perhaps been inevitable. But she said reassuringly, "I'm sure once they come to know you better things will be different."

"I wish I were so hopeful. I am telling you all this because I have come to fear I have brought you here under something of a false pretense. Don't misunderstand me. I still wish for nothing so much as to make you my wife. But I wanted you to have an opportunity to judge for yourself whether you could make your home here. It is the major reason I agreed so readily to your suggestion. Given the temperament of these people, and the cold welcome they have shown me, I confess I would not in the least blame you if you discovered you could not."

She honored him for his candor, and was in fact a little intrigued by the problem he had set her. "I promise you I am not such a coward. And I am convinced that with time things will change. It has been—what? Only eighteen months since you came into the title? That is a very short time, after all."

"I wish I might think so," he said a little gloomily. "But you do not know these people. They are the most stubborn, backward, illogical . . . but there! I fear I am allowing my English upbringing to prejudice me. And I feel all English when I am here, despite my Scots birth. It's doubly ironic that in England I am considered a Scot, and in Scotland very much the opposite. But I fear you will soon see what I mean for yourself. To the English mind it quickly becomes apparent why the country has remained so backward for so long."

He shrugged and went to stand before the fireplace. "To add to it, I fear my uncle was representative of everything that has held Scotland in the dark ages in the past. He ran his little corner of Scotland like his personal kingdom, and was pretty much the last word on any issue in a way that no English landlord would be permitted to be in this day and age. It would at least be excusable if he had had their well-being at heart, but he and my cousin between them seem to have squandered what little fortune there was on costly and ruinous extravagances, with little care given to the poverty-stricken condition of their tenants. Which makes it all the more galling that I am regarded with such suspicion."

Then he shook his head as if to clear it, and went on in a more positive tone, "But I don't wish you to think I am discouraged. The Duke of Argyll, whose estates are not so very distant from here, has achieved wonders even in this poor part of the country, and is one of the few truly modern and forward-thinking Scots. And even he has met with ridiculous resistance and superstition. Between us, we hope . . . but that is for another day. I fear I have tired you too much already with my complaints. But I wanted you to understand what I face here—and what you yourself will see when I show you around. After England, you will find the condition of the people here dismaying. The absurd part is that they seem to take their poverty very much for granted, and resist any hint of change, even for the better."

"Well, it is not only the Scots, surely, who resist change?" she asked sensibly. "You should have heard the uproar at home when it was merely suggested that we might change and modernize the church building, which is sadly ancient and beginning to be unsafe, as you know. You'd have thought we'd suggested bringing in devil worship at the very least."

He smiled rather perfunctorily. "Did they? I can well imagine. But compared with these people, your village is a haven of modern thinking. The majority of Scots are ignorant and superstitious, and care for little but their own feuds. Even the English are still much resented here—another reason why I wished you to see the situation for yourself before you consented to marry me. If you do find yourself able to make me the happiest of men, you may be sure you will not be condemned to spending much time here."

She could not believe the Scots could all be as universally bad as he was painting them. "Well," she said lightly, "I appreciate your honesty, but I confess I do not yet despair of the situation. It is only natural that they would be a little suspicious at first, particularly since you replace so romantic and much-loved an heir. Keep in mind you are still very much a stranger to them. But at the very least I can promise you that my decision will not be based on what you have told me. If nothing else, I am far too stubborn myself to be defeated by a handful of illogical locals."

He came to her quickly and again raised her hand to his lips. "Ah! You don't know how much you relieve my mind. I have come to fear, as I said, that I may have brought you here under false pretenses, for I won't try to hide from you that things are not as pleasant as they should be. And then to have you held up so near here! It would be no more than I deserve if you had insisted upon going home again immediately."

"My dear James," she said in some amusement. "You have allowed all this rain to make you melancholy. I confess it always does me. Either that or you underrate me shockingly. If you but knew it, you could not have told me a thing more inclined to pique my interest, for I can never resist a challenge, you know."

He pressed her hand warmly again. "Thank you. If I underrate you, it is because you possess a gaiety and warm courage I had never thought to find in a woman. It is what I most love in you. But now I have kept you up too late. Go to bed, and we will talk again tomorrow. And for both our sakes we will hope for better weather tomorrow. I have not forgotten that you are an intrepid horsewoman, and I long to be able to show you around."

She was indeed by then finding it difficult to keep her eyes open, and so smiled sleepily at him and accepted her bedroom candle from him at the foot of the stairs. But as she tumbled gratefully into bed a short time later, she reflected that she was still glad she had come. She had no idea yet whether she would accept Kintyre's offer or not—though she could envision far worse lives than working with him to win over the loyalty and respect of the locals, and improve their standard of living. But she had the oddest feeling, unfelt since she had been a child, that she was on the brink of some wonderful new discovery, and that her life would never be the same again. Life at home seemed unbearably dull by comparison.

It was only much afterward that she was to remember that easy confidence and sense of excitement, and laugh at her own naïveté. But as yet she knew nothing of the complicated resentments and loyalties she would soon find made up the average Scot. Or how much of a trick fate still had in store for her. She went to sleep with the sound of the rain drumming on the windows, and for once even it sounded unexpectedly comforting.

Chapter 4

THREE interminable days later, Gillian sat ruefully remembering that feeling of contentment and easy confidence. It had continued to rain, keeping them all indoors, and she had come to see at least a little what Kintyre had been talking about.

It was not that the servants were sullen or overtly resentful. They went about their duties quietly and respectfully, from Mrs. MacDonald down to the lowest scullery maid, with downcast eyes and monosyllabic answers.

It was natural, of course, that they might be curious and even a little suspicious about her. Servants always knew their masters' secrets, and she would have been surprised if the reason for her presence there were not generally known. But it was more than that. There was nothing one could quite put one's finger on—no open insolence or disrespect. One's orders were obeyed and the house was obviously run smoothly. But there was no friendliness or welcome, and no life in the comfortable rooms.

She did not normally think of herself as fanciful, but she felt very much an outsider, despite Kintyre's obvious welcome. In the light of day his house had proved to be a pleasant, mid-Georgian building of largish rooms and considerable comfort. If it were true it was in disrepair eighteen months ago, Kintyre had accomplished something of a miracle in so short a time. Gillian would have found it easy to imagine herself mistress there had there not been that faint chill permeating the place that had nothing to do with actual temperature or the still-prevailing rain.

The rain had not helped, of course. Though Kintyre had insisted upon taking her all through the house, she had still seen almost nothing of the countryside, and quickly grew tired of the endless vistas of fog to be seen from every streaming windowpane.

Sir Giles was still nursing a growing cold, and was short-tempered with it, and Gillian began to think in amusement that if it didn't stop raining soon, they would all be at each other's throats. Kintyre himself did his best to entertain his guests, and promised them a ride to the sea as soon as the weather should clear. But he admitted ruefully that even in summer it was a rare day that did not see at least some rain.

He had made no attempt to disguise that he was conscious too of the unwelcome atmosphere in the house, or that if she consented to marry him he would not expect her to spend much of her time there. He retained his estate in England and divided his own time between the two, though he frankly admitted he himself spent as little time in Scotland as his affairs would allow. She had thought him too critical before, when he had explained it on her first night there; but now she began to understand why he did so.

It was absurd, of course, and a part of her resisted the notion that rational people could be driven away by the unspecified behavior of their servants. But she found herself not looking forward to a prolonged stay in that gloomy atmosphere.

As for the earl himself—and she had to keep reminding herself it was he she had come to get to know better, not his home—Gillian found more and more to admire in him as the days passed. He possessed a pleasant disposition that allowed him to listen gravely to her grandfather's grumblings and not lose his temper, and despite everything she had never heard him be anything less than patient and courteous with his servants. It was evident as well that he had a strong sense of responsibility toward his Scots dependents, despite their treatment of him and the fact that he could not love them.

In fact, on the first long rainy afternoon, he took Gillian into his study and showed her his plans for the estate. As she already knew, that part of Scotland was riddled with lochs, and he showed her on a map where his estates lay. Kintyre Hall was some fives miles from the sea, which he assured her was an advantage. Nearer the sea one endured gales and fog and almost incessant rain, and little grew but gorse and the ubiquitous heather.

"I believe the original house lay much nearer the coast, for you must know there have been lairds of Kintyre here for a thousand years. But this house was built some hundred and seventy years ago, and it was decided then to build farther inland. Since it seems to rain most of the time anyway, I am glad they did."

He made no attempt to hide the fact that the west of Scotland was still pitifully poor and lagged a hundred years behind the more prosperous parts even of the rest of Scotland. "I fear there is precious little employment except for fishing and kelp-gathering. Most of the locals live in abject poverty, as I've already said, and seem to consider it only to be expected. But if I am successful in my plans they may find themselves dragged into modern times, even if against their wills."

She noticed that he looked faintly excited, and was very willing to encourage him. He showed her a point on the map below Kintyre Hall, and said, the excitement even more apparent, "This is still Kintyre land. With the backing of the Duke of Argyll—I told you about him, I believe. One of the only great families in this part of the country, or indeed, all of Scotland. I hope you will be able to meet him while you are here. But anyway, together we mean to build a canal across here. It is badly overdue and will prove a boon to shipping. At present, anything shipped north from the Clyde estuary or Loch Fyne has to use the hazardous passage around the Mull of Kintyre, which adds unnecessary miles and expense to anything sent from the booming industrial centers in Glasgow. You may not realize it, but Scotland is presently leading the field in steam navigation on the Clyde, which we hope our prospective canal will be able to take advantage of."

He grinned, looking suddenly younger. "It will without doubt increase jobs locally, but I won't hide from you that my main motive is a purely selfish one. If we are successful it should add considerably to my own personal fortune. I haven't disguised from you, I hope, that my means at the moment are fairly modest. I've no fortune to offer you, at least at present. But I believe I may offer you an almost unlimited future. In ten years' time, if we're successful, I should be so wealthy you might choose anywhere you'd like to live. Even an English title is not out of the question, if you'd prefer it. It is another reason I wanted you to come here and see everything for yourself before making up your mind."

She could not help but be impressed, though she had no particular desire for a great fortune. She had an income of her own from her late parents, and had never been determined to marry merely for money. But what she liked was his enthusiasm and his ambition. It was certainly yet another point in his favor.

In fact, if she wanted a challenge and something worthwhile to do with her life, it seemed more and more clear that she need look no further and might accept Kintyre's offer immediately.

And yet she held back, not entirely certain herself why she hesitated. The attitude of the servants and the isolation of the place had something to do with it. But she had come to make a reasoned decision, and she saw no urgency to rush into anything after only three days.

But as the days passed she had to acknowledge that she was more and more eager to escape the atmosphere in the house, if only for a few hours.

Her opportunity arose on the fourth day. Kintyre was called away on some unexpected business, and Sir Giles had gone up after lunch to rest. Gillian looked up from a rather boring book to discover that, almost miraculously, the clouds had suddenly parted and a watery sunshine was trying to break through.

It was astonishing what a difference it made, both to the countryside and her own mood. From a wall of almost complete gray, she could now see a good distance, and the country was unexpectedly attractive. The sky had taken on a deep blue, the light was soft and golden, and when she threw open the window the breeze was inviting. Abruptly she closed her book and refused to stay indoors any longer.

Feeling unexpectedly lighthearted, she went upstairs and changed into her habit. She was aware that Kintyre would not have wished her to ride out alone, but surely on so narrow a peninsula she could scarcely get lost, and she had a sudden desperate desire to ride to the sea, and shake the atmosphere of the house off completely. She was convinced that the constant rain had much to do with it, and that if she could but get away for a little while, she would be able to come back and laugh at her earlier fancies.

Even so, she had a foolish temptation to creep stealthily downstairs again, for fear someone would try and stop her. Unfortunately, it did not occur to her until much later to remember the lesson she should have learned on their journey there: that this was not safe and familiar England, and she little understood the dangers that could lie in wait even in broad daylight and on so lovely and peaceful an afternoon.

The Scots groom who came out at her appearance did show considerable reluctance to saddle a horse for her. But she had no intention of being thwarted at that point, and in the end he shrugged and went away to do her bidding. To his even more reluctant suggestion, made in the broadest of Scots, that he should accompany her for fear that she should get lost on her own, she returned a firm negative answer, reading in his tone a condemnation of all English and probably of all women, and having no intention of having her adventure spoiled by the presence of so taciturn and obviously disapproving a companion.

He was a thin, dark young man with a not-unpleasing countenance—though like most of the servants she had met so far, he looked as if he feared a smile might crack his face in two. But he shrugged and gave her a leg up into the saddle, making no more attempt to dissuade her.

She knew the general layout of the peninsula by then from Kintyre's description, for it was scarcely ten miles wide at most points, with the Atlantic on one side and Loch Fyne on the other, and the Firth of Clyde not very far to the south.

At the moment she was mainly interested in catching a glimpse of the sea at last, and perhaps even of the islands that she knew lay both to the east and west; part of the fabled Hebrides. Kintyre had assured her that on good days Jura and even Mull could be seen to the east, and Arran to the west, and had promised her an excursion to one or all of them once the weather cleared.

In light of the groom's disapproval she had not liked to ask directions, but doubted she could go seriously wrong if she followed the sun. And she soon forgot everything in the pleasure of the ride. After so many gloomy days, it was indeed a sparkling afternoon, and indeed her only dissatisfaction was that the mare the groom had saddled for her proved to be a patient and far-from-spirited hack, chosen no doubt as a "suitable" lady's mount. It offered her little in the way of exercise, but picked its way uninterestedly at scarcely more than an amble.

But even at that slow pace her patience was soon rewarded, for as she topped a small rise she was able to get her first real glimpse of the sea, still some miles in the distance. The country she was riding through proved to be largely flat, and Kintyre was undoubtedly correct that the thin, marshy soil would grow little but bracken and heather. And yet the air was clear and tangily salt-laden, and her spirits rose the closer she got to the sea. There was even something about the smell that was strangely familiar, as if she should know what it was.

And then of a sudden she knew. The tall highwayman had carried just such a tang about him, of the sea and heather and open moor. Just thinking of it brought his image abruptly before her with unexpected clarity.

It was an unwanted reminder, for she had largely been able to put the incident out of her mind over the last few days. She deliberately forced back the reminder and urged her mount to a faster trot.

Even the mare lifted her head as they got closer to the sea, and put forward her ears in something approximating eagerness. Even so, it took longer than Gillian had anticipated to reach the shoreline, and the sun proved to be unexpectedly hot. By the time she did arrive she was feeling both hot and thirsty herself.

The shore proved very rocky, but the view was more than enough to make up for it. The sea, gray and forbidding despite the weak sunshine, was clearly falling, and the beach, though uneven and not particularly inviting, was nevertheless easily accessible.

Gillian hesitated only an instant before sliding from the saddle, welcoming the cool breeze in her face and the taste of salt on her lips. After one glance along the empty shore she left her horse cropping contentedly on some sparse grass and picked her way down toward the water.

An empty shore is a temptation to anyone, and after her hot ride she was strongly inclined to remove her boots and stockings and paddle. It seemed unlikely she would be discovered in that isolated spot, and she had never outgrown the childish liking for freezing water and sand between her toes.

But the difficulty of removing her boots by herself—and still more daunting, putting them back on again—and the fear of being discovered by some local fisherman in so compromising a position restrained her. Instead she contented herself with removing her fashionable hat and opening the tight collar to her habit, the sun feeling warm and welcome on her bare skin.

Still, she thought she could easily make her way to a large outcropping of rocks, a little way from shore, where she might sit undisturbed. As a child she had spent many happy hours at the seashore, and she had never tired of staring out to sea, or exploring tide pools.

But it was her very virtue in resisting temptation that managed to undo her in the end. She had looped the tail of her habit over her arm, and it proved more difficult than she had anticipated to negotiate such slippery rocks thus encumbered and in her stiff boots. She had managed to cover not quite half the distance to the rocks that were her destination when a flat stepping stone twisted treacherously underneath her. Before she could regain her balance she found herself falling backward, flailing her arms helplessly, but wholly unable to save herself.

Even so, the mishap was merely ludicrous and not in any way dangerous, for the sea was not deep at that point. All that happened was that she found herself suddenly sitting down hard and unexpectedly among some rather sharp rocks and in about a foot of icy water. The tide was still low and she was never in any real danger, but the sea was unexpectedly cold and the rocks bruisingly hard beneath her, and it was a humiliating enough situation to find herself in.

For a moment or two she just sat there, gasping against the cold, while the icy seawater quickly soaked her heavy skirts and reminded her that this was, after all, the northern Atlantic. Sitting in it almost up to her waist while fully dressed, the tide bubbling and sucking around her, dragging at her skirts, it was easy enough to remember that the water came straight off the ice and snow of the far northern regions.

After a moment she said a fairly unladylike word, culled from her grandfather's vocabulary, and then began to laugh. Of all the absurd situations to find herself in. At her age she should have learned not to be so impetuous, and it would undoubtedly serve her right when she had to ride all the way back to Kintyre Hall in wet boots and icily clinging skirts, courting the amused contempt of all Kintyre's servants.

She had been so very sure the shore was deserted that

when an amused voice spoke from behind her, she nearly jumped a foot. "Is that some new way of swimming, Mistress? It's a braw enough day for it, I'll grant you, but I'd suggest you rid yourself of a few of those petticoats first, or you're likely to find yourself carried with the tide all the way to Ireland."

Chapter 5

SHE was more than annoyed to be caught in so humiliating a situation. But when she turned her head sharply to find the source of the voice, she began to understand how she had missed him before, so naturally did he blend into his surroundings.

He looked, indeed, as if he had been in for a swim himself, for his gleaming white shirt was open almost to the waist to expose an expanse of strong brown chest, and his buckskins and boots were the exact same shade as the bracken near the shore. He was standing, legs spread apart in a sturdy stance, regarding her in amusement, both fists on his hips and an unmistakable twinkle in his eyes. His voice was obviously Scots, for it had an indefinable lilt that Kintyre's so conspicuously lacked, but it was clearly educated, and not that of the almost unintelligible servants which were all she had yet met in the country.

This much she took in in that first glance, and then her own sense of humor reasserted itself. It was a ludicrous enough situation to be caught in, and he was entitled to his amusement. "I confess I had been longing for a paddle on such a hot day," she said ruefully. "But I'd intended to at least remove my boots first."

His laugh was uninhibitedly attractive, and he came toward her then with a lithe grace there could be no mistaking, as if he were as much a part of this wild and unfamiliar scene as his clothes suggested. Another moment and he had confidently traversed the stones that had so ignominiously defeated her, and stood above her, the laughter still in his face and his gray eyes unabashedly inspecting her. "Ah, I thought it some new English fad we'd not yet heard of," he said in amusement. "You're a long way from home, Mistress. But however hot a day it is, you may have noticed that the sea is always cold here, unlike your Southern waters. So unless you wish to court pneumonia, you'd best curtail your pleasure."

There was something half-familiar in his deep, amused tones, but after a puzzled moment she put it down to the lilt of his accent. "Yes, I had indeed noticed. Is Ireland what lies to the west of here?"

"Aye, but doubtless you'd fetch up first on Jura, and be taken for a strange sort of mermaid there," he said easily. "It's doubtful you'd be so lucky as to make it all the way to Ireland."

He held a strong brown hand down to her and she accepted it gratefully, for the tide was sucking at her skirts so strongly by then it was doubtful if she could have extricated herself easily alone. He clasped her hand and pulled her up with seeming ease, standing braced there on the rocks above her, though the water gave up her skirts only reluctantly.

But she gave a sudden gasp and would have sat down again in the icy water if his strong hand had not been supporting her. It seemed that the tumble had wounded more than her dignity, for there was a stab of agony in her left ankle, and she discovered too late that it would not bear her weight.

"Oh—! I . . . would seem to have twisted my ankle." She managed through bitten lips. "Pray, don't move for just a second."

He did not obey her, but without warning slung her up over his shoulder as if she had been a bag of potatoes. It was a highly undignified mode of transport, especially since her sodden skirts were dripping down his front and making him almost as wet as she was. But she seemed at the moment in little position to object as he made his way confidently back toward shore.

He reached the more solid sand easily enough, and there lowered her onto a convenient rock. She felt light-headed and ridiculous, sitting there in her soaking habit with her ankle throbbing painfully. Nor was she one who much relished being made to feel helpless. But before she could prevent him or even guess at his intention, he had gone down on one knee before her and without hesitation tossed up her bedraggled skirts and petticoats and bent to inspect her ankle.

She opened her lips to object, and then closed them again in resignation. Here she was, stranded miles from home and soaking wet, her ankle hurting so much by now it was making her a little sick, and there was no doubt all of it was the result of her own folly. It was clearly past time to be worrying about propriety.

"What a devil of a lot of clothing you foolish women wear, to be sure!" complained her unconventional rescuer. But she noticed that his fingers were surprisingly gentle, and the top of his dark head, with an endearing hint of curl in his thick hair, was near enough to touch as he bent over her.

Then she caught herself up with a start, wondering what on earth had put such a mad thought into her head. Kintyre, in the past few days, had been much closer to her, and yet she had never wanted to touch his hair. It could only be the cold and the pain making her giddy.

He looked up then to say briefly, "Yes, you've doubtless sprained it, for your ankle's swelling rapidly." Then he took a harder look at her, and abruptly thrust her head down between her knees with as little ceremony as he had done all else.

"I should have some strong usquebaugh to give you, like any respectable Scot, but I've come out without my flask," he said in amusement. "But you'll be well enough in a minute or two."

She was discovering that irritation was nearly as good a stimulant as smelling salts. "I am not in the least faint!" she mumbled indignantly. "And I must protest, you have a provoking habit of laying hands on me in a most improper manner, sir."

He laughed without sympathy. "And you've the foolish

pride of all giddy women. But I'll confess I've little use for propriety. Now, that boot should come off, and the sooner the better. Then we'd be able to determine if anything is broken."

She sat up hurriedly, alarmed by this program. "No! I mean—I thank you, but I've no need to trouble you further. I can make it back on my own."

He sat back on his heels and regarded her frankly. "Don't be daft. You'll not get far on your own as you are, and it will scarcely help matters any to have you faint and break your neck as well as your ankle. Besides, I'd not have guessed you were a coward, somehow."

"A coward—! Of course I am not—Now look—!"

But she might once more have spared her breath. He had watched the no doubt transparent emotions chasing each other across her face with some amusement, and then, taking the matter into his own hands in a way he seemed far too prone to do, produced a knife from somewhere about his person and set about slitting her boot along its seam with an unexpectedly delicate precision.

He was deft and quick, but even so it hurt abominably. She ought to have asserted her independence over such maddening arrogance, but all too quickly she found it all she could do to keep from disgracing herself by crying out. She could taste the salt of her own blood from her bitten lip, and she felt oddly hot and clammy at the same time, despite her sodden skirts.

"There, I'm done," he said with unexpected gentleness. "And you're a brave lass for all my words—and your own foolish pride. You'd have done better to swear at me."

For some reason his praise brought foolish tears to her eyes, as his earlier insults and ministrations had not been able to. She blinked them back furiously. "I am much more likely to swear at myself, for my own folly. But I am curious, sir. Are you by any chance married?"

She had for once the satisfaction of taking him by surprise, though the quick laughter was back in his eyes. "Married? What's that to do with it? No, I'm not married."

"I thought you could not be. Had you a wife, she would

clearly have murdered you long since. You have a most infuriating habit of getting your way against all odds that would lead any female to thoughts of violence."

He threw back his head and laughed, and she could clearly see the strong column of his brown throat. "Aye, I've little time for women, I confess. They've an infuriating habit of setting traps for a man, and seldom saying what they mean."

She opened her mouth to refute the accusation, and then shut it again. He was looking up at her, his amused brown face very near her own, casually holding her wet stockinged foot in his strong hand as if he had the right, her skirts still indelicately raised to reveal her soaking petticoats. And whether because of that, or her shaken wits, or for some other reason she afterward had no wish to explore too closely, the moment seemed to spin out as if time stood still around them.

He was indeed so close she could see the texture of his skin and the small laugh lines around his eyes. He was not conventionally handsome. His face was too strong, all planes and hard angles and taut brown skin. Kintyre was by far the better looking, if it came to that. And yet she would have been lying to herself if she had not acknowledged, with a sort of dazed astonishment at herself, that she far preferred this man's bold, arrogant face to Kintyre's more civilized features. It told her a great deal about herself she had not known before—and was not sure she had wanted to learn.

And still the moment stretched out, giving her time to take in every small detail about him. His eyes were as gray as the distant cold sea, and the mocking amusement in them was still very much in evidence and seemed to be more or less habitual. The faint lines at the corners of his eyes might have been from straining his eyes against the sun, but in such a rainy climate might as easily have been from laughing frequently and finding an odd amusement in much of the world around him. His nose was strong, his mouth unyielding, though at the moment curved with some private amusement; and his hair was very dark and with the faint curl she had noticed earlier accentuated by the strong breeze.

She stared at him, thinking, absurdly but inescapably, that life had a way of making nonsense of even one's most careful plans.

But it was only for a moment that the strange spell held, after all. She blinked, as if surfacing from some distant place, and he released her foot, remarking casually as if he had been wholly unaware of that strange moment, "There. I don't mean to boast of my handiwork, but with a little luck a bootmaker will be able to stitch up your boot as good as new again. Though I'd not venture to say the same for your habit."

Instantly the memory of that strange moment fled in renewed annoyance, and she stiffened, thinking it was like him to have reminded her of what she must look like, with her skirts soaking and hiked up about her in a most improper manner, and her face no doubt shiny and her hair coming down.

But again as if reading her thoughts with insulting ease, he managed to slip beneath her guard in the manner of the skilled duellist he so obviously was. "Nay, you've little need to worry, Mistress," he remarked assessingly. "Even in sodden skirts and a twisted ankle, you'd still take the breath away from a poor man. And it's just like a woman to be thinking of her appearance at such a foolish moment."

She closed her lips firmly before she could make even more of a fool of herself. He had the most infuriating habit, she'd noticed, of insulting one and then casually issuing a back-handed compliment, the net effect of which was to keep one constantly off-balance. Conversation with him was like a game of tennis, or walking a narrow cliff, never sure when one might plunge over. "Yes," she remarked thoughtfully after a moment, when she had controlled her burning cheeks. "You should clearly never marry."

He laughed again, in no whit insulted. "Under the circumstances it's unlikely I shall. But I confess I've a weakness for a lass with a ready tongue. And now we've talked enough nonsense. It's time to get you back before you turn to a block of ice. You're already blue enough."

Again he had managed to issue a compliment and take it back again almost in the same breath. She was resigned to it by now, but there had been something in his earlier words that had struck a faint chord, though she could not for the moment place it.

But before she could pursue the elusive memory, he had again swept her up into his arms without warning—though at least it was not over his shoulder this time, which had been as painful as it was humiliating. He carried her to her horse, still patiently cropping, and set her up in the saddle with annoying ease, though a spasm of something crossed his face, so quickly she was not sure she hadn't imagined it.

She thought with resignation that no man had ever manhandled her so carelessly or so often; but it seemed useless to point the fact out to him again, as well as the extreme impropriety of it all. He had clearly spoken the truth when he said he had little use for propriety.

"I now know something of what a sack of meal must feel," she remarked dryly. "But I suppose I must be grateful to you. Now if you'll hand me my reins, I need not trouble you further."

She was by no means sure it was true, for she had already discovered she could not bear to place her injured foot in the stirrup, and so was perched more than precariously in the saddle.

But she need not have worried. Instead of answering her, he calmly stowed her boot in her saddlebag, and set out on foot, leading her.

He had not asked her identity, but she supposed that in so small a place the fact that the local laird had English visitors must have been known to everyone. But she had a sudden mental image of being tamely led back, bootless and disheveled, by this brown and arrogant devil, to the amused enjoyment of all Kintyre's servants. It was a scene she scarcely relished, and so she said more firmly, "Surely you cannot be proposing to walk all that way? Besides, I've no intention of putting you to any more trouble."

He glanced up at her with a certain mockery. "Whether or not you wish it, I begin to think you'll prove a fair amount of trouble before all's said and done," he remarked unexpectedly, and walked on.

He strode easily, whistling somewhat tunelessly between his teeth, and wholly ignored her after that. Short of wresting the reins from his grip, which would be an undignified and probably futile business, she saw no way of stopping him. She had, perforce, to sit there seething, thinking that if all highlanders possessed such remarkable manners, she was indeed glad Kintyre had been reared in England.

It took her a moment to realize that the man was not, in fact, leading her back the way she had come, but north, along the shore. Perhaps it was an easier way, particularly by foot, but still she could not prevent exclaiming a little suspiciously, "Where are you taking me? This is not the way back to Kintyre House."

She might not have spoken for all the attention he paid to her. He continued to walk easily, whistling tunelessly. It was ridiculous. She did not seriously believe he meant her any harm. And yet she refused to be treated any longer like a foolish child or an even more foolish woman, needing to be rescued from her own folly.

But even as she debated her best course of action in the face of his frustrating intractability, she saw that they had rounded a curve in the shore. Unexpectedly, there before her eyes stood an ancient keep, standing as it must have since the middle ages, guarding the shore. It blended so naturally into its surroundings of gray rock and sea that she had not even guessed a habitation stood so close, but that had doubtless been a good part of its value in days gone by.

It could barely be called a habitation however. It looked well on the way to joining the many ruins she had seen on the road in Scotland, and only the lazy curl of smoke and the massive door standing ajar gave any hint that it might be occupied.

She was, in truth, a little curious to see inside such a place, but still, she had no intention of being taken there so meekly, as if she had no say in the matter. Aside from the impropriety, she had little liking for having her wishes so wholly ignored. She took a deep breath, and said as calmly as she could manage, "This has gone far enough. Pray hand me my reins, sir."

At least she got an answer from him that time. "You've no need to screech," he protested mildly. "I heard you the first time."

"I'm not screeching—!" She heard the shrill indignation in her own voice and was irritated by it. "And if you heard me the first time, there is no excuse for ignoring my wishes."

He did not even turn to look at her, but continued on his way, still whistling between his teeth.

It was then a squat figure emerged from the keep, his face ill-shaven and his hair a fiery red. He stared at their approach with scant favor, and it flashed into her mind that there was something obscurely familiar about the way he stood there, disapproval evident in every line of his body. "So ye found her, then?" he observed gruffly.

Before she could react to that remarkable statement, her escort answered lazily, "Aye, I found her. Landed her like a mermaid, as it happens."

The other looked her over in what she could not mistake for anything but disapproval. "Aye, and it's a bedraggled enough mermaid ye've landed, by the looks of it," he said frankly. "Had ye to wrestle her into the sea and half-drown her to subdue her? I'd no' thought ye so clumsy, Rory. And sma' reward to ye if ye've opened up your wound again," he added disapprovingly.

It was then Gillian knew. She sat there, looking between the two of them speaking as if she weren't there, and felt numb and foolish, and more than a little afraid, for she should have guessed long since. No wonder she'd had such a sense of familiarity with both of them.

But then she had no one to blame but herself, after all. It seemed she had forgotten, despite all the warnings, that this was not safe, tame England, but a very different country indeed, where it seemed the normal rules of civilized behavior scarcely applied.

"*You?*" she managed faintly. "Oh, what a fool I am! It was you who held us up."

Chapter 6

HE made her a sweeping bow. "I'm flattered I had such a place in your memory, Mistress. And you must admit, Lachlan, that it's a bonny enough fish I've landed, for all her draggled petticoats. She was foolish enough to paddle without removing her boots first, and has a sprained ankle to show for it."

"Ye had no need to tell me that," retorted Lachlan. "All women are foolish to one degree or another."

The man called Rory stood back so as to observe her better, his fists once more on his hips. "Aye. But I fear we are giving Mistress Thorncliff a poor idea of Highland hospitality. She is cold and tired and probably hungry, and her ankle needs wrapping. Have the lads left anything to eat? We must be on our best behavior with so distinguished a guest in our midst."

It would not have been true to say she was not frightened. Visions of rape and murder flashed inexorably through her head, and she thought they had every right to call her a fool. She had been an easy enough fish to reel in, in all conscience. But at least she had no intention of being taken quite so tamely.

Rory still held her reins, but his step back had given her the maneuvering room she needed. Without warning she reached forward and grabbed the cheek-strap and jerked the mare's head round sharply. At the same time she slapped her furiously on the rump. "Go on! Get up! *Go!*"

It would have been too much to expect the mare, notoriously stolid, to break into panicked flight. But she did the next best thing. Understandably startled, she tossed her head and succeeded in jerking the reins from Rory's loosened grasp. At the same time, in a piece of luck that Gillian hadn't anticipated, she swung her hindquarters around, buffeting into the man and sending him off-balance.

It was no more than a second's advantage, but Gillian gave him no time to recover. She kicked the mare sharply, at the moment caring neither about the risk of falling off nor the danger of her still dangling reins, and merely cursing her sidesaddle and present precarious perch. Foremost in her mind was the determination to best an infuriating and unscrupulous thief in whatever his plans might be for her.

Indeed, she actually thought for an exhilarating moment that she might succeed in her escape. The frightened animal, thus given the bit, took a few running strides, hampered by the dangling reins and Gillian's own damp skirts.

But the moment of victory was pitiably brief and over almost as soon as it had begun. Rory snatched at the reins as she passed, and caught them again with ridiculous ease, although with considerable risk to his own safety. The next moment she had been unceremoniously pulled from the saddle, with scant regard for her dignity or her tender ankle, and was tumbled into his arms again, ruffled and furious.

He grinned down at her, holding her with seeming ease despite her struggles. "It seems you've an unlucky way of falling into disaster, Mistress Thorncliff," he told her mockingly.

"And I begin to think its no' a mermaid, but a spitting cat ye've captured," observed Lachlan.

"Aye, but I'll tame her soon enough." Without further hesitation he strode with her through the door into the ancient keep. Gillian had a vague impression of a large, rough hall, clean enough but carelessly cluttered, and then she was being borne swiftly up a worn pair of stone steps. If his wound were bothering him Rory gave no sign of it, and she found herself wishing that her grandfather's aim had been truer, after all. She might have been spared a most terrifying ordeal if it had.

But of that she preferred not to think. She had ceased her struggles, realizing that even if she were to break free she could scarcely hope to escape on her injured ankle. For the moment she was well and truly netted, and could only bide her time, hoping for another opportunity.

Nevertheless, she had to resist the temptation to close her eyes like a frightened child, as if that would make it all somehow less real. At the very least it would wipe out the brown face so close to her own, at the moment registering nothing but mocking amusement.

But since she suspected that was exactly what he wanted, she made herself keep her head up, refusing to scream or faint or plead with him. There might come a time for that later, but that, too, was something she preferred not to think about now.

At the top he paused to kick open a door, and carried her into what was clearly a bedroom, hung with faded velvet. There he sat her down easily on the edge of a huge tester bed, and then stood before her, looking very large and intimidating, his arms folded and that look of amusement very much on his hard face.

When she returned his stare as best she could, he grinned. "Aye, you've a cool head on your shoulders," he remarked approvingly. "And a haughty way of looking down your nose at the rest of your fellow creatures that effectively reduces us to our place. You won my admiration initially by not screeching or falling into hysterics at the sight of such armed and dangerous ruffians as we were, but instead calmly ordering us not to disturb your trunks. Even Lachlan was impressed, and he despises all women."

"I am naturally delighted to have won Lachlan's limited approval," she managed steadily enough. "But you can never hope to get away with this, you know. Kintyre won't rest until he sees you hung."

"Perhaps. He can only hang me once, however. But I'm curious. What is it you imagine I brought you here for?"

She took a deep breath. She did not really believe he had anything more in mind than holding her to ransom. That was humiliating enough, considering she had no one but herself to blame, but she had little enough to fear, after all.

"I imagine you mean to ransom me back to Kintyre—or

my grandfather, or both. But you will scarcely succeed. If I don't return shortly I will be searched for, and they know the direction in which I rode. However, if you release me at once, and unharmed, I will forbear to tell Lord Kintyre of my treatment at your hands."

"Aye, that's a tempting offer," he agreed gravely. "But you are an unconscionable liar, Mistress Gillian Thorncliff. Kintyre is away on business and will not return until late, and you left the house without telling anyone of your plans. You even declined the escort of the groom who saddled your horse for you. It will be hours yet before you are missed, and still longer before they think of searching for you. I've little enough to fear."

She almost gasped. "Are you telling me someone on Kintyre's staff is in your pay?"

"I've no need to pay him. But we're wandering somewhat from the point. I hold no brief for Kintyre—the best thing I know of him to date is his taste in women, by the way. I'd not have expected him to choose so well. But you're right. I've little doubt he would pay handsomely to have you restored to him."

When she remained defiantly silent he went on, "And then there's your grandfather, as well. A braw old fool, with more guts than sense—it would seem his granddaughter takes after him in that. But I'm told Sir Giles Thorncliff is a wealthy man in his own right. It would seem you are a most profitable mermaid I've landed for myself."

Her hands curled tightly into fists. Her grandfather was a stubborn and infuriating old man, but news of her being abducted and held to ransom might well kill him. "And you are excellently informed. You must indeed have a spy within Lord Kintyre's household. But they are not quite as efficient as they should be, or you would know that I am not yet betrothed to Lord Kintyre. That might upset your plans slightly."

"Not in the least. It merely gives me a better opinion of your intelligence. And if you've so little regard for his affection or honor, I would certainly recommend you think twice about wedding him. Whether or not you are betrothed to him should make no difference to his willingness to ransom you."

She flushed for some reason, and said stiffly, "I have every confidence in Lord Kintyre's honor."

"Then if you are right, and I mean to hold you to ransom, you've nothing to worry about, have you?"

"*If* you mean to hold me to ransom? What else am I to think? Don't forget, I know you for a thief already," she told him contemptuously.

"Aye, but you've overlooked one possibility." He went to stand before the fire and turned his back to the flames, looking her over insolently in a way that made her cheeks burn hotly and her palm itch to slap him. "In fact, I will confess you present me with something of a dilemma, Mistress Thorncliff. I will admit the thought of ransom is tempting, but on the other hand, it would seem it has been too long since Duntroon Castle has entertained so charming a guest, and I find myself suddenly envious of Kintyre's good fortune. A lass—even an English one—with locks the color of rich mahogany, and bewitching green eyes, could tempt a man to forget so paltry a thing as a fortune in ransom."

Her heart had begun to beat rather sickeningly in her breast, but she would not let him see he had frightened her. She suspected, anyway, that his threats were no more than a ploy to drive up the price. He would be a fool to risk harming her and thus the ransom she might bring. "And do you expect me to feel flattered?" she demanded scornfully. "Or to beg you to spare me from what is popularly considered to be a fate worse than death? I fear I must disappoint you."

But he was still only amused. "But then, I would naturally not consider it a fate worse than death. And being somewhat vain, I suspect you might even find it less horrifying than you imagine."

"Your crudeness is only exceeded by your conceit! But if you force me against my will, I can promise you will find little joy in the taking. In the end you might come to regret the fortune in ransom you had thrown away, for I doubt

Kintyre would any longer be willing to pay your price. But that is your own choice, of course."

He laughed out loud, standing there before her in his buckskins, looking the very picture of a maurauder, a man out of step with his civilized time and making no apologies for it. "And I'm thinking you can know little of the subject, Gillian Thorncliff, if you believe I would have need to force you," he said with an even greater conceit that left her gasping. "As for the ransom, do you truly rate your charms so cheap? Even if you had suffered that fate worse than death that you speak of, I think Kintyre might still be persuaded to ransom you, and even marry you, if you played your cards right, if for no other reason than his own pride's sake. So you see, it is not quite such a dilemma after all— for either of us."

"And do you truly think I would hold him to marriage after—that?" she demanded contemptuously.

He shrugged and his gray eyes narrowed as if he were seeing pictures only he could see, and none too pleasant ones at that. Then he shrugged. "I'm thinking that it's little you know of him after all, if you can ask me that. It would gall him past bearing that I had enjoyed you first, but in the end it would only make him the more determined to wed you. So you need have no fears—on that score at least, if I cannot be so sanguine about other things you might come to regret in the fullness of time."

She had not, until that moment, really believed he might actually rape her instead of claiming the ransom, despite his words. But now she stared at him, seeing the truth in his eyes at last. "You hate him!" she whispered. "That's what this is all about, isn't it? It's nothing to do with me at all."

But she might have known by then she would get no straight answer from him. "I told you, you underrate your charms shockingly, Miss Thorncliff. And overrate Kintyre's importance, as well. I've no energy to waste in hating him."

Even so, she did not believe him. She knew an absurd impulse to laugh, for there was no escaping the irony of her present predicament. "And to think I came to Scotland hoping for adventure," she exclaimed before she could prevent herself.

"Aye, it's dangerous to wish for something for fear you might get it," he agreed, unconsciously echoing her own earlier thoughts. "And this is not England, Gillian Thorncliff. You'll find we are far simpler around here, and more basic in our emotions. I'd not need the excuse of hating the present Earl of Kintyre to find pleasure in your arms."

She still had a ridiculous urge to laugh, as if none of this could be happening to her. Only a few weeks ago she had been lamenting that life passed her by. Now in a very short space of time she had been held up, abducted and threatened with rape. It seemed she was ungrateful enough not to appreciate her good fortune.

But at least she could not fail to believe him capable of everything he threatened. He stood there before her, tall and formidable-looking and very much at ease. In that moment she was ashamed to remember she had ever been attracted to him.

Nor, clearly, could she hope for any help from below. The man Lachlan had looked disapproving, but he had made no move to prevent his master from carrying her upstairs, and would doubtless not trouble to come to the rescue of a foolish Englishwoman who had only herself to blame for her present predicament.

But at least she was resolved not to go tamely to her fate. She lifted her chin proudly. "You will find little enough pleasure in my arms, I promise you! And if you touch me— if you dare to come one step closer, even—I will not wait for Kintyre to avenge me. I will kill you myself, no matter how long it takes me to do it, or how far you go to hide from me. And that you may count on, Englishwoman though I may be."

He threw back his head and laughed again, his hands on his lean hips and his brown throat bare and strong in his opened shirt. And it was in that fraught moment there was an unexpected interruption at the door.

"Rory, will ye no' ha' done wi' yer teasing?" the stocky servant said disapprovingly, standing with a covered tray incongruously in his hands and a scowl on his ugly face. "Mistress Thorncliff will die of an inflammation if no' out o' those wet petticoats shortly, and then ye *will* ha' Kintyre to deal with."

Chapter 7

"NOT she," said the man called Rory easily. "She'd not give in to anything so tamely, even an inflammation. But you're right. The teasing's gone on overlong."

It took Gillian a stunned moment to take the truth in. "Teasing?" she repeated as if she had never heard the word before. "*Teasing—?* Are you telling me you were only teasing me with all your threats?"

"Aye, it's an unfortunate habit of mine," he conceded without a trace of remorse. "But I had no intention, when we started, of anything but binding your ankle and drying your skirts for you. It was your own imagination that was my undoing."

"My *imagination*? I was terrified! What else was I to think once I realized who you were?"

"I will admit I'd not expected that. You've unexpectedly sharp eyes, lass."

She was still trying to take it all in. "But this is ridiculous! It was *not* all my overactive imagination. You threatened and manhandled me! Or do you mean to deny that as well?"

"If I manhandled you, it was only to keep you from doing yourself an injury," he told her virtuously. "But I made no threats. If there's a scrap of honesty in you, you must admit it was you who jumped to such instant and unflattering conclusions."

"I—!" Gillian felt a little as though she had wandered into a madhouse. She had been through too many conflicting and violent emotions in that short hour—far more than she could remember experiencing in a year in her usual safe world. And yet, when she later reflected back on that frightening conversation, she was forced to acknowledge that it was just possible a very different construction might be placed upon his words. It was certainly her knowledge of his identity that had colored all her subsequent perceptions.

And yet she could not believe she had been so completely mistaken. "Now wait a minute. What did you mean when you admitted you'd 'found' me? You came deliberately in search of me, don't try to deny it."

He grinned. "Only because Ewan was concerned for you. He's the lad who saddled your horse for you, incidentally. He knew Kintyre was away, and feared you'd get into trouble on your own, being unfamiliar with the country. And you must admit he was correct. You'd be halfway out to sea by now if I hadn't come to rescue you."

"I had never known highwaymen were such paragons of all the virtues!" she retorted sarcastically. "In fact, you only had my best interests at heart when you molested and terrified me?"

"Aye, we've an unwarranted reputation. 'Tis sad to see how we're misjudged."

She felt foolish and furious and unsettled. But she possessed just enough of a sense of justice to see that it could conceivably have been her own overactive imagination that had indeed triggered the ludicrous scene. Still, she found that she could not forgive him for the fear and horror she had experienced, and so said coldly, "And you really expect me to believe that you, an admitted thief, mean nothing more harmful than to succor my wounds and see me honorably home? I was wishing I had had the forethought to bring a pistol with me. If I had, I would gladly have put a bullet through you. Did you consider that when you were playing your elaborate jest on me?"

"Mayhap then he'd learn his lesson," observed Lachlan, setting his tray down on a bedside table. "I've warned him his sense of humor will some day be the death o' him."

Rory was still grinning. "Aye, but in my defense, if you'd shown a hint of fear, instead of merely looking at me as if I were a bug that had crawled out from under a rock, I might have drawn back sooner. You're quite a lass, Miss Gillian Thorncliff. I said Kintyre showed unexpected good taste."

"I wish I *had* had a pistol! Are you telling me it was all lies? You don't even mean to hold me for ransom?"

Then she cheerfully could have bitten out her tongue, for even to her own ears there was just the faintest hint of disappointment in the words.

She should have known he would not miss it. "I'm willing to oblige," he told her audaciously. "I'll admit it's a tempting enough thought. But aside from the fact it's no' a Scots custom to make war with women and children—you would have to look to the English for that—I confess I've developed a certain grudging admiration for you, Englishwoman though you are. You shall be returned to your doting fiancé as soon as your ankle has been strapped and your clothes are dry. I trust our rude hospitality will suffice until then."

Her cheeks had crimsoned, and she could have cursed her unruly tongue. "Nevertheless, even if it was only the kindest of hospitality you intended to offer me, I believe I will not trouble you. Pray have my horse brought 'round at once."

"For the first time I can see you might do very well for Kintyre. That's quite in his style. It's just so he speaks to the uncivilized and slow-witted fools he finds himself surrounded with here, as if he had not a drop of anything so much to be despised as Scots blood in his own veins. But you'd be fainting long before you reached Kintyre House. Besides, I owe you something for teasing you overlong. You will find that even a thief has some rudimentary knowledge of hospitality. Lachlan has brought you some tea, and though he's an ugly enough ruffian and a thief as well, you'll find he's not a bad cook. This was my sister's bedchamber, so I don't doubt there's something here you can change into while your skirts are drying, and then I'll be back to bind up that ankle. After that, you are free to go when you will."

"Sister?" she repeated foolishly, finding the notion hard

to reconcile with all that she knew of him. "You have a sister?"

He grinned knowingly. "Oh, aye. Two of them, if that reassures you. You'll find even rogues and highwaymen have families like everyone else. Did you imagine we sprang straight from the devil's horns, like Aphrodite from the head of Zeus?"

She was becoming resigned to being thrown from emotion to emotion in this infuriating man's company. Certainly he admitted openly and cheerfully to being a highwayman, and had threatened her with the direst of fates. Even more certainly, she should refuse to remain in such a den of iniquity.

But it was true that the tea smelled delicious and she was wet and cold and her ankle still throbbed painfully. And for some absurd reason the mere existence of sisters reassured her, however foolishly. Besides, the thought of dry clothes was becoming irresistible, and despite her bravado, she had no real desire to present herself at Kintyre House in her present bedraggled state and have to explain to her host what had happened to her.

As if taking her acquiescence for granted, Rory had gone to rummage in a chest against one wall, and now emerged, even more incongruously, with an armful of glowing green velvet. "Aye, this should suit you," he said, looking her over with far too bold and knowing an eye. "I regret we've no maids here at Duntroon, but Lachlan has a surprisingly fair hand with an iron. He'll return for your wet skirts and do what he can to dry them. Unless you'd like me to stay and help with your laces? You'll find I make a decent enough lady's maid myself, when I've a mind to."

When she didn't dignify that with an answer, he grinned, and in another moment they had both gone, shutting the door behind them. Gillian was left with the rich velvet spilling on the bed beside her and a pot of tea gently steaming on a nearby table, as if that frightening scene had never taken place and she had not been terrified for her life and virtue.

* * *

Even so, it took her a good while to calm herself, and she gave utterance to a number of choice words culled from her grandfather's vocabulary before her first hot fury was expended. While reluctantly prepared to acknowledge that she might have been, at least in part, in some way to blame for the scene, she still was determined not to let her tormentor off too lightly, and had she not been shivering with cold by then, she might well have refused to change. The man called Rory was far too free with his orders for her liking, and it was time someone taught him a lesson.

Of course the trouble with that was that she was the only one likely to suffer from such a lesson. After a short, sharp struggle with her conscience, she gratefully stripped off her sodden habit, and huddled into the rich velvet.

It turned out to be a dressing gown that was as warm as it was improper. It looked far more like a garment for a light-o'-love than a sister, and Gillian did not doubt that the infuriating rogue downstairs had infinite experience with the type of woman who would wear such a gown.

She should doubtless have been shocked by such a garment, but she was ruefully aware of a certain guilty pleasure in it. She herself owned nothing so impractical, and she could not help wondering if Kintyre would enjoy seeing her in something similar after they were wed.

But, if she were honest, it was not the thought of Kintyre seeing her in it that had the blood rushing suddenly to her cheeks and which did as much as the fire to banish the last of her chill.

She caught sight of her reflection just then in a mirror across the room, and had to look twice to recognize herself. Her cheeks were still flushed, her hair, usually worn smooth, had been tossed by the sea-laden air into a riot of curls about her face, and her eyes seemed to glitter mysteriously between her lashes. The emerald velvet gleamed dully in the firelight, and seemed to suit the creature she saw in the mirror, and none of it had anything to do with the sober and respectable Miss Gillian Thorncliff.

She turned away from her image quickly, not liking what

it revealed about her, and reflecting that it was just as well her annoying host could not see her now. Instead she sipped gratefully at the strong tea, as unsettled in mind and spirit as she could ever remember being.

She was almost grateful when Lachlan returned to carry away her sodden habit, promising to set it before the kitchen fire. He looked at her oddly, but made no comment at her transformation, and she weakly handed her habit over to him, wondering as she did so if she were indeed a fool to give up her clothes so meekly.

But it seemed she was already in too deep to turn back, and now that she was so deliciously warm she shuddered at the thought of donning her soaking habit once more. Besides, she was far too comfortable to want to stir for the moment. The long ride and the sea air would seem to have made her sleepy, and it was all she could do to prop her eyes open.

It didn't help that the bed was proving extremely comfortable. After another sharp struggle with herself, she lay back on it, just for a moment. She had never met a man like Rory before and couldn't begin to understand him. He boasted of being a thief and a rogue, had played an unforgivable jest upon her, and was altogether despicable. Any sensible woman would not know a moment's safety in his disturbing presence.

She absently pulled a pillow under her head, and nestled her cheek into it. And yet, if she were honest, for some reason there had existed between them from the first one of those indefinable tugs of liking, or perhaps recognition, that now and then sprang up between two people and had no rational explanation. Even when he had robbed them she had been aware of an odd sympathy for him, masked and heavily muffled though he had been, which had made no sense. And when her grandfather had shot him, she had been more horrified than a mere general dislike of violence could possibly explain.

Even now, though she had sworn to be revenged upon him for his humiliating jest, she found little comfort in the thought that she might all too easily do so. One word to

Kintyre and both Rory and Lachlan, and whomever else the "lads" might be that Rory had spoken of, would be arrested and sent in chains to the nearest jail, undoubtedly to be hung for their crimes.

That brought her heavy eyelids temporarily up again. He must be as well aware of that as she was. And that being the case, why on earth had he risked being recognized by bringing her here? Was he so sure of his charm? That brought a brief resurgence of her resentment. Or could it be that despite his words he had no intention of allowing her to leave once her skirts were dry?

But if so, surely he had no need for this even more elaborate jest. Her lids drifted down again on the thought as of their own accord. In fact, it was becoming more and more difficult for her to believe him a highwayman. She had naturally never known a highwayman before, but she had imagined them to be rough, surly creatures, wholly abandoned to vice.

Well, the man called Rory certainly had the look of one who had seen his share of vice, and even enjoyed a good deal of it. But he was obviously educated and of good birth; he was handsome, charming, amusing, everything that should have made him a pillar of the community. And yet he lived in this ancient and tumble-down keep, held up coaches for a living, and openly boasted of the fact.

She had to sternly resist the temptation to weave a romantic tale about him to account for such an apparent anomaly. Instead she should be roundly condemning him, and reminding herself that she had no proof at all that she was not still in danger of losing her virtue or her life, or perhaps both.

Yes, that was better. He was a rogue and a thief and a liar, and obviously without an ounce of shame. To see him hang should be the ambition of every civic-minded person.

And yet, she drifted to sleep wondering what it would feel like to live a life above the law and the shackles of society. Her own life had been so hedged 'round by conventions and the limitations of her sex from the moment of her birth that she could not really even imagine it.

And when she dreamt it was that he was holding up Kintyre's coach, not her grandfather's. But this time it was not gold he was after. It was her he laughingly snatched from beneath Kintyre's very nose, to carry off across his saddle-bow in the best fairy-tale tradition.

Oddly enough, in her dream she was aware of many emotions. But none of them had anything to do with fear.

Chapter 8

WHEN Gillian woke, she was still caught in the web of her dream. Her unconscious mind seemed reluctant to let it go, and for a moment or two she drowsed on, with no remembrance of where she was or of all that had happened.

Then a voice said lazily, "It must have been an uncommonly pleasant dream, lass. I'm sorry I woke you."

The pleasant drowsiness fled and she came bolt upright. At the sight of him leaning against the doorjamb as if he had all the time in the world and every right to be there, memory of her dream sent the hot blood to her cheeks.

"I did knock," he went on in amusement. "But you were so deeply asleep you didn't hear me. Either you've a clear conscience, or I frightened you less than you'd have me believe."

Then he simply stared at her, and the blatant admiration in his cool gray eyes and the amused knowledge that quirked his mouth had her cheeks burning even hotter. She became confusingly aware that in that very improper robe, and still warm and tousled from sleep, she must present a very different picture from the practical and poised woman she showed the world.

She did her best to gather the scattered mantle of her dignity about her, fearing it was a hopeless effort by then. "What do you want?" she demanded.

"Lachlan says your habit is dry—though I'm loath to see you put off what you're wearing for so practical a garment," he admitted. "But then mayhap you don't realize that the fire glints off the red of your hair and the velvet brings out the green of your eyes in a way that makes me forget all my good intentions."

Her heart leapt in her breast in an annoying fashion—but again, it was not with fright. It was ridiculous, and she should clearly put a speedy end to so dangerous a scene. But all she could find to say, and that shakily, was, "Don't be absurd. My hair is not red."

"Not a blatant red, I'll agree, but you'll admit, I hope, that we Scots have some small experience in the matter. And you've no need to feel any shame to admit it, for we've no unnatural prejudice against the color here. It denotes temper and spirit, and we've admiration for both of those qualities in man or woman. My own name means 'red-haired one' in Gaelic, though I fear my parents were overly optimistic when they christened me. I grew up blackbrowed and sinful with it, no doubt to their acute disappointment."

He shifted his wide shoulders from the doorway and came toward the bed and she drew a deep breath for some reason. But all he said, prosaically enough, was, "And now I have come to bind up that ankle. We've no women at Duntroon, as I said, but I trust you will find me a deft enough nurse. In my line of work I've necessarily some experience in such matters."

"Yes, I would imagine that you must have." Her voice was ironic, though she had to clear her throat first to speak at all. "Who tended your shoulder, by the way? It would seem to have healed speedily enough."

He grinned. "Oh, aye. For all his courage, I'm glad to say your grandfather's aim was lamentably poor. The ball did no more than graze me."

"And the next time?" she inquired steadily. "When you hold up someone who's a better shot?"

After a moment, he shrugged. "I'll be dead, and no great loss to the world, as I think you'll readily admit. It will save the government the cost of hanging me. As for my shoulder, Lachlan dressed it for me, but I doubt you'd prefer his ministrations to mine. He's a rough nurse with but scant gentleness or sympathy."

She wanted to refuse to have him wrap her ankle, but since he had already once tossed up her petticoats most indecorously, and carried her bodily up the stairs, it seemed a little late for a show of modesty. Besides, she knew her objections had little to do with modesty. And so she endured his inspection of her swollen ankle and its subsequent tight wrapping.

Again, for all his mockery, he showed unexpected gentleness. In fact, to his credit he behaved throughout as impersonally as if he had indeed been a doctor, or the aging Lachlan.

But for all the pain he was inevitably causing, her mind was not on her ankle. She asked after a moment, almost against her will, "And are you really so indifferent to your own death, or was that mere boasting?"

The quick laughter sprang to his eyes again, though he kept them on his work. For some reason she again had to almost physically resist the temptation to put out a hand and touch his crisp black hair. "You've a lowering way of deflating a man's ego, I fear. But then we all must die sometime. All of life's a risk—as you have no doubt recently discovered for yourself, Miss Gillian Thorncliff."

When she found no ready answer to that, he deftly completed his task, whistling the same cheerful tune under his breath she had heard before. "It seems unlikely anything is broken," he said at last, rising to regard her with his knowing gray eyes. "With any luck you'll be able to walk on it by the end of the week."

"I . . . thank you."

He heard the stiffness in her voice and was amused by it. "Now I am instructed to say that Lachlan has dinner laid below." He once more gave her a very creditable bow, as he had when he'd held them up. "Will you do me the great honor, Mistress Thorncliff, of dining with me?"

That made her sit up more sharply. "Dinner? Good God, what time is it? How long was I asleep?" She saw now that the shadows had indeed lengthened across the pleasant chamber and that it was much later than she had realized.

"It's close on five. But it will be light for hours yet, and it would be a shame to disappoint Lachlan. He's been all aflutter in the kitchen for the last hour, for its seldom we have the opportunity of entertaining so distinguished a guest. In the usual course of events he has little enough scope for his talents in the kitchen, for we're an oafish lot and little appreciate the finer delicacies. I think he sometimes regrets the absence of women at Duntroon, though he's a confirmed misogynist otherwise."

She had to laugh, and the sound surprised her. "I somehow cannot see Lachlan in an apron whipping up a dainty dish. He seems more at home robbing coaches."

"Aye, but for all his gruff exterior, he's no' an easy man to categorize, as you will find of most Scots. In your honor he's whipping up a batch of his speciality, mushroom fritters. In fact, we are all indebted to you, for it's seldom we can coax him into taking the trouble. And you've an attractive laugh, lass. You should use it more often."

It was only then, too late, that she realized her tactical mistake. By letting his nonsense amuse her, she had subtly altered the situation between them, and abandoned at least some of her moral high ground. If nothing else, it would be increasingly difficult to remain on her dignity.

Which was no doubt exactly what he had intended. But it was true that now that the worst of her fears had been allayed—and it was with something like shock that she realized she no longer believed he meant her any real harm—she had to acknowledge that she was growing more and more curious about her unconventional host.

Even so, she knew without a shadow of a doubt that she should insist upon being taken back to Kintyre House immediately. There were more dangers than merely physical ones, and she was finding the impossible man before her all too fascinating for her own peace of mind.

But she also knew, with something like inevitability, that if she did she would regret for the rest of her life the lost opportunity to stay and eat mushroom fritters with an avowed highwayman. Put like that it sounded ridiculous, of course, but hadn't she come to Scotland in the hope of finding adventure? Surely it would be almost churlish to refuse when it was handed so patly to her.

Not that she believed for a moment that the gruff Lachlan had whipped up mushroom fritters for her delectation. That was just more of her host's nonsense. But it at least served to make her realize that she was indeed remarkably hungry.

As if sensing her weakening, Rory laughed and without warning scooped her up into his arms again. "But I've been overlong and now I fear we must hurry. Lachlan's fritters are best eaten straight from the fire, and I must admit I am fairly sharp-set myself. I've not eaten since early this morning."

She should protest this habit he had of manhandling her at his whim. But instead she allowed herself, perforce, to be carried downstairs again, the improper green velvet trailing in rich folds over her host's strong arm. And the only useful thought to emerge from the fairly breathless experience was the unpalatable realization that she was not nearly so strong-minded as she had always fondly imagined herself.

To her surprise, there were indeed mushroom fritters and they were delicious. Rory carried her not into a dining room or hall of some sort, but to a library, unexpectedly well-filled with books. It was as shabby and old-fashioned as the rest of the ancient castle, but was made unexpectedly attractive by the fire gleaming on the worn leather chairs and the bindings of the books, and by a small table set near the fire, dressed amazingly with formal candles and snowy napery. He lowered her into an ornately carved chair at one side of the table and arranged a footstool for her injured ankle before taking his place opposite.

For the first time she realized that he had changed for the occasion, and looked amazingly formal and handsome in breeches and an elegantly cut coat. But not even the customary attire of a gentleman succeeded in making him look like any man of her acquaintance. His face was too hard and brown, his shoulders too broad, and his tall figure too careless for that. It was as if he wore the clothes as a concession to her, but was far more comfortable in his worn buckskins and an open-throated shirt.

But his unexpected change of dress made her feel even more conspicuous in her improper emerald velvet. She would not have put it past him to have done it merely to put her at a further disadvantage.

As if unaware there was anything the least unusual in this unlikely tête-à-tête, he had picked up a decanter and inquired casually, "Will you have wine with me, or lemonade by yourself? And before you answer I should perhaps warn you that I take great pride in my cellars, and will take it as a personal affront if you refuse to do justice to my palate. Besides which, I shall be disappointed in you. As Scots we've no silly prejudice against women drinking strong spirits, you know. Most Scotswomen can drink their menfolk under the table, and do so frequently."

She knew she ought to demand lemonade, but it seemed a day for giving in to dangerous impulses. Besides, he had issued a direct challenge and she was in no mood to refuse. So she lifted her chin and allowed him to fill her glass with a rich ruby liquid.

Nor was she even very surprised by then to realize, when she took a sip of it, that the wine was a rich deep burgundy that her grandfather, also a considerable connoisseur, would not have scorned to serve, and that the glasses were of Venetian crystal.

Once she had begun to notice, she could not mistake other subtle touches of luxury around her. The heavy silver of the candlesticks and cutlery were old and valuable, a painting glowed above her host's dark head with the quiet colors of a master hand, and the books, she had no doubt, would turn out to be rare editions. The supper ultimately laid before them by a dour Lachlan could indeed have graced the finest table in London and was served on the most delicate of porcelain.

The man opposite her sat watching as she sipped her wine, the mockery in his face still very much in evidence.

"I congratulate you," she remarked dryly. "It would seem

that highway robbery pays better than I would have thought."

"Aye, I've no complaints. We are no' all savages in Scotland, as you see. I've as much taste for my creature comforts as the next man."

Her eyebrows went up. "I doubt your victims would be particularly comforted if they could see to what use you've put your ill-gotten gains. But then I'm sure you have developed a most convenient conscience by now."

He grinned lazily. "You are one of my victims, and yet you seem to have little difficulty in swallowing the fruits of my ill-gotten gains, as you call them. Or does hunger serve as an excuse to overcome your scruples?"

She was annoyed, for she had indeed launched absently into the delicious food set before her, and he was right that she found it difficult to appear morally superior with her mouth full of roast chicken.

He laughed at her expression. "Never mind. Doubtless you'll find, like the rest of us, that your own conscience will grow less troublesome with practice."

She swallowed the chicken with difficulty. "I do not mean to have any more practice, I thank you. My conscience has been tried enough already."

"You must have a mighty weak conscience, in that case, for your exposure to sin will be brief enough."

He was mocking her, she knew. But she could not prevent herself from asking the question that had been occupying more and more of her mind. "That I can guarantee. But why do you do it? There must surely be other ways of making a living here, poor as the country is. And you are obviously a man of birth and ability. Nor would it seem, looking about me, that you are in any particular want. However well it pays, it would not seem to be worth the risk." She could not quite keep the sarcasm out of her tone.

"Ah, but want and desire are seldom the same thing. And all of life is a risk."

She was somehow absurdly disappointed. "You do it for nothing but *greed* then?"

He shrugged. "Aye, and the excitement. You look absurdly disappointed. Did you expect some noble tale to explain my fall from grace? You are more of a romantic than I had expected."

That was undoubtedly well-deserved. "And does the excitement outweigh the danger?" she demanded scathingly. "Or is highway robbery not a crime in Scotland as it is in England?"

He grinned unabashedly. "Aye, it's a crime punishable by hanging, even here. But as you will soon discover if you remain long in Scotland, there are crimes and then there are crimes—and besides, they have to catch me first. Why? Would you enjoy seeing me dancing at the end of a rope?"

She had a sudden mental picture of the scene, and had to suppress a shudder. For all his annoying arrogance, it was not a pleasant thought. "Believe it or not, I would dislike seeing any man at the end of a rope," she said quietly.

Rory's face softened for a moment. "Aye. You've a dangerously soft heart, Miss Gillian Thorncliff. It will get you into trouble one day, I fear."

Her chin went up at that. "Don't let the notion run away with you. I've still no sympathy for common thieves."

"But then I protest the word *common*. Rieving is a fine and respected tradition in Scotland."

"Not so very respected if it is punishable by hanging."

"But then one can't have everything. And what of you? For all your stiff conscience, it would seem you know something of greed yourself."

She was taken wholly off guard. "*I* do?"

"Oh, I've no doubt you have another word for it. Most of us dislike the unvarnished truth. But I am told you possess a handsome fortune in your own right, and are your grandfather's sole heiress besides. And yet you could not resist the opportunity to add a title to your name. We all have our price, it would seem."

She was unaccountably stung. "I assure you that isn't why—" Then she was furious at herself for having allowed him to get to her, and made herself shrug. "Perhaps you're right. Women lack your freedom, I regret to say, and there are few enough avenues open to us. And what is your price? A purse and a few gold snuffboxes? I would not have thought this area would prove profitable enough to satisfy your obvious taste for expensive living."

"Oh, I've a few more quivers to my bow."

"I don't doubt it, Mr. . . ." She stopped, realizing she still did not know anything but his first name.

He raised his glass in silent mockery. "Forgive me for not presenting you with my card before I pulled you from the sea. I have no doubt in England it would have been considered most improper of me. I am Rory Kilmartin, very much at your service, Mistress Thorncliff."

He seemed determined to annoy her. "You will forgive me for doubting that last. After all, to date you have robbed me, abducted me, frightened me, and threatened me with bodily harm. It would seem you will have to enlighten me on the particular code of conduct that governs your profession."

He laughed again, in no whit touched by her sarcasm. "I dislike all codes of conduct. But you have reminded me of an oversight. These belong to you, I believe."

And to her astonishment, he calmly handed over her pearls.

Chapter 9

S HE gaped at him, then accepted the pearls weakly. "It seems I will never understand you."

He grinned. "But then you've the unfortunate English habit of jumping to conclusions. Put them on. They should go well with emerald velvet."

Instead, she tucked them in her pocket and put her chin on her fist to study him gravely. "Why did you bring me here, if it was not to hold me to ransom?" she demanded abruptly.

"I would have thought the answer to that was more than obvious. Or have you not looked into your mirror lately?"

Then, before the unexpected flattery could go to her head, he added offhandedly, "And I must confess I'd a desire to discover what sort of woman would wed the Earl of Kintyre."

So that was it. She thought it a far more truthful answer than his first, but it still stung. "I see. But would not a simple invitation have sufficed in that case?"

"Under the circumstances, I doubted it. Even before you recognized me, you should have seen your own face. You looked at me in your ridiculous wet skirts with your green eyes cool as glass and about as trusting, and made it clear you'd had your head filled with tales of the barbarity of the Scots. It seemed clear I would have to over-persuade you a trifle."

"So you decided to abduct me. And my eyes are not green, they're hazel."

"You're remarkably free of vanity, lass. Your eyes are

hazel except when you're angry, or amused. Then they glow as green as any emerald."

"And which are they now?" she demanded dangerously.

"Now they are a cool and critical hazel, befitting so obviously practical and independent a young woman," he said mockingly. "I imagine it is just the way you look when you put an impudent servant in his place—or accept a proposal of marriage from the Earl of Kintyre. Your brain clicks away behind your eyes and misses very little, did you know? I suspect you pride yourself upon making reasoned, practical decisions without allowing yourself to be too swayed by messy emotions. Isn't that right?"

She was again unaccountably stung. "And you are clearly a cultured, educated man, who robs coaches for a living, and will undoubtedly end up on the gallows. It seems to me you could use a better acquaintance with reason."

He threw back his head and laughed, a sight she was discovering appealed to her far more than it should have. "Touché. But I'm flattered by your description. And while I no doubt deserve to end up on the gallows, you will forgive me if I hope your gloomy prognostication will be delayed as long as possible."

He had an answer for everything, it seemed, but she suddenly found it was no longer a jest to her. "I am glad you find the thought so amusing."

"Oh, aye, I find most things in life amusing, I confess," he said lazily. "It makes it easier to bear. But to get back to the subject at hand, now that I have seen you for myself, I confess I find it hard to believe you really mean to wed Kintyre."

There was something in his voice that put her on the defensive immediately. "And why should I not?"

He shrugged and sat back in his chair, playing with his glass and very much at his ease. "No particular reason. I have no doubt he is a most worthy man, and will make any woman an unexceptionable husband." His voice was bland.

"I agree. And what of you? Have you dipped a toe in

such dangerous matrimonial waters? For all I know, you have ten wives tucked away somewhere."

He laughed. "You flatter me. Not even one. I'm not nearly the catch Kintyre is. Besides, we've no women at Duntroon for a reason. However bonny they start out to be, most have a distressing habit of growing less bonny in time and more of a scold. I've no wish to regret my bargain once it was too late and I was stuck with her."

She was again stung. "You are not very gallant. But doubtless you are wise, for your chosen profession would hardly seem to lend itself to domestic tranquility. I can only pity any poor woman condemned to sit and wait patiently for you to return, never knowing whether you were alive and merely out amusing yourself, or shot dead in a gutter somewhere. Or even in jail and about to be hung for your pains. It seems a thankless enough life."

He grinned. "You sound as if you had given it some thought. But then life's seldom fair to women. I have often noted it and been glad I was born a man. And it is undoubtedly the reason I have remained single. But in my defense, it is just possible that some women are less practical than you, and would manage to find at least some compensation in such a lopsided bargain. I only hope you may find as much in the bargain you're about to make for yourself."

"I have no doubt you mean something insulting. But I know Kintyre's good nature well enough by now not to doubt it," she retorted.

His fine mouth curled a little, but the amusement was still in his eyes. "Aye, we are just coming to know his good nature here in the west. But I am curious. Did you really come all this way merely to weigh all the factors before giving Kintyre an answer?"

She shrugged. "Of course. It is a strange and foreign country to me, after all, and I wished to see it before I made up my mind."

"I'd give much to know what you've concluded. But I must congratulate you. It is not many women who possess so much forethought, and refuse to be swayed by the usual feminine considerations. But then, it is a fool who buys a piece of horseflesh without, er, trying it out first. All women should follow your example."

He was again mocking her, but she chose to ignore it. "Why so I think. You are right that life is often unfair to my sex. We are even more at risk if we should—buy a bad horse, so to speak. And like you, I have no wish to find myself, too late, saddled with a commoner or one touched in the wind."

He gave another shout of laughter. "No, by God! Or a confirmed limper! And have you determined Kintyre to be sound in all his paces? For myself, I would have said he was showy enough, but not a stayer. But then perhaps I'm prejudiced."

"I have little doubt you are. I am well aware how he has been received here, for all he was born a Scot," she said stiffly.

But he was once more untouched. "Aye, we've little liking for a Scot who forgets where his loyalty lies."

"And it seems to me you are all even more prejudiced than you accuse the English of being! He can scarcely be blamed for the fact his father removed him to England when he was no more than a child. Or that he is not the wild young heir everyone seems to lament so much."

"So you've heard that story, have you? I am surprised he cared to tell it, for it's scarcely edifying—or suited for feminine ears, come to that."

"He found it necessary to make some explanation for the way he is treated here, even by his own servants, for I could scarcely have missed it. And it seems to me monstrously unfair. In fact, if you must know, it has given me an even better impression of him than I had before I came. Despite the treatment he has received here—and it seems to me the locals could learn a thing or two about loyalty!—he still means to do his best, and has the welfare of his dependents, and indeed the whole district, very much to heart. But I am sure you will sneer at that as well."

"Nay, I'll not sneer. He is fortunate to have so warm an advocate in you" was all Rory said. "And has he told you of his plans for the district?"

She was suddenly wary, for though the question seemed absent enough, she had no intention of betraying Kintyre's plans in case they were not generally known. "Only in general," she answered vaguely. "I know he is appalled by the poverty he finds here and means to do something about it. But then I also suspect, from what I have seen so far, that the average Scot is so prejudiced and stubborn he would prefer to cut off his own nose to spite his face rather than accept anything from an outsider, even help."

He grinned. "And you are clearly an expert, after only four days. But it's true enough we've a stubborn pride that often gets in our way. And knowing all this, will you be content to live here once you are married? Or will we see even less of him than we do already?"

It struck her, for some reason, that this question was the sole reason for the odd twist the conversation had taken. And that he was more interested in her answer than his casual attitude conveyed. And so she said even more offhandedly, "I've no idea. I thought we had agreed I came only to try out his paces, so to speak."

"Aye, so we had." Again he seemed neither disappointed nor in any way abashed by her snub. "But I'm curious. What made you choose a Scot—even so dubious a one as Kintyre? Surely one of your charm and fortune must have had any number of suitors at home, and though I'll grant you the title must be tempting, it would seem you have little enough love for my country."

She found herself wishing she had put an end to this absurd conversation long ago. "I do not know your country, and so am ill-qualified to judge," she said stiffly. "And as for Kintyre, I would have thought his many excellent qualities must be evident even to someone like you. I have no need to enumerate them. Any woman would be lucky to possess such a husband."

"Of course," he agreed, only one corner of his mobile mouth betraying him. "But enlighten my ignorance. Not being a lass, perhaps I have missed some of his lordship's excellent qualities. He has wealth, of course, which must weigh with any forward-looking female such as yourself."

"Of course." Despite herself her chin was tilted defiantly. "I thought you had already decided it was nothing but greed on my part."

"But then one may find some things not worth the price," he pointed out. "There is the title as well, of course. Even a Scots one is not to be sneezed at in these perilous times."

"Especially when you add to it the fact that he is responsible, kind, generous, and good-natured. Surely even you will admit those to be qualities any woman must value in a husband?"

"For myself I am reserving judgment, but I will duly note them down," Rory agreed gravely. "We see so little of him in these parts I have not yet had an opportunity of proving or disproving your claims. But if you are right, I can only wonder at your hesitation. You should clearly snap up such a paragon at once. Which reminds me, I can only assume Kintyre agreed to having his teeth inspected in this fashion?"

He was making it all sound ridiculous, but she refused to give him the satisfaction. "Of course. We are both mature, reasonable people, after all, and have no intention of being rushed into anything."

"Aye, but this is Scotland," he said mockingly. "Here you may perhaps find that such sane, sensible plans have a way of turning on you when you least expect it."

She lifted her chin. "I do not anticipate it," she said deliberately.

"But then one seldom does."

It was ridiculous, and she was more than tired of the conversation. "But you still have yet to tell me your conclusions. You said you had sought me out of curiosity. I hope your curiosity has been satisfied?"

"Aye," he said unrevealingly after a moment. "It has."

When he said no more, she was left in little doubt what his conclusions had been—or that they were exceedingly unflattering.

Abruptly he grinned. "Aren't you going to ask me what they are?"

"No, I thank you! I doubt my vanity could stand it."

"Nay, I'd not thought you a coward, whatever else you may be, Gillian Thorncliff. And it's like a lass to ask a question and then be afraid of the answer she might receive."

"I am not a coward!"

"That at least I will grant you," he told her unexpectedly. "But you've no need to worry, the truth is no' so painful as you seem to think. I was curious to discover what manner of woman would wed Kintyre, and see for myself what sort of changes we might expect if an Englishwoman took up residence amongst us."

She made a wry face, no longer certain she wished to hear his conclusions. "And?"

"I concluded Kintyre had done us more of a favor than he may know," he returned surprisingly. "You are not the disapproving Englishwoman with her nose in the air I had been expecting, finding nothing but fault with our poverty or our ways. Nor yet are you the well-bred Scotswoman who has little more understanding of the Highlander, and perhaps even less liking."

He had once more managed to catch her off her guard. "And you determined all this in a few hours' acquaintance?" she countered, a little weakly. "I must congratulate you on your insight."

"It required little enough insight, at least to satisfy my original reason for seeking you out today."

That brought her head up. "Original? Are you saying your reason changed?"

Again he smiled down into her eyes, and she found she could not look away, however much she knew she should. "You are not so modest as all that. You know it did. After all, I might have had an answer to my question within ten minutes of meeting you. I had no need to take you home and dress you in velvet or give you supper by candlelight."

She feared what her face might reveal to him, and so dropped her gaze to her glass. "No, that was merely icing on the cake. A chance to amuse yourself at my expense."

"Aye, it was amusing," he said. "But not for the reasons you imagine. And that is as much as I am going to minister to your vanity today," he added lazily, "except to say, I have of a sudden turned prognosticator, and I will predict one thing."

"And what is that?" She had, perforce, to lift her eyes, and tried to make her voice sound normal, but feared she scarcely succeeded.

"That for all your coming to look him over, you will not wed the Earl of Kintyre," he said calmly.

That brought her head up dangerously, for this was conceit of a remarkable order. "Indeed? And why is that?"

"Because, for all your practicality, you will find that one does not choose a husband as one buys a horse. I might have believed it once of you, but not after seeing you in that velvet robe."

And then, before she could find anything to reply to that, he added carelessly, "And that being the case, it is time you changed back into your sober habit, Cinderella, before I am tempted to forget all my good intentions, and you find yourself with more experience of sin than I had intended for your first taste of it. It's growing late, and it would never do to put too much of a strain on your over-rigid conscience all at once."

It was only then that Gillian realized with a guilty start how late it had grown, and that she had wholly forgotten her earlier fear, or that her grandfather and Kintyre must long since have begun to worry about her.

Chapter 10

RORY insisted upon escorting her back, despite her protests.

"Nay, we are not such barbarians as you seem to think," he told her in amusement. "Besides, surely you of all people must know by now, Mistress Thorncliff, that Scotland abounds with rogues and vagabonds, and 'tis not safe for a woman to be out alone?"

"The only rogue and vagabond I know of around here is yourself," she retorted. "And if you must needs hold up coaches for a living, I would advise you to choose a less remarkable mount."

He grinned and patted the arching neck of his roan. "Aye, but not all victims have such sharp eyes as you do. Besides, I've a special fondness for Cuileann here."

She discovered that for all her words she was not ill-pleased with his escort. "What does that mean?" She tried to pronounce the unpronounceable Gaelic word.

"Hmm? *Cuileann?*" he asked rather absent-mindedly. "It is Gaelic for holly. It was Christmas when I first got him. But if you're to marry a Scot, you must learn some of the language, lass. There are enough of Kintyre's dependents who have little or no English."

She concluded resignedly that the roan was also stolen, and that for all her vaunted sensibility, for some reason she was in constant danger of allowing herself to forget the admittedly disreputable character of her companion. It was almost as if she willfully chose to overlook it, despite all she knew to his discredit.

That was inexplicable enough, for she had always prided

herself on being clear-sighted and far too level-headed to be swayed by her unreliable emotions when it came to dealing with people. But what was even more unfathomable was that Rory seemed as determined she should be confronted by the truth at every turn.

They rode on in silence for some moments, he in seeming ease and she with her thoughts buzzing and bumbling about in her head like clumsy bees. For all his arrogance, it was clear he faced the truth more clearly than she did. All in all, it had been a most unsettling afternoon, and the sooner it was over the better.

Even so, she was unprepared for the moment when he halted once again. "You'll understand why I don't escort you all the way to the door of Kintyre House," he said in amusement, "so I'm afraid I must leave you now. You have only to follow this road for another quarter mile or so."

She halted her own horse, aware that she was unlikely ever to see this amusing rogue again. "I am not certain whether to thank you for your rescue or not. But at least I can say that it has been an experience I am unlikely to forget."

He took her offered hand and held it, grinning. "Delicately put, though I note you are careful not to say whether for good or ill. I am in something of the same boat, I confess. I have yet to determine for myself whether it will prove a blessing or a curse that I have discovered the real lass behind the reserved face you show the world."

When she remained silent, after a moment he added, "I have only one favor to ask of you."

Her heart was beating fast of a sudden, for she knew what he was going to ask. How could she not? She had been expecting it from the beginning, and yet she was still not sure she knew the answer. Or perhaps the only thing she feared was giving voice to the answer she knew had been made long ago, without her conscious volition.

But again, he succeeded in surprising her. "I would ask you not to give the lad away who saddled your horse for you. He's a mother and several brothers and sisters to support and he needs the pittance Kintyre pays him."

At last she said dryly, "And am I to ignore the fact that one of Kintyre's servants is in your pay?"

He grinned. "If it eases your conscience any, Ewan is not in my pay. You little understand the west of Scotland yet, I can see. He merely obliges me now and then out of friendship."

"I see. Is that his name? Ewan?"

"Aye." He sat his horse easily, neither pressing her nor appearing in the least anxious. But then for all Rory's talk of friendship, it was not his mother or brothers and sisters who would starve if the lad were to lose his job. She was suddenly a little angry with him. "Then if he is indeed a friend of yours, I wonder you should so risk his livelihood for your own ends?" she retorted.

"Aye, but I warned you once, I believe, that things are seldom as they appear around here. You've no way of knowing, so I cannot blame you for little understanding us. I would never ask it of him, and what he does he does freely, of his own will."

"And yet you benefit from this convenient arrangement. Could you not find full-time employment for him yourself if he were to be dismissed for your sins?"

"I could," he agreed gravely, the amusement once more lurking in the back of his eyes. "But he'd be obliged to be away from home more than he would like, and as you so rightly surmised, it suits me well enough to have him where he is."

After a moment she said ironically, "Then your conscience may rest easy. I never had any intention of betraying him."

He bowed his head in grave acknowledgment. "Thank you. I am in your debt."

She sat regarding him, wondering if she would ever understand him. He had not asked the one question she had expected, and after a moment she said unwillingly, "But what of you? It would seem to me that you are in even more danger from me than the lad Ewan."

He grinned. "Aye, you've only to tell Kintyre of the way I've ill-used you, and he will be doubly eager to see my head in a noose. If you played your cards right, you might even still be here in time to see me hung."

She was suddenly sharply angry with him, but refused to add to his already colossal vanity by letting him see it. "That is a considerable inducement for remaining, I will confess," she said coldly.

He laughed. "In that case, I am loath to disappoint you. And certainly all things are possible in this world. But some, I will admit, are more possible than others. Were you to tell Kintyre of my presence in the neighborhood, he might contrive to have me arrested in a day or two, once he could find sufficient men he trusted to accompany him, and overcame the locals' disinclination to stir themselves. But by then I would have received warning long since and would hardly have waited around for him."

She was more relieved than she liked to admit, even to herself. But it annoyed her somewhat that he had no need of her silence. For some reason she had wanted him to have to ask it of her. "By Ewan, no doubt? I do indeed begin to see the way of things here," she responded with some sarcasm. "It is little wonder you are able to continue your illicit activities in this region with such impunity. Is the whole of the peninsula in your employ?"

"Nay, lass, I've no' such grandiose notions as all that. It would be unnecessarily expensive, and I've no real need for such a network."

"Especially since I've little doubt that, among the local feminine population at least, you'd have little need to pay them."

He put back his head and laughed. "Your flatter me, I fear. I've no admiring throng, nor like to."

She could have bitten out her tongue for having uttered so revealing a thought. Nor did she believe him. There might be no women at Duntroon, but she would not believe him inexperienced in the ways of women—of all sorts and classes. It seemed to her that he was exceedingly dangerous, in fact, and likely to find it insultingly easy to fascinate any woman he chose. For some reason, the thought made her even angrier.

As if her feelings were woefully transparent to him, abruptly he reached out one gloved hand and took her chin in his fingers, forcing her willy-nilly to look at him. She was angry, and ashamed of the reason for her anger, which, absurdly, only made her angrier. But she found she could not look away from that brown face, from which all hint of amusement had unexpectedly fled.

"Nay, lass," he said almost gently. "If you wish for me to beg for your silence, I will. But I've no need of it."

"You've made that more than plain!" she retorted, stung once again into unwise speech.

He smiled. "But not for the reason you are imagining. I've no wish to overburden so innocent a conscience. But why do you think I placed my safety and that of my men in the hands of a foolish prating woman?"

"But then you have already said you are in little enough danger! You would contrive to disappear long before you could be arrested." She no longer cared that she undoubtedly revealed far too much in the petty words.

His smile grew, but his fingers tightened on her chin. "Aye, but it would be more of an inconvenience than you know to be obliged to do so. And this is a missish game I had not expected of you. Do you wish me to admit that my future lies in your hands?"

Shamed and sickened by her spurt of jealousy—for she could find no other name for it—she at last managed to look away. "No," she said quietly at last. "But you may rest easy. I suspect you know I never had any intention of telling either Kintyre or my grandfather about this meeting."

She could not see his face, but there was a little silence. "I had not expected you to make me a present of the information so easily," he said after a moment. "Most women would have teased and threatened and tried to barter for such a promise. I will admit you have once more succeeded in surprising me."

She doubted that, for she feared she was being humiliatingly predictable. But she said merely, "Then it will be worth it. I somehow doubt many things manage to surprise you—especially in women."

He was once more amused. "They are the most inexplicable of all."

She dared finally to look at him again. "And I think you know us very well indeed," she retorted. "I suspect you knew that if you had asked for my promise, I doubt I would have given it. And I think it is long since time I took my leave of you. For the sake of my conscience, if nothing else, it is better that we not meet again."

He grinned. "Ah, but then I warned you all of life is a risk, Mistress Thorncliff. And this is a sma' enough place, in all truth. If you should ever have need of me, you have only to send word through Ewan."

She frowned. "And why should I have need of you?"

"I've no notion. But then life is full of surprises, as I've already noted. And if you should ever feel the need just for companionship, you have only to put yourself to the trouble of riding out again, unescorted."

She knew she was tempted, for he had shown her a side of life she had never dreamed existed. But she shook her head quickly. "Blinking once at your illegalities is one thing, but don't run away with the notion that I approve of anything you do," she said truthfully. "I will keep silent about today, for my own sake as well as yours. But I cannot pledge the same if we should meet again. I am, after all, supposed to be a sensible, law-abiding Englishwoman."

He did not protest, but instead gave her a mocking salute. "As you wish. Though I suspect you do yourself an injustice in so sober and dull a description."

"No. I suspect I have not been myself today. I am far more sober and dull a creature than you seem to believe. And though I will confess today has been unexpectedly— entertaining, if nothing else, I will be glad enough to regain my familiar self again."

But when he shrugged and turned his horse away, she could not help a small stab of regret that he could so easily accept her verdict. But then what had she expected? She was no doubt but one of a succession of lasses, as he called them, that he had trifled away an afternoon in teasing and provoking. And that being the case, she was indeed more capable of foolish delusions than she had ever suspected herself of being. If she weren't careful, much more acquaintance with the annoying and provoking Rory Kilmartin might upset all her careful plans and change her life in ways that she was by no means prepared for or willing to have happen.

Even so, she was grateful that her sprained ankle would keep her indoors for at least a week, and she would thus be spared all temptation.

It did not help that when she at last reached Kintyre House, tired and bedraggled, it was to find Kintyre on the point of setting out in search of her, with a small party gathered to help hunt for the foolish Sassenach who had managed to get herself lost in broad daylight on her first day out, to the no doubt annoying inconvenience of Earl and servants alike.

They all watched her ignominious return, not with the obvious relief to be found in Kintyre's eyes, but with unmistakable appreciation, making her feel exactly like a child caught out in some misdeed and about to be publicly scolded.

Besides, it was annoyingly near to the truth. Her guilty knowledge burned as if blazoned on her forehead, and it merely added to her indignation to discover that one of the search party proved to be the youth Ewan, who had every reason to know where she had spent the afternoon. But at least he had the grace to keep his eyes discreetly lowered— though even he could not prevent a slight touch of amusement, and no doubt scorn,— at her feeble excuses.

But to his credit, Kintyre seemed merely relieved at her return. He immediately dismissed the servants, and listened to her halting tale, of having missed the way and dismounting to slake her thirst at a small stream, where she twisted her ankle and had been helped by a kind woman at a bothy nearby, with more patience than she herself felt the story merited. He even failed to scold her for having foolishly ridden out unescorted, and indeed seemed inclined to blame himself for her mishap. Had he but known it, he could hardly have hit upon a better way to add to the guilt she was already feeling.

He insisted himself upon carrying her back to the house, where her story had to be repeated before a far more skeptical Sir Giles. Her grandfather, no mincer of words, read her a sharp lecture on the folly of worrying everyone and setting the household about its ears; but Gillian suspected he had been little worried himself. In fact, he confessed afterward that he had slept through most of it, and only learned of her disappearance a bare half hour ago.

Gillian was amused, but it was Kintyre's attitude that was making her feel bad. She would far have preferred a scold from him. "I am merely glad you are safe," he told her simply, pressing her hand. "Indeed, I blame myself for having driven you to risk your safety. If I had put aside my business and dedicated myself to entertaining you as I should have, none of this might have happened, and you would have been spared what I can't help but think was a most unpleasant afternoon. I only hope it may not have given you a distaste for the whole district."

"My dear James," she said with deliberate lightness, "I unwisely went out without an escort, and have no one to blame but myself for my mishap. At any rate, my dignity is far more damaged than my ankle, which will heal itself within a day or two. Pray don't make me feel any worse than I already do."

But it seemed his was not a disposition to let it go so easily. "It is like you to say so, my dear, but I feel myself very much to blame—especially after so frightening an incident earlier. I am beginning to think Scotland a most dangerous place for you."

"What earlier inciden—oh! You mean the holdup," she said, feeling foolish. "The two are hardly comparable. Anyway, I assure you I had already forgotten it."

"I fear my memory is not so easily regulated, for I have certainly not forgotten it. And now to have this happen on top of it. I naturally do not mean to scold you—indeed, it is not my right, even if I were inclined to do so, which I assure you I'm not. But I fear I must request you not to ride out again alone. As you have discovered, this is not England, and indeed anything might happen."

That at least was more true than he perhaps guessed. But she discovered she was growing a little tired of the subject—prompted, no doubt, by her guilty conscience. "You are making far too much of a trifling incident for which I am wholly to blame. Pray let us drop the subject."

Sir Giles, having vented his spleen, had now settled back with a paper before the fire and lost interest in the whole. "I agree!" he said testily. "She's returned, more or less safe and sound, and has no doubt paid the price of her own folly with a twisted ankle. If *I* am not upset, you've no reason to be. Besides, I learned long ago that she does exactly what she pleases, and seldom comes to any harm."

For once Kintyre looked momentarily annoyed, but quickly covered it. "That may be true in England, sir, but we unfortunately are not in England now. Besides, she has come to harm on this occasion. Which reminds me, I must make it my business to seek out this woman you speak of and reward her suitably. I have every reason to be extremely grateful to her, and indeed I am delighted to discover she treated you with kindness. As you know, it might well have been otherwise, but you give me reason to hope that I am at last making myself accepted and trusted."

That was an unexpected danger, and indeed merely added to her guilt. Gillian said quickly, "There is no need. I had my purse with me, but she would take no reward from me. And indeed, I was so turned around I suspect I would be hard put to describe the location to you. But she certainly spoke respectfully enough of you. I think you may have exaggerated the distrust you think you find here, for I saw no example of it."

He looked relieved, but said in some surprise, "She spoke English, then?"

Gillian was annoyed at her slip. Rory had every right to mistrust her, for it seemed she was but a poor conspirator. "No. That is, she spoke some. If you must know, I was in too much pain when my boot was being cut off to pay much attention. But we somehow managed to make ourselves understood."

She was grateful when he said no more, and insisted upon carrying her upstairs. But Gillian was belatedly discovering that she knew Kintyre less well than she had thought. His manner remained polite and solicitous, but she had no idea what he was really thinking. Her own guilty conscience made her fear he suspected more than he was revealing, but she told herself that was ridiculous. He had no reason to suspect her story, and indeed gave every indication of believing it implicitly.

But she decided it was perhaps time she dedicated herself to what she had come for, and set about discovering what lay behind her host's calm face and habitual good manners. It seemed that after a week spent almost constantly in his company, she knew very little about him.

And it might serve to take her mind off a far more difficult and inexplicable a character, which was all to the good.

Chapter 11

KINTYRE insisted, despite Gillian's objections, upon sending for a doctor to examine her injured ankle. When she protested that it was but a slight sprain and she had no need or desire to have a doctor brought all that way merely to tell her that, Kintyre said with one of his rare smiles, "No, no, my mind is made up. Humor me, if you will. I wish McTavish to reassure me there will be no lasting harm—for which I would never forgive myself, if there were. He is scarcely up to the standards of a fashionable London doctor, I fear, but I believe him to be a sound enough man."

Gillian found herself wishing that for all his touching concern, Kintyre had taken the matter a little more lightly. She had been foolish and suffered the consequences, and that should have been the end of it. For the first time it also occurred to her that though she had found his attentiveness and consideration during her stay pleasant, on the whole, if he were to wrap her in cotton wool all their married lives, she would soon be tearing her hair.

But then, perhaps she was only unfairly comparing him to a certain careless highwayman who had mocked her for her folly and showed not the slightest inclination to place her on a glass shelf or acknowledge her dignity at all. Why that should be so appealing to her in the face of Kintyre's quiet kindliness, was more than she could explain, and showed a sadly unstable character, she feared. But the more Kintyre fussed, the more she had to bite her tongue to keep from losing her temper with him.

Nor was she prepared to give him her promise that she

would not go out riding again without an escort. She was sorry for the worry she had caused him, but whether or not she married him she had no intention of giving up so much of her independence. And it seemed to her wise to settle the issue once and for all.

So, when he gently raised the question again, saying with a smile, "Remember, I hope soon to have the right to consider your safety and happiness very much my concern," she thought it best to be honest with him.

"My dear sir, if you must know, I would far prefer that you were to scold me or even take a stick to me, both of which I fully deserve! But as to giving you such a promise, I might be tempted out of contrition now, knowing I had unnecessarily worried you. But I fear it is one I could not keep. You must know I am of an independent nature that little likes either being checked or even gently guided. There! I have admitted the worst. It is just as well you know that of me before matters progress any further between us. Now, pray, pray, make no more of it! I fear that is another fault of mine, that I can never bear to have my follies continuously exclaimed over. You see how frank I am being with you? It is out of necessity, perhaps, having exposed myself so grievously, but I hope you will admire me for my candor."

"On the contrary, I hold it very much a virtue," Kintyre said in his grave, warm way. "And I will say no more, if you wish. Clearly, I must see to your safety by putting myself at your disposal from now on. I only wish all duties were so pleasant. I am so seldom here, that there is inevitably a great deal to attend to when I am. And I won't attempt to conceal from you that I am still anxious, just at present, to prove myself to the locals. But I will be glad enough for an excuse to put off such tedious business while you are here. And I can only think you must have been very bored indeed in my absence to venture out so far on your own. I hope the somewhat . . . uncomfortable atmosphere within the house did not drive you away?"

These were, on several counts, even more dangerous waters. She had felt the need to escape the atmosphere of the house, but it was something she had no desire to confess to him. He was concerned enough about his reception there—and if Rory Kilmartin were to be believed, with good reason. She had no desire to add any more to his worries.

But in addition, this would clearly have been the time to mention her afternoon's adventures if she were going to. She could even have done so lightly, dismissively, in a way that would not have made Kintyre suspicious. But she remained silent, partly out of a wish not to appear even more foolish than she did already, and partly out of a reluctance that even she could not name. The man called Rory Kilmartin was a rogue and a thief, but he had amused her, and however guilty Kintyre might make her feel with his genuine concern and generosity, she did not wish to see Rory in jail or dangling at the end of a rope. It might be the product of an inconsistent and undoubtedly feminine logic, but there it was, and she did not even try to talk herself out of it.

She had endured the ministrations of the taciturn Scots doctor, who bound up her ankle for her with a certain dryness as if he thought her behavior no more than to be expected of a foolish female, and an Englishwoman at that. He prescribed a week of absolute bedrest.

She determinedly dismissed a week's bedrest for no more than a sprained ankle, but she thought it was just as well she would be tied by the heels for some appreciable time, and thus unable to ride. Not betraying the man was one thing, courting disaster by meeting him again was quite another. But she had to admit the temptation was strong. He had frightened and infuriated and provoked her, but for whatever reason the tug of liking between them could not be denied, and as the tedious days passed, seemed only to grow stronger.

Nor did it help that the weather had decided to turn glorious after almost two solid weeks of rain, while she was tied to her chair and unable to go out.

She came downstairs again in two days' time, with the aid of a cane and her grandfather's arm. And true to his word, Kintyre abandoned whatever business he might have had and devoted himself to her entertainment.

But though she continued to like him very well and respect his plans for the neighborhood, for some reason she came no nearer to making her mind up about whether to marry him or not.

Her grandfather was right that it was inconsistent and unlike her to be so wishy-washy. Nor could she imagine what else she could be looking for. Kintyre had shown himself in every way a worthy, even a generous man. His tolerance in the face of her folly, and his tendency to place the blame on himself for neglecting her rather than her own folly in riding out alone, showed uncommon restraint, to put it no higher. She knew very well that the average male's reaction to a crisis was exactly like her grandfather's: to first resent being made to worry, and then, after the reason for concern was over, to shift the blame as quickly as possible to the cause of the worry itself.

By that measure, Kintyre had consistently shown himself to possess, to a large degree, the qualities that any woman of sense would desire in a husband. If he had proved himself a touch overprotective, she acknowledged that most women would find that a virtue, not a fault. And she was honest enough to realize that it was perhaps no more than her guilty conscience that made her reject his concern now, rather than any innate dislike of being made to feel coddled and cared for.

Why, then, did she still hesitate? She was not in love with him, it was true. But he did not seem to require such an emotion in his prospective bride, and it seemed more than likely that a strong liking was a better basis for a marriage than that more elusive and transitory emotion would ever be. Besides, such liking might well turn to love in time.

And yet she somehow doubted it. For all his kindness, there was a lack of openness about Kintyre that she was only just coming to realize. He spoke frankly of his position and his hopes, he paid her pleasant compliments and neither talked down to her nor seemed to despise her intelligence and independence. But she seldom had the impression of knowing what he was thinking, or reading his deepest feelings. She was coming to know what he liked and disliked, what he ate for breakfast, and how he preferred his tea—surely all important details to know about a man one was considering spending one's life with. But she knew little of his hopes and dreams, his fears and insecurities, whatever made up the real man beneath the polite mask.

She resolutely dismissed the notion that her present hesitation sprang from her unexpected acquaintance with one who, for all his mystery and unpredictability, took little trouble to disguise what he was thinking or feeling. Compared with Rory Kilmartin, Kintyre was a pale glass whose smooth silver surface reflected only oneself and never allowed others to get beneath the surface at all.

But that was an unfair comparison, no doubt. However likable a rogue Rory Kilmartin was, she did not fancy herself to have fallen in love with him after one—no, two meetings, any more than she believed herself in love with Kintyre. That would be unforgivable folly indeed. Nor was she young enough or impressionable enough to imagine that a person of her rank and upbringing could ever forget the gulf that lay between herself and Rory, or that he was an outlaw and likely to come to an unfortunate and most unromantic end sooner or later. If he were not captured and hung for his crimes—which seemed painfully likely—some irate victim might one day succeed in putting a bullet in him and he would die ignominiously in a ditch somewhere.

Well, if the thought of so grim a fate for so amusing and infuriating a man could not fail to depress her, it went no further than that. Besides, it was clearly her duty as a law-abiding citizen to deplore his crimes and his obvious belief that he was outside of the law and might do as he wished. She did deplore it, even if she would do nothing that might help to bring about his inevitable downfall.

And yet, though she had come to make up her mind about Kintyre and must clearly come to some solution soon, it was not Kintyre who too-often dominated her thoughts as she lay wide awake night after night, long after the candles had been blown out and everyone else was asleep. She would not believe so likable and polished a man no more than a common thief, and she could not help speculating about his past. What had brought such an obviously educated and cultured man to such a pass? Surely some tragedy must lie at the root of it, for what else could account for such a fall from grace?

She amused herself for a time by making up improbable stories for him. He was some noble, perhaps even royal figure, brought low by perfidy or betrayal. The lending library abounded with such tales, and if they were to be believed, the world was overcrowded with wronged heroes needing only the help of some virtuous and trusting female to win back their rightful places.

But even as she indulged herself in such nonsense, she could not help but be amused by her own absurdity. There was little about Rory Kilmartin to suggest a tragic hero wronged by the world. Nor did he seem to be in want. In fact, he made no bones about enjoying the illegal fruits of his labors, and she had seldom met anyone with fewer excuses or moral justifications for what he did.

And that was perhaps why she liked him so well, in spite of herself. He did what he chose, without excuses, and thumbed his nose at the rest of the world. She knew few men who were as free, despite their birth or wealth, and she envied him that freedom.

The thought surprised her, and brought her fully awake again. She was reasonably content with her own life, wasn't she? She had, admittedly, come to Scotland seeking out some slight adventure, and she had enjoyed both her brief tastes of it, but she was well aware she was far too conventional to let it go any further than that. The life of an outcast was not for her, however appealing it might sometimes seem. The very fact that she was here, in this house, calmly considering the idea of marrying a man she did not love, should show her that. For all her complaints against the constraints of her life, she lacked the courage or even the will to ever do anything about it. Rory Kilmartin was right about her to that extent, at least. The knowledge, though undeniable, was far from pleasant.

Surprisingly it was her grandfather, not Kintyre, who began to grow impatient at her lack of decision. Sir Giles had not favored the match, if for no other reason than that it had not been his own idea, but he came scratching on her door one night, when the rest of the household had long since gone to sleep.

She knew he required very little sleep at his age, and so was scarcely surprised to see him stick his head 'round the door, already in his dressing gown and with his white hair ruffled. "Hmmph!" he said, "so you weren't asleep. Fool of a doctor said you were wholly knocked up, but he don't know you. Light some candles, girl! Light some candles. I'm coming in and I can't see in the dark."

She did so in amusement, wondering if he had come to ask the sharp questions about her adventure that Kintyre had failed to. He had seemed to have lost interest in it, especially in the face of Kintyre's continued concern, but he knew her very well, and might have his own suspicions.

As if to bear out her fears, he said now, abruptly, "Well, missy, and what have you to say for yourself?"

"S-say?" She tried to pull herself together, for fear he would indeed suspect something of the truth, at least. "Why nothing. What should I say, except that I am sorry to have put everyone to so much worry."

"I'm not talking of that," Sir Giles retorted impatiently. "Lord, I've better sense than to fret about what mischief you might get up to. Known you all of your life, haven't I? The question is, when are you going to stop shilly-shallying around and give the man a straight answer?"

"Man?" She was wholly taken aback. "You mean Kintyre? I thought you didn't want me to marry him."

"I don't," he said with grim satisfaction. "But the sooner you give him an answer, the sooner we can go home."

She had always, in the past, dismissed his dislike of the match as pure insular prejudice, but now she began to wonder if it might be more than that. Recalling her own recent doubts, she asked abruptly, "Grandfather, tell me truthfully what you have against Kintyre. I really want to know."

"I've nothing against Kintyre!" he said contrarily. But he ceased his rather restless pacing, and sat down in the chair before the fire. "Except that he never puts a foot wrong, or says the wrong word. I never trust a man who's always right."

She was amused at that, coming from a man who had seldom admitted to being wrong in all his eighty-three years. "I thought it was the fact he was an uncivilized Scot you had against him? You go too fast for me, Grandfather. But never mind. What else?"

He snorted. "Nothing, if you've a taste for a husband who'll consent to be led around by your petticoat strings, miss! And if so, all I can say is I've misjudged you all these years."

"That's helpful. First he's uncivilized, then he's petti-coat-led."

"Don't be pert, miss! As for the notion you can choose a husband as you would a hat—"

"Or a horse," she put in irrepressibly.

"What's that? Don't interrupt me, my girl! It throws me off. As I was saying, the notion that you can choose a husband as you would a hat, or a horse if you prefer, is ridiculous! Mark my words, all your careful calculations will come to naught in the end. Life has a way of twisting on you when you least expect it, and of making a fool out of all of us. And so it will with you, missy, just you mark my words."

He had once more managed to surprise her, for it was curiously reminiscent of what Rory Kilmartin had said. But Gillian merely kissed her grandfather's cheek with unwonted affection. "I will make up my mind about marrying Kintyre when I'm ready to, and not before."

"Hmmph!" said her grandfather triumphantly. "You've doubts of your own or you wouldn't be hesitating."

She ignored that. "Now pray cease scolding me as if I were six years old, instead of six-and-twenty, and go to bed. You know it is very late."

"Sometimes I wish you were six again, and I could paddle some sense into you," he said bluntly. "As for sleep, you will find, if you ever reach my age—which at the moment I take leave to doubt—that sleep is an overrated commodity. Nor do I know how anyone could be expected to sleep in a country where anything might happen, and, it seems, frequently does."

"Don't talk to me of your age, for I'm convinced you'll live to be a hundred," she told him truthfully. "And whether or not I agree to marry Kintyre, you must admit there is something about this country. I'm not sorry we came."

But as she lay awake some time later, after her grandfather had at last shuffled back to his own room, she wondered if it were true. It seemed to her that ever since she had come into Scotland things were happening that were as unsettling as they were unexpected. She was not sure she would ever be the same again.

Chapter 12

IT had occurred to Gillian, given the general attitude of
Kintyre's servants, that others besides the groom Ewan
might know of Rory Kilmartin's presence in the neighborhood and were keeping silent for their own ends. Having
herself lived in a restricted community all her life she knew
how quickly gossip could travel, and given everything she
was coming to learn about the Scots, it was entirely likely
that they would not betray one of their own to an outsider
like Kintyre, whatever his crimes.

Consequently, when Mrs. MacDonald, the housekeeper,
brought up her breakfast one morning, Gillian could not resist the temptation to question her.

Mrs. MacDonald was a round, energetic woman with
slightly less of a pronounced brogue than many of the
lower servants, and seemed, by all appearances, to be an
excellent housekeeper. She had been polite enough but
scarcely warm in her manner toward Gillian; though
whether that was because the Scotswoman shared the general distrust of her employer or was merely regarding
Gillian in light of a prospective mistress who might usurp
her authority, it was difficult to tell.

Mrs. MacDonald set down the breakfast tray with her
usual efficiency, stopping only to inquire whether there was
anything else that might be wanted. There was certainly no
thaw in her manner, but on impulse Gillian said abruptly,
"Yes. There is something. I met a curious man the other
day when I was out riding and thought you might perhaps
be able to tell me who it was."

She knew instantly by the housekeeper's demeanor that

Mrs. MacDonald knew exactly whom she was talking of. But all the housekeeper said was "One may meet all sorts o' strange men in these parts, I'm sure, Miss."

"Yes, but he is not easily missed. A tall man with laughing eyes and an annoying habit of having his own way, despite anyone else's wishes in the matter. Do you know him?"

But the housekeeper was still not giving anything away. "Och, it's a sma' place, Miss," she said unrevealingly. "'Tis hard to hide, even if ye've a mind to. And such a man as ye describe would have more trouble than most remaining unremarked, it would seem. But the master is right that it's no' a safe place for such as you to go about alone in."

Gillian was watching her closely, trying to discover if the housekeeper approved or disapproved of Rory Kilmartin. "Do you mean because I am English, or a friend of the Earl of Kintyre's?" she asked more boldly.

The housekeeper shrugged, but showed no sign of wanting to put an end to the interview. "Either would suffice. This is no' tame England, Miss."

"Why, so I am beginning to understand. And yet, I would have said it was safe enough. The . . . the man I am speaking of has an annoying trick of appearing more dangerous than he is, I think. But in the end I found him . . . kind enough."

She knew then that the housekeeper knew the whole story of her day's adventure. But again all Mrs. MacDonald said was, with a certain dryness, "Aye, he has a way of appearing kind when it suits his purposes."

"You are saying then that I should not trust him?"

"If it comes to that, few men are to be trusted where a lass is concerned," said Mrs. MacDonald with a certain cynicism. "It seems to me a woman must decide that for herself."

"Yes, I would agree with you." Gillian was of a sudden engrossed in pleating the counterpane between her fingers and no longer wished to meet the housekeeper's too shrewd eyes. "You do know him, then?"

Mrs. MacDonald seemed to decide to drop the game,

whatever it had been. "Aye, I've known him a' his life, though that's little enough to boast of, when all's said and done," she said more directly. "May I ask if ye told the master of this meeting?"

Gillian looked up quickly. There was a silent message passed between them then that she had not intended, but would not withdraw. "No," she said softly. "So . . . casual a meeting seemed of little moment. But I confess I am curious about him. In fact, I would give a good deal to know how he arrived at his present way of life."

She thought there was a certain relief in the housekeeper's face, though again it was hard to tell. "Who can say how any o' us come to the life we lead?" she asked with a shrug. "The good Lord works in mysterious ways, I'm sure."

It was like pulling teeth trying to get any information out of her. But then it had been the same with the man Rory Kilmartin. Gillian wondered if all Scots were naturally perverse. She tried again. "And yet surely you must have some idea, if, as you say, you have known him all his life."

"Aye, since he was a bairn," conceded Mrs. MacDonald at last. "I won't say I made a career o' watching him grow up, but it was only natural I should see a good deal o' him, seeing as how he was a friend of the young master's. A'most inseparable, they were—and both a rare handfu', even then."

Gillian was staggered, for she somehow had not expected that, though she saw now she should have. "Of the young master's?" she repeated quickly. "You mean the son of the old earl? He didn't tell me that."

"Aye, he's no' like to boast o' it," said the housekeeper dryly. "And as things turned out, it's like to be more a handicap than a blessing to him now, for all they were like brothers. But that's the way o' the world, and we've a new master now, as ye have every reason to know, Miss."

Gillian let that pass. "They were like brothers," she repeated slowly. "Good God, that is the one thing I never . . . but of course! It explains everything. Mrs. MacDonald, I've never heard the whole story. Would you tell it to me? I can't tell you why it's important to me, but it is. I would like to know the truth of what happened."

Mrs. MacDonald shrugged again, but fortunately asked no awkward questions. "Och, though there's little comfort in the telling, and that's a fact. Terrible popular around here, was the young laird."

"I had heard he was wild."

"Wild enough, but it's seldom that's to be held against a man, at least in the Highlands, miss. His ain father had been wild as well, and we're seldom ones to grudge a bit o' spirit in the young. Perhaps it is different in your country." She spoke as though she had little expectation that the cold English might understand so basic a thing.

"No, not so different after all," Gillian admitted. "Is that why the new earl is so resented?"

"We've been pleased enough wi' him, if it comes to that. He seems a kind enough man, and we've no complaints," said the housekeeper dismissingly. "It's hardly our place if we did, but since young Master's dead, it's all one to us."

Gillian saw in those few dismissing words more than perhaps the housekeeper intended. Poor Kintyre. It seemed clear he was resented by his new dependents precisely because he was a good and reasonable master, and not a hot-blooded and highly romantic young Highlander. They might find themselves more prosperous because of him, but it was perhaps human nature to prefer the romance over the staid reality.

And, after all, wasn't she guilty of almost the same thing?

But it was not the moment for such thoughts and she quickly returned her attention to the matter at hand. "You said Rory Kilmartin had been like a brother to the young master. Was he involved as well in the . . . the events that led to the tragedy?"

Mrs. MacDonald seemed to have abandoned a good part of her reserve by then, and seemed willing enough to recount the tale, though it proved a familiar enough story in the end. The young heir, Master Alexander as Mrs. Mac-Donald called him, had always been inclined to wildness,

as his father and his grandfather had been before him, back
to the first laird of Kintyre, a thousand years ago. The late
earl and the young Master had had dunamany arguments
over it, for they were both hotheaded and quick enough to
temper. Fair shouted each other down, often enough, and a
miracle it hadn't come to blows, for the old earl had remained a strong and braw man, praise the Lord, almost
until his death.

And it was true enough that for all their brashing, they
had been fond enough of one another. Too alike they were,
when all was said and done, and that had been at the root of
their troubles.

Rory Kilmartin had more or less grown up with the
young Master, and been his constant companion, though
there were many, the late earl included, who did not believe
the friendship a fortunate one. Both were high-spirited and
unbroken to bridle, which was perhaps scarcely surprising
since young Kilmartin was a distant though poor connec-
tion of the family, and had already come into his modest estate, which he was even then in a fair way to squandering.

The long and the short of it was that they had both gone
away to university in Edinburgh, with predictable results,
and the late earl had dispatched letter after angry letter,
threatening to cut off his heir's allowance and refusing to
pay any more of his debts. No one really expected him to
do so, however, and by all accounts the letters had had little
if any effect. The young laird had continued down the slippery path of his own choosing, and to do him justice, no
one doubted that it was precisely the path the old earl had
himself followed in his day, as rumor had it Master Alex
was quick enough to point out.

Well, things had gone on pretty much in that way, even
after the two left university. They had lingered on in Edinburgh, ignoring the earl's demands that his heir return
home, and it was perhaps little wonder they found Edinburgh more amusing than the bleak far west coast of Scotland. By all accounts, wenching and gaming had been the
order of the day, though both had been racing mad as well,
and young Alexander had squandered a fortune—won at

the dice tables so it was said—on a yacht that they used to take out in the worst of weather, the *Braw Lass* he had named her. For of course both had been at home on the sea since before they could walk. They had both been addicted to danger and excitement since they were but bairns together, and seemed to have remained inseparable even now that they had grown up.

The first word they had in the Mull of the events that were to prove so disastrous was that the young Master had gotten mixed up in some dangerous political movement, which also was perhaps predictable enough in a wild young Scot whose ancestors had spent their lives fighting against the English, down to his grandfather who had perished at Culloden. A meeting had been raided, and rather than allowing himself to be arrested, young Alexander had lost his head and fired on the soldiers. One had been killed, but the young laird, with Kilmartin's help, had managed to get away in the *Braw Lass* and flee to France, and things had never been the same again.

The old earl, crushed with shame and rage, had refused to have his son's name spoken ever again in his hearing, and had died soon after, no doubt of a broken heart.

For a time no one in the household had known what was to become of the title and the estate. The young Master was under attainder and would be hanged if he returned to Scotland, but even so, a private attempt was made to locate him, somewhere on the continent. The English crown, predictably enough, had petitioned to have the title declared empty, so that it might pass on to the nearest heir, the present earl. But before that could be completed, word had come that the young Master, the wild and tragic Alexander, was dead, killed in a squalid gaming-room brawl in Vienna. Thus had a most painful chapter been closed at last, and few cared to speak of it any longer.

"And did Rory Kilmartin remain with him abroad?" asked Gillian very softly.

"No one knows, miss. It was not until . . . afterward . . . that he returned here, at any rate. But he's hardly quick to boast of it, since that might put his ain neck in a noose. And he's never been one to risk himself unnecessarily." The last was said with a certain dryness again.

Gillian found that hard to reconcile with the man she knew, but she said merely, "Thank you. I think I begin to understand a great deal more than I did. But was Kilmartin himself never implicated in the shooting of the soldier?"

"Not that we ever heard," shrugged the housekeeper. "Nor was he one to waste his time on futile causes. I understand he was off wenching on the night in question, which was predictable, but he was able to be found by his servant in time to spirit the young Master away. He's tolerated around here for that reason, though few really approve of him. It was bad enough, but at least the old earl hadn't to see his only son and heir tried and hanged for murder and we're grateful to Kilmartin for that. But he's a bad penny, like enough, and I've heard tell of some of his doings lately. Still, it's no' likely anyone around here will turn him in, when all's said and done. And now, I've stayed too long, Miss, fashin' wi' ye, and must be about my duties. Was there anything else ye'll be wanting?"

Gillian dismissed her, having learned far more than she had expected. It certainly explained much of the reason for Kintyre's limited acceptance. She still felt that with time he would manage to win over the Scots' loyalty, but it would not be easy. He himself must know most of this, and find it frustrating to have himself always measured against a romantic youth whose death had accomplished what his living might not have been able to. Dead, he had become a legend, whereas alive the locals might quickly have tired of his wildness and extravagance.

And yet it was but another factor in the difficult decision facing her. She had said she wanted challenge and adventure, but she was no longer so sure she could face a lifetime of suspicion and resentment, as she inevitably would if she married Kintyre. It seemed the old tragedy still had the power to affect too many lives: Kintyre's, Rory's, and now even her own.

But if the truth be known, it was not of Kintyre's plight and her own forthcoming decision, nor even of the tragic young heir nor the old earl that her thoughts kept returning. It seemed to her they were by no means the principle victims of the tragedy.

Well, at least she could understand now why Rory Kilmartin led the life he did. And if she could not help but grieve a little for the wasted promise, all that bright charm and humor and loyalty to a friend squandered in a tragedy not of his own making, why then it was no one's business but her own. She knew well that even he would be the last one to thank her for it.

Chapter 13

KINTYRE, oblivious to these thoughts, carried on very much as before. He seemed to have no suspicions of her lost afternoon, and indeed, whiled away some hours that very afternoon showing her the plans for the proposed canal and explaining its details to her. Gillian was genuinely interested, and after what she had seen of the poorness of the country, very much applauded his scheme and did not hesitate to say so.

He looked pleased. "Yes, I hope it will bring a much needed prosperity to the region. I may not have grown up here, but I have fond enough emotions toward it as my birthplace, that I would like to do what I can to improve the lot of the locals—which, as you saw for yourself, is pitiful enough. I regret to say that they are, at present, merely suspicious of my schemes, but that's only to be expected, and I hope the added employment for men and generally increased revenue in the region will do much to convince them of my sincerity."

"I am sure it will," she said warmly.

He shrugged. "I wish I were so optimistic. I'm afraid my uncle was very much one of the old school. I understand the scheme was put to him some years ago, and he did not hesitate to refuse it. It seems it little mattered that his people were starving so long as things went on as he had always known them and he needn't suffer the inconvenience of a canal cut across his lands. It spoiled the hunting, you see. Well, I am English enough in my outlook to deplore such willful blindness."

"Your uncle would certainly seem to have been a most

colorful man. But why did the locals admire him so if he was such a bad landlord?"

Kintyre shrugged. "I daresay it is all tied up in the ancient clan system of the Highlands, though I confess it is something the English mind can little grasp, and I have trouble enough myself with it. He still operated under the notion that the laird, or head of the clan, stands in something like the position of a father to his people. And in his defense, he does seem to have treated them all as his children—neglecting them all equally and settling quarrels among them like some ancient potentate. It is absurd nowadays, of course, and was anachronistic even in his own time. For one thing, the idea is wholly impracticable in modern times, and few forward-thinking Scots, like Argyll, still hold with it. He pays his workers a regular wage and can hire and fire them at will. I applaud him for it, for it seems to me the clan system merely breeds dependence in these people instead of teaching them to take responsibility for themselves. It is little wonder they have been destitute for centuries, and have made nothing of themselves. The system absolutely discouraged it."

He grimaced. "Though that is another thing that is resented in me, I don't doubt. I am an outsider, and have no intention of becoming a father to them. I do hope to make them self-supporting some day, which would seem to me to be far preferable to being dependent upon the whims of anyone else, however benevolent, and by all accounts my uncle was seldom that. But I'm not at all sure they see it that way."

What he said made sense to her. "Give them time. As you say, it is a system that has worked for them for a great many years. I am sure they will see the advantages of what you are doing once they begin to benefit from it."

She could not help but admire his dedication to the same people who held him in such suspicion. A great many men might have given up out of anger or pique, but he merely seemed more determined in the face of such obstacles.

But when she said as much to him, he smiled and shook his head. "No, I will benefit as well, as you know. And I confess to possessing more ambition than can be satisfied by the possession of a threadbare Scots title. Would you object very much to finding yourself married to a politician, my dear?"

She had not considered it before, but could not deny there was an appeal in the idea. "Why, no," she said truthfully. "I think I would enjoy it."

"And I am convinced you would make an excellent political hostess. Will you be offended if I say it is one of the first things that attracted me to you? Even Argyll does not possess so charming and cultured a wife. I envision that you will prove a strong asset to me." He smiled faintly. "As witness, I have only to look at the way you have managed to win my servants over. You have aroused more interest in them already than I have been able to inspire in all these months."

She flushed a little, for some reason. "Now you are being ridiculous. If they are curious about me, why that is merely because they are wondering what sort of mistress I would make. But it seems clear you admire this Duke of Argyll very much. I will indeed look forward to meeting him."

"Yes, and I am quite certain he will approve of my choice," he said, with another of his warm looks. "I won't disguise from you that that was a consideration as well. Scotland owes a great deal to his family. The third duke, the present Argyll's grandfather, has done much to show what can be done in this country with only a little ambition and perseverance, and he has carried on the process admirably. The third duke built a model village in Inverary when he built the present castle, and has done much to establish sorely needed industry here on the coast. I merely follow his example, but I have hopes that the canal, and the exploiting of the kelp harvests and herring, will do as much to improve the lot of my dependents as he has managed to accomplish for his. And, I might add, it has made him a very rich man. When your ankle has recovered, I will take you over to see it."

"I will look forward to it."

It might have been a logical moment to press her for an

answer to his suit, and she had feared for some days that he must be growing impatient. But he did not. He merely smiled warmly at her and said no more, a discretion that did him no disservice in her eyes—especially since she seemed no nearer to knowing what answer to give him.

Once her ankle grew stronger, Kintyre drove her and her grandfather around the estate, pointing out improvements he wished to make, and took them to the site of the proposed canal. They were full and interesting days, and despite her doubts Gillian began to picture herself as a part of such ambitious plans. It would feel good to be doing such worthy work, and if she found herself no nearer to loving Kintyre, at least she was coming to respect him more and more, and that was probably worth far more in the long run.

But she was beginning to realize as well that he was graver than she liked, of a serious rather than humorous turn of mind. That was an admittedly foolish thing to base the choice of a husband on, but she herself tended to see the humor in most things, and she was not sure that so much worthy gravity would not begin to pall on her after a while.

She would not admit that her discovery had anything to do with that other Scot, who certainly could not claim gravity as a fault. For all his tragedy he had a jest for everything. She told herself firmly that that would grow tiresome as well, for one must take life seriously some time. It was all very well to find his story touching, but it had nothing to do with her, after all, and she certainly had no intention of ever seeing him again.

And yet she was unprepared for her reaction one morning when, over breakfast, Kintyre informed them matter-of-factly that he had a lead to the highwaymen who had held them up, and hoped to hear that an arrest had been made within a day or two.

Gillian looked up sharply, and had to make herself wait until she was certain her voice was steady before she inquired, "I must congratulate you. How did that come about?"

"I have had inquiries put about, but I must admit I had not hoped for much success. These people all stick together against outsiders, no matter what the crime. But I have been hearing rumors lately of a suspicious band of scoundrels living nearby. I have every reason to suspect they may be our men."

She again had to make an effort to control her voice. "But surely they would not be living here openly?"

"I told you these people all stick together. But I have developed a few sources of my own. As I said, I have hopes of hearing of the arrest of such impudent villains within the next few days."

"Hmmph!" Sir Giles put down his knife and fork. "Small good it will do us, for it's doubtful we'll see our valuables returned. Still, I daresay it will prevent them from preying on some other hapless travellers."

Gillian felt the presence of her pearls, carefully hidden in her wardrobe upstairs, as a guilty secret, and feared she must somehow betray herself. But the conversation turned then, and nothing more was said on the subject.

She had to exercise all her control to act normally and force herself to finish her breakfast, though the meal seemed to drag on interminably. She was grateful when Kintyre himself folded his napkin and rose, saying apologetically, "My dear, I'm afraid I must leave you to your own devices this morning. I must attend to a pressing matter with my gamekeeper, who informs me the poaching has increased recently. I can only wonder how it could increase any more, for none of the locals seem to pay any heed to fences and posted warnings. But still, I suppose I must attend to it. Which reminds me, sir. You may wish to take out a gun some morning. I myself scarcely have any time for hunting while I am here, but I am informed the local grouse offer particularly challenging sport."

"I might," acknowledged her grandfather grudgingly. "But there's apt to be little enough challenge if the locals have been allowed free rein, destroying all your coverts. You'd best treat it harshly now if you hope to have any game remaining. Once poaching becomes rampant only the most stringent methods will succeed in putting a stop to it. And even then it takes years to rebuild any decent game."

They chatted on for some few moments about gamekeepers (whom Sir Giles was convinced were all dishonest), the trouble with maintaining one's coverts, and the best methods to use for discouraging and trapping poachers. Gillian listened to it all impatiently, reflecting that if Kintyre himself admittedly never hunted there, it could scarcely matter if the locals poached on his preserves, especially considering how poor they all seemed to be. But then she had little doubt that was one of those masculine subjects she could never hope to understand fully. And at the moment she was merely anxious for breakfast to be over.

Kintyre lingered to inquire about her plans for the day, and to promise that tomorrow he would make up for his truancy by escorting her into Oban, if she cared to go and thought her ankle would withstand it.

"Oh, yes," she said brightly. "I shall look forward to it. In fact, I thought I would just have a quiet day today, writing letters and reading."

He looked pleased. "You relieve my mind. I fear you have been doing too much lately, and that I have selfishly allowed you to overtax your ankle by taking you around so much. I am anxious to have you see everything, naturally, but the doctor warned me it would be weak for some weeks, and you must take care not to overdo it. And tomorrow, you know, you may see much of the village from a carriage, of course, for it is scarcely large or interesting enough to require extensive walking. I fear you will find it a disappointment after English towns."

She managed to reassure him, but only by promising to spare her ankle and rest up for tomorrow's activities. She was almost dancing with impatience by then, but when he at last took his leave, and her grandfather had gone off to the library to read the Edinburgh papers, she went up to her room not to rest her ankle, as she had promised, but to change straight into her habit.

It was by then a full week since her accident, and though her ankle was still tender, and riding was probably not a wise idea, she was able to walk to the stables under her own power and request that a horse be saddled for her. It was not the groom Ewan who appeared, or she thought she might have entrusted a message with him.

But as she waited, she was ruefully aware that she was glad for the excuse to go herself. She felt a little breathless, as if she faced some danger or excitement, but that was ridiculous, of course. All she meant to do was to ride to the coast and warn Kilmartin of the danger he was in.

The ethics of what she was doing occurred to her briefly, only to be dismissed. He might be a highwayman, but she liked him too well to wish to see him at the end of a rope. Nor did she perceive her actions as being disloyal to Kintyre. It was just that she could not sit idly by and allow his trap to be sprung.

Her only fear was that she might already be too late, and so she waited in a fever of impatience for a horse to be saddled. But even as she waited, the youth Ewan came into the stableyard, carrying a bucket of water.

When he saw her, he put the water down slowly some distance from her and pulled his forelock in respect.

She was aware that the other stablelad might be within earshot, and so said impersonally, "Good day to you. I've seen you before, haven't I? Didn't you saddle my horse for me the last time?"

He inclined his head. "Aye, Mistress." His expression was carefully impassive, but to his credit he neither looked afraid of her nor revealed that he knew his future was in her hands. And in truth, he got something of his own back again, for he added a little audaciously, taking in her habit, "And will ye be riding alone again, Mistress?"

She said, still carefully. "Yes. I've no expectation of meeting with the same mishap twice. In fact, I thought to go in the same direction I rode last. I found it oddly pleasant, despite my foolish accident."

He glanced quickly at the stablelad bringing out the saddled horse for her, and then said noncommittally, "It's a fair eno' ride. But are you certain 'tis wise to risk it so soon?"

She was also very aware of the groom who had returned with her horse and was regarding her quizzically. "Perhaps not. But then I shall be more careful this time. I feel sure I am in no danger."

He vouchsafed no answer to that, but stood watching as she mounted and waited patiently to have her girths tightened and the stirrup arranged so that it would be more comfortable against her injured ankle. But she was relieved to see, even as she herself rode circumspectly out of the yard, that he had quietly disappeared. She hoped he might somehow get a message through to Kilmartin so that she would be spared going all the way to Duntroon, which further impropriety would only add to her present guilt.

Chapter 14

WHETHER or not Ewan got a message through, Gillian had gone little more than a mile or two when she was relieved to see a mounted rider ahead, calmly waiting for her.

The sun was in her eyes, but she had no difficulty in recognizing that lazily insolent figure, sitting his horse so casually, one knee thrown over the saddle as if he had all the time in the world and begrudged none of it. Her heart began to beat a little fast, but then she was annoyed at so telltale a sign, and determinedly disciplined it.

He did not trouble to come forward but sat there waiting for her to reach him. "I began to despair of you," he said by way of greeting. "Was your ankle so slow in mending, or did Kintyre forbid you to venture out alone again, after your last unfortunate adventure?"

Her chin went up at that. "Neither. Did you really imagine me so spineless as to be tamely ordered about?"

He smiled at her, and she was aware of a sudden absurd happiness. "Nay, lass," he said unexpectedly. "But I did fear your overactive conscience might prevail. I am delighted to see that it didn't. How is the ankle, by the way? I trust my wrapping did it no irreparable harm?"

Her unexpected reaction to him gave her ample warning. She knew not what magic he possessed, but it seemed he had only to smile at her and she forgot everything she knew against him and all her own previous sensible decisions. It had been foolish to come after all; and if she were wise she would deliver her message and depart as quickly as possible. Only a fool continued to flirt with danger once it had been recognized and acknowledged.

And yet she found herself saying, as if they had met innocently on a village street somewhere and were engaging in the most idle of chitchat, "It is almost wholly healed, I thank you. I can walk on it now without much pain."

"I'm glad. And even more delighted that you ventured out today. I must confess I have missed you since last I saw you, lass. Lachlan says I've been like a bear with a sore paw. But then I suspect he's been missing you as well."

Despite her obvious weakness where he was concerned, she was determined not to be taken in by his flattery. "Lachlan! He frowned the whole time I was there, and clearly disapproved of me. Don't pretend he didn't."

"Ah, but he's a surly knave, and never knows when he's well off," said Kilmartin audaciously. "I, on the other hand, am well versed in pleasing myself, and so am not so easily misled. But you have yet to tell me the end of your adventures last time. I hear you had an unexpected audience for your return."

"I have no doubt Ewan entertained you thoroughly with the tale of my humiliation. It must have amused you greatly."

"Nay, he assured me you held your chin in the air and carried it off in high fashion, so that even the few snickers were silenced."

"And I suppose he has a great admiration for me as well?" she inquired ironically. "If so, he hides it most successfully."

"Nay, lass," he said more gently. "You've earned nothing but admiration here, even if you are all but betrothed to the new earl. We're sometimes hard to fathom to an outsider, but I won't have you running away with the notion that we're all against you."

Then, before she could adjust to this, he once more threw her off-balance. "And did his lordship read you a lecture on the evils of riding out unescorted once he had you safely alone?"

"No," she said stiffly, not wanting to discuss Kintyre with him. "He was most kind."

"Aye. You've told me before of his kindness. And guilt is often a better whip than the most thundering scold. In fact, I had feared it would keep you safe indoors and out of harm's way. I was beginning to think I would have to storm the fastness of Kintyre House myself if I was ever to see you again." He spoke almost idly, watching her in a way that brought the blood abruptly to her cheeks. It was as if he had forgotten what she looked like and it was of some urgency that he reacquaint himself with every line of her features. Or he wished to be reassured that his first impression had been the correct one.

But his words inevitably reminded her of her errand. Besides, it was clearly past time to put an end to such dangerous foolishness. "I am well aware you are not serious. But it is just as well you did not come to Kintyre House to see me. I fear you would have received a somewhat warmer reception than you expected."

His gray eyes switched to sudden interest, though the amusement was never very far at the back of them. "Did you imagine I meant to ride boldly up to the door and hand in my card to the butler? Even having admitted I am more delighted for a glimpse of your disapproving face than I had expected, I'm not quite so foolhardy as that, I promise you."

"No," she retorted rather shortly. "I should have known you would have your own way of gaining access. After all, I am sure that so accomplished a thief as you might come in through any convenient window you chose."

He grinned, in no way abashed. "Aye, but I doubt I'd receive a warm welcome if I were to venture into your bedchamber one night at midnight—tempting though the idea may be. Your indoctrination into sin is still too recent for that."

"Will you be serious? I am trying to tell you that Kintyre now knows who held us up. He means to have you arrested in the next few days."

But she might have expected that his reaction would not

be any of the possible variations she had imagined. He looked neither alarmed nor angry, but merely curious. "Does he indeed? And how does he know that, I wonder?"

"Not through me, if that is what you fear. For some foolish reason I have kept my word to you. But he knows it all the same. It would seem you have not quite managed to acquire everyone's loyalty hereabouts, for someone informed him of your presence in the neighborhood."

Still he did not look alarmed. "And you have come to warn me? I'm flattered, lass. But what do you expect me to do?"

She was long past considering the tatters of her pride. "It seems more than obvious! You must get away before he can find and arrest you. You said once you had only to disappear, so you must have some plan of escape."

He still looked faintly amused, but she was grateful that at least he forebore to press her any further on a topic she had no desire to be taxed on. But all he said was, "Yes, I have a plan. Would you like to see it?"

Her warning delivered, she certainly should have turned and left him then. She had revealed herself far too much already, and risked both her reputation and her honor if she were discovered. Instead she asked ironically, "Are you sure it is wise to trust me with it?"

"Aye. I'll trust you. You have only to go a little way further with me. Besides, it would be a shame to return without your ride, now that you have come so far."

After a brief, sharp struggle with her conscience, she weakly turned to accompany him, unable to deny her curiosity. Besides, he would be gone soon enough. Surely it could not hurt to give in to temptation this one last time? But even as she asked herself the question, she was afraid she knew the answer to it all too well.

If he felt a certain triumph at her ready acquiescence, at least he had the grace to hide it. Instead he rode leisurely beside her, as if the law might not even at that moment be bent on arresting him, and they were out for nothing more than a pleasant afternoon ride.

When he showed no signs of breaking the silence, at last

she remarked a little dryly, "At least I know a great deal more about you than I did the last time we met."

He looked interested, and in no way concerned. "Do you? And which one of the many gossips at Kintyre House has been entertaining you with tales of my murky past?"

"Mrs. MacDonald."

"I'm flattered that you bothered to ask, but I would not believe everything you hear, even from her."

"I don't. But I found her honest enough, if somewhat foolishly inclined to overlook your more obvious faults. And I will confess it explains a great deal. But not why you chose to throw away your promise by stooping to become a common highwayman."

He burst out laughing. "I am even more flattered at the assumption I ever possessed any promise. And as for being a common highwayman, I thought we had dispensed with the term the last time we met. I protest I am not in the least common."

There was clearly no penetrating his colossal vanity. "At least I understand now why the locals feel they owe you a certain loyalty. And I will spare myself the lecture on your chosen profession, since it will obviously be a waste of my breath. But do you really think your late friend would have approved of what you are doing?"

"It must have been a highly colored version Mrs. Mac-Donald told you, if she left you with the impression that Alex would have balked at much of anything," he said in amusement. "But then I daresay he is still something of a hero up at the house. It is amazing how death washes one free of all faults and leaves only the pious—and usually misleading—memory behind. Alex would be as amused at that as anything, for he heard enough lectures in his lifetime to make it unlikely he would become such a hero after his death."

She knew she would have done better to ask him no more, but she could not resist saying softly, "And were you with him until he died? That must have been . . . hard for you. Mrs. MacDonald told me you'd grown up together."

He shrugged. "Aye, I was with him. I often marvel at the

tricks life can hold, for neither of us had envisioned that particular one, I'll grant you. But I've long since ceased to weep for him, if that's what you mean."

"And yet you came back here."

"It was my home, when all's said and done, and I'd had enough of foreign parts. But what a gloomy discussion this has turned out to be, when it's too fine a day to steep ourselves in melancholy."

They rode for some further distance in silence, until she was moved to demand, "How much farther is it? I hope you do not propose to abduct me again, for I should warn you I have the use of both legs this time, and have no intention of being carried off against my will."

He grinned. "I'm tempted, I'll confess. And yet a wise man never makes the mistake of repeating himself, especially with a lass. No, you'll be home in excellent time to allay Kintyre's fears, unless you are woefully accident prone and tumble into the sea again. And we are there. If you put yourself to the trouble you may see her already. Straight ahead of us."

"Her?" she queried, narrowing her eyes to scan the distance. They had ridden toward the sea, but she could see nothing but the rough coastline and the blue sea beyond. "I can see nothing. Is this some kind of a jest—Oh!" For she had caught sight of a mast, almost hidden among the cliffs. "Do you mean the boat?"

He was grinning and watched her with lazy appreciation. But he chided her at that. "I can see you are no sailor, lass. She's a ship, not a boat. A schooner to be exact, and as lovely a lass as you could hope to see. She's just back from a quick trip to France, and will be away again before dawn, so you see, you almost dallied too long playing Lady Invalid, and nearly missed her."

She looked at him straightly, knowing the answer even before she asked the question. "France? We are at war with France. How could she . . ."

He was once more amused. "You've a touching innocence, lass, but a woeful knowledge of the world." He clearly waited for her to come to the right conclusion herself.

She did, resignedly. "I might have known. You're a smuggler as well as a highwayman. There seems to be no end to your accomplishments."

"Why so I think," he said in amusement. "I must confess I usually captain her myself, but I'd some other business on shore of late, so she's made a few runs without me. Would you like to come aboard the *Braw Lass*?"

To stall, for she knew beyond doubt that she should do no such thing, she said dryly, "I do not recognize you in so conciliating a mood. I am not used to having any say in the matter where you are concerned. You have a high-handed way of forcing others against their will with scant consideration for their wishes."

He grinned. "If so, I apologize. I have no intention of forcing you against your will this morning, Miss Thorncliff. You are free to turn back and enjoy your ride in peace."

She was perversely annoyed with him again, for he had a positive genius for putting her in a bad light. Or for handling women, come to that. She had resisted his calm assumption that he had the right of ordering all to his pleasure, but now that he had given her leave to go, she was strangely loath to take it. She knew she should have repudiated the suggestion immediately. Any sensible woman would have been shocked at the idea of going aboard a smuggler's vessel.

But then any sensible woman would not have come along so meekly with a known thief and highwayman. She said weakly, still stalling, "The *Braw Lass?* Isn't that Alexander's yacht? Mrs. MacDonald told me about it."

He laughed at that. "Bless you, it's clear I shall have to educate you, lass. Aye, I named her after the other, but Alex's yacht was a plaything, though she was lovely to handle and we had some amusing times in her. My crew would not appreciate your so slighting this second lass."

It was indeed a beautiful ship, though as he said, she knew next to nothing about sailing. She wondered how he had obtained it, if it was not Alexander's yacht, and then as quickly doubted she would appreciate the answer she was likely to get if she asked. With a man like Rory Kilmartin, ignorance definitely seemed best on occasion.

As if reading her thoughts, which he seemed to do with annoying ease, he laughed, and took her compliance for granted. "Come," he said. "Lachlan will see to the horses."

She saw that the dour Scot had indeed emerged from somewhere and stood ready to take their horses. She weakly allowed Rory to lift her down, thinking disparagingly that she seemed to possess a spinelessness she had never guessed at and didn't much like. As he set her on her feet, he said, "Are you sure your ankle is fully recovered?"

"Quite sure. Good day to you, Lachlan," she offered gravely.

The other scowled at her. "Good day to you, Mistress. I'd feared his high-handed ways had given ye a sufficient distaste of us that he'd no' lure you out a second time. But then he a'ways had a rare way with the lassies."

"If you mean a habit of giving them little choice in matters, I would agree with you."

"The two of you may abuse me later to your heart's content," said Rory goodnaturedly. "Now we've little time. Though you're right. 'Tis doubtless dangerous to come aboard a smuggler's ship, I'll not deny, for so upright and law-abiding a citizen as you are."

"But then I seem to have ceased to be either upright or law-abiding since I met you," she returned truthfully, and weakly abandoned all further protests.

Chapter 15

GILLIAN might still have hesitated, however, had she realized the mode Rory would use to convey her to the ship. He eyed the boat bobbing some distance from shore, and the few feet of seawater between them, and then without hesitation picked her up bodily and strode out to toss her into the longboat.

She reflected resignedly that she should by now be used to his free and easy way of handling her. And it was true she had no real relish for wading out to the boat, as the others did. Returning bedraggled and with a ruined habit to Kintyre House once was bad enough, but she had best not do it again.

She had never been on a boat of any kind before, and even the small longboat, rowed by a pair of brawny Highlanders, was something of a thrill to her. They seemed to skim with amazing speed and lightness across the water, and long before she could have believed it possible, they had reached the ship, lying gracefully at anchor.

Up close it appeared much larger than she had imagined, and she saw with something of a shock that only a rope ladder led up to the much higher deck of the *Braw Lass* above them.

Kilmartin sensed her dismay and said, grinning, "Don't worry, lass. I'll toss you over my shoulder and carry you up. That way your modesty will be preserved."

"To the detriment of my pride. No thank you," she returned firmly. "I have no doubt I can manage on my own, if you will oblige your men to turn their eyes away."

He laughed and did so, and thus she was able to climb

the ladder by dint of tucking up her skirts and firmly closing her mind to the picture she must present below. It was somewhat alarming to find herself dangling from the side of a ship on nothing more substantial than a rope, but she supposed that were she to fall Kilmartin would catch her, and so managed to arrive on the deck of the ship at last, a little breathless to be sure, but with an absurd sense of pride at her accomplishment.

Two more sailors lifted her aboard at the top, and the next moment Kilmartin had joined them, and said warmly, "Well done, lass. I'd made sure I'd have to haul you up like a landed herring. You've a head for heights, I see."

She was again immensely and absurdly pleased by his praise, but said merely, "And have there been many lasses you've hauled aboard like a landed herring?"

"Aye, dozens. Sometimes it's a chore keeping them away. But now that you're here, you've yet to say what you think of my *Lass*. I must warn you I'm immensely proud of her and like her to be properly appreciated."

She looked around curiously, surprised to see that the few sailors she saw were all very young, and neatly dressed. They greeted Kilmartin with surprising informality, but it was easy to see they were fond of him, and when he gave a command, it seemed to be obeyed with alacrity.

He allowed her to explore at will, amused by her obvious interest and pleasure in the well-made ship. At last she said in puzzlement, "But she's beautiful. She doesn't look at all like a smuggler's ship."

"And what do you imagine a smuggler's ship looks like?" he inquired in lazy amusement.

"I don't know, of course. But I wouldn't have thought like this—sleek and well cared for and everything in perfect order. Why, you might sail anywhere in her and use her for legitimate purposes. Why don't you?"

He was even more amused. "Did you expect my ship to be filthy and in disrepair, and the crew in rags, with a skull and crossbones flying from the mast? It's obvious you've read too many romantic novels and know precious little about sailing, lass. Whatever the cargo, a ship requires discipline and order or you're inviting disaster. And as for legitimate purposes, do you see me earnestly plying back and forth with her decks filled with herring and counting my guineas?"

She considered it and realized she could not, but she was too stubborn to admit it. After a minute he went on, "Anyway, there's far more money and excitement to be found in goods that have paid no duty on either coast. And thanks to the war and the American blockade, such runs are more profitable than ever at present."

She guessed shrewdly that it was the excitement, probably even more than the money, that attracted him. Mrs. MacDonald had said he and Alexander had been addicted to danger, and it was obviously still true of the one remaining member of the twosome.

Still, she could not condone such open flouting of the laws, whatever the motive. "And what happens when you are overtaken and arrested?"

"But then it is the job of a good privateer to see that that doesn't happen," he countered.

"Privateer. Riever. You always have some romantic name for what you do, don't you?" she exclaimed impatiently. "Why don't you call it by its real name? But then smuggling and highway robbery don't sound quite so noble, do they?"

He shrugged, in no whit troubled. "I've no particular liking for harsh reality, if that's what you mean. It would seem I lack your Puritan strain, lass."

She was stung, however foolishly. "It is not Puritan to possess respect for the law. Where would we be if we all embraced your free and easy interpretation?"

"You're asking the wrong man," he said carelessly. "I've no wish to see any man—or woman—do aught against his will."

"And does that vast tolerance apply to Kintyre as well?" she demanded.

"Certainly. He is master here, and no one mistakes it, believe me."

"That's not an answer."

"It is the only one you are likely to get from me, however."

She was suddenly angry, without quite knowing the reason. "It seems to me that if you have such influence over the people here, you might use it in his behalf instead of sneering at him."

"Now when have you ever heard me sneering at him?" he inquired mildly.

"Even that was a sneer. It seems to me that he means nothing but good for all of you, but he is greeted everywhere with suspicion and dislike, merely because he is not the man you wanted."

"Aye, I have already noted him down as a great benefactor."

"There! You are doing it again. The truth is, you were closer to the mark when you claimed to hate him. And it is so unfair. In fact, I have yet to hear a kind word spoken about him hereabouts."

"It's true we are a suspicious lot," he acknowledged gravely. "Mayhap we've missed something of his good intentions, or done him an injustice. But he should be delighted he has so eloquent a defender in you."

"Oh, you are impossible! You claim the English are intolerant, but it seems to me you Scots take the prize. The canal he means to build will provide jobs for hundreds, and provide a boon to shipping in all Scotland. And he has told me of other schemes he has in mind, like harvesting the kelp locally to be used in industry, and making the herring fishing more efficient. Surely even you can see that that will bring nothing but good to the region?"

"A most impressive list. But I protest. Why do you say 'even' me? To my knowledge I have yet to say an unkind word against his lordship."

She realized in frustration that she was wasting her breath, but she could not let it go at that. She liked him enough that she did not care to see him behaving so blindly, and so said more quietly, "Because you clearly have not forgiven him for standing in your friend's shoes."

There was a hint of amusement behind his eyes, but he said gravely enough, "I am jealous of him, then. Is that it?"

"I don't say what you feel is not natural enough. But surely you can see that it is unfair to blame Kintyre for what he can't help? And he does mean nothing but good here, if you can only open your mind enough to acknowledge it."

"I see. Now I am closed-minded as well. I thank you for the compliments, lass. But I'll confess I did not seek you out on such a fine day to discuss Kintyre, however worthy and misunderstood he may be."

That was far more dangerous ground, as far as she was concerned. But she was woman enough not to be able to resist asking quietly, "And why did you seek me out?"

"But then we have had this conversation before," he pointed out with patience. "Are you really so lacking in vanity that you could believe my only reason was to get back at Kintyre?"

She knew a stab deep in her heart, but made herself say steadily, "No, but nor am I blind—nor do I possess your own brand of inimitable conceit. And you have as much as admitted it any way, by talking of your 'only' reason."

"I should learn to avoid clever women," he said in amusement. "But you overestimate the importance of Kintyre in my life, believe me, lass. I didn't wait for the last three days in the vain hope you would venture out again merely to score off Kintyre. But you must come to your own conclusion about that. There is nothing I can say that will convince you if you have so little faith in your own ability to attract a man."

And there it was in a nutshell. She readily admitted that part of her desperately wanted to believe him. But the cold, rational part of her brain, the one she was far more accustomed to listening to, pointed out unanswerably that he still had not answered her question, and that by seducing her he might indeed hope to get back at Kintyre for any real or imagined injuries.

Not, of course, she assured herself hastily, that she had any intention of allowing herself to be seduced.

And yet, she was admittedly playing with fire. Out of loyalty to Kintyre, if nothing else, she should have refused to ride out again with the laughing man who stood before her, amused comprehension in his face at the struggle so patently going on within her. And to have come aboard his ship, which he openly admitted he used for smuggling, was even more inexcusable.

Why had she, anyway? Because, that same voice whispered, however logical and sensible she might believe herself to be, there was a part of her that found unexpected excitement in the company of so dangerous a man. Nor, it whispered even more deceptively, was she yet wed to Kintyre, or even betrothed to him. Once she was, there would be no further chance for even such mild adventure as this. She would be a wife and then a mother; and however much she might value her independence, or how considerate Kintyre was, she would have others to answer to and her life would never again be exclusively her own.

For some reason the thought depressed her mightily. She had set out to find a husband who would limit her independence as little as possible, but she saw now that that had been folly. Rory was right that you couldn't choose a husband as you would a hat, or a horse. More important, marriage must inevitably change her as well, whether she liked it or no. Doubtless she would become like the majority of her married friends, forever preoccupied with her husband and children and household, and dwindling rapidly into a grandmother, with her life over and her youth gone, and any hope of adventure behind her.

But where had this sudden yearning for adventure and freedom come from? She had lived a pleasant, peaceful life and thought that was exactly what she wanted. She had thought herself long past the age of romantic dreams and a girl's foolish fantasies of excitement and danger. These new feelings disturbed and discomfited her.

As if guessing at the turmoil going on in her brain, Rory remained silent. She feared he saw too much, and wondered how he had come to know women so well—and then shrank at the obvious implications of that. She scarcely realized she was speaking aloud when she said softly, and a little sadly, "But if I am being a fool, it is destined to be over soon enough. You will have to leave to avoid being arrested and it is unlikely we will ever meet again."

He was still watching her, with that annoying amusement still deep in his eyes. "Aye," he said carelessly. "As temptations go, 'tis a safe enough one. One last fling before you marry Kintyre and have respectability thrust upon you. My Lady Kintyre cannot go jaunting about with a known highwayman, nor come aboard smugglers' vessels. Besides, she will soon have too much to occupy her to feel their lack. Counting linen. Respectable females seem to spend an unconscionable amount of their time counting linen, I've noted. And playing hostess to the neighboring gentry."

For some reason foolish tears stung at her eyelids at the picture he painted, but she would not let him guess. "Both of immense importance," she said valiantly.

"Oh, aye, I don't doubt it. And then, of course, in a year or two you will be the mother of a hopeful brood, all cast in Kintyre's image. Or at least I hope so. You will find that this kindly picture of him you have may suffer a setback if you should prove to be indiscreet."

"You are coarse!" she answered, making a fast recovery.

"But then I am nought but a coarse highwayman, when all's said and done," he countered promptly. "Now where was I?"

"You were trying to show me that marriage to Kintyre will be dull and change me forever! I thank you for your concern, but a woman's lot is regrettably not so free as a man's."

"Nay, lass, I know it." He had a disconcerting trick of being unexpectedly gentle at times. "But perhaps they have more choices than you have yet acknowledged."

"What? To cast my lot with a bunch of smugglers and vagabonds? How long would that last? And what would become of my reputation when you had tired of the novelty of teasing me? Oh, there is little you cannot tell me about the tyranny of my sex. I have weighed all the choices and found them equally unpleasant. But unlike you, I cannot choose simply to ignore what I dislike. Or sail away to France when life grows too real for me."

"Aye, 'tis a hard life for a woman. I have always thought so. But all those dire consequences we just spoke of are still in the future, and I have always thought opportunities were meant to be grasped. Would you like to go out with us?" The question was put with supreme casualness.

She looked at him unbelievingly, hope and reality warring sharply within her. "Go out with you?" she repeated in astonishment. "You mean *smuggling*?"

Chapter 16

RORY laughed at the horror in her tone. "We've a preference for the term *free-trading*. But yes. We mean to make a run in the next couple of days."

The very suggestion was preposterous. But she discovered that after her initial reaction she was not as shocked as she should no doubt have been. Worse, she recognized in that instant that she desperately wanted to go. It might make all her dull life afterward at least bearable, and if she turned down such an opportunity it would certainly never come again.

She tried to wrestle sternly with her conscience. But to her shame, even she could hear the unexpected longing in her next question. "To France? You're going to France?"

He smiled sympathetically down into her eyes, as if he understood far more than she wanted him to. "Well, no, lass," he said apologetically, as if having to disappoint a child. "We could scarce make it to France and back in a day, and while I've no objection, I suspect that annoying propriety of yours would never consent to be gone longer than that. I was thinking of a run to Ireland, where we've some consignments to drop off and a few things to pick up, including a horse or two that might interest you. We could be there and back in a good day and night of sailing."

"Of course it is out of the question." There, that was better, though in truth she wondered which of them she was trying to convince more. And she rather spoiled her effect by adding, "Besides, how could I possibly explain my absence for so long a time?"

"Why surely the independent Miss Thorncliff need not ask permission of anyone? Remember, you are not yet betrothed to his lordship. You've as yet no linen to count or bairns to grab at your skirts, holding you back."

"And I'm unlikely to, if I undertake such an adventure," she pointed out dryly. "Besides, there is my grandfather to be considered."

She didn't know why she was still discussing the matter. It was clearly out of the question, as she had said. It only made her feel worse to realize how impossible it was. She was not like him, willing and able to throw away all respectability in a fine, defiant gesture. She had her grandfather to consider, and her own future. Male-like, he little understood or cared how different were their situations, and how lamentably a woman must pay if ever she lost her reputation in the eyes of the world.

He said idly, as if it little mattered whether she came or no, and yet still with that odd gentleness in his voice that disconcerted her now and then, "But surely you are clever enough to feign an illness for the required time? I won't believe you so lacking in ingenuity that you can't think of something."

She glanced up, no doubt betrayed into revealing just how much she wanted to go by then. It was just possible, for her maid might be trusted. In fact, her quick brain was already toying with various stratagems. Not that she had any intention of putting them into effect, of course. That went without saying.

What she actually did say, however, was "When are you going?"

He was having trouble hiding his amusement. "Let us say day after tomorrow. That should give you ample time to perfect your excuses. We shall be leaving at midnight. If you're not here by then, we sail without you."

She had no intention of committing herself. Or of coming on such a journey, come to that. It was all just talk. "And why on earth should I care to risk my neck and reputation on such a voyage?" she inquired righteously. "If there is any justice in the world you will be seized for the outlaw you are and the next I shall hear of you, you will be languishing in jail."

He was grinning openly now. "But then the nearest jail of any size is Edinburgh Castle. Nay, lass. You may lie to me—though you make a poor enough job of it, I confess—but you're far too honest at base to continue to lie to yourself forever. Come or not, as you choose. But if you do come, we shall have done with any more of your muddled conventions and outraged virtue. It ill suits you, and we've no time for it between us. And now I must get you back or Kintyre will send out another search party, and begin to suspect you have more of an affinity for the wild Scots on his lands than either of us wish him to guess."

His words at least succeeded in bringing her common sense belatedly flooding back. "It was all but a dream, anyway. Have you forgotten that Kintyre means to see you arrested within the next few days? You must get away from here immediately."

Even she could hear the aching disappointment in her voice. He laughed and pinched her chin. "You look like one of my wee nieces when a promised treat has been denied her. I cannot bear to disappoint a lass—especially one who looks at me with jade eyes and tries so hard to disguise her disappointment. You will find, if you remain much longer here, that things are not so predictable as they are in England, and that what Kintyre intends and what actually happens may be two different things."

"But he has been informed of your presence here! I tell you he was in deadly earnest. I have long realized you held us up merely to irritate him, but you tweaked the wrong nose that time. He is an important man in this district and means to be an even more important one. And he will not rest until he has seen behind bars any man who dares humiliate him just when he is beginning to gain the respect of the locals."

She was a little surprised at her words, and wondered when she had reached such a conclusion. She had sung his praises primarily to irritate the annoyingly conceited man before her, but she had, until that moment, largely believed Kintyre a man of virtue. She still did so, of course. But from nowhere had come the realization that it was his vanity, and not his duty as a law-abiding citizen that had driven his hunt for the highwaymen, and she was more than a little surprised by it. It made him look ridiculous to have his chosen bride held up almost on his own lands, and did nothing to help in his battle to win over the respect of the locals. She had no doubt they were chuckling over it among themselves, and he must be very aware of it.

She seemed to have surprised Rory as well. "Accept my congratulations, lass. If you've realized that, you're in less danger than I thought you. But even so, he will have a hard time pinning the crime upon me. I can produce a dozen witnesses who will swear I was at home on that day, and nowhere near his lordship's carriage."

"Lachlan, I presume?" she inquired dryly. "Since he is equally a suspect, I somehow doubt he will be believed."

He laughed. "Aye, but every man in the Mull cannot equally be suspected. You've no need to fear for my neck just yet, though I'm flattered by your concern. Which leads us back to the question at hand. Will you come out with us? I've no intention of persuading you against your will. It must be your own decision. What is it to be?"

"Yes," she said recklessly, feeling as if she were burning her bridges behind her. And yet once it was said she felt an enormous sense of excitement and even liberation, so that she could not have withdrawn her answer even if she tried. It seemed she was still bent on flirting with the devil, however dangerous and foolhardy it might be.

He grinned, looking pleased, but of a sudden became immensely practical. He instructed her on what to wear and how to slip out of the house, and promised to have an escort waiting for her. The details made her suffer a slight setback, for it made her fine adventure sound less fine all of a sudden and more what it was: a piece of madness that she would no doubt one day come to regret. But she refused to invite Rory's further scorn by vacillating and withdrawing her answer, so obviously suffering from belated cold feet like the weak-willed woman he no doubt already thought her.

She wondered then if that was why he was spelling out all the sordid details to her, to give her an opportunity to back out now before it was too late. But that thought merely served to stiffen her spine, and so she listened to his instructions coolly, as if she was very used to bribing her maid and waiting for the servants to go to sleep so that she could sneak out of the house. She tried not to think that it was madness indeed, and would very likely spell total disaster for her.

He insisted that she should go back then, curtailing her tour of his ship, since he reminded her unwillingly that no one knew where she had gone. With unwonted meekness she allowed him to return her to shore, prey to far more conflicting emotions than she wanted him to guess.

But then she had the awful fear that he somehow knew anyway, and in his own way sympathized with her for her plight.

Her conscience warred with her all the next day, but oddly enough it did not seem able to shake her resolve. It was folly, dangerous folly, and she knew she risked far more than Rory guessed. No man, especially one as free as he was, could possibly understand the shackles of convention and reputation that bound a woman, or the disaster that could overtake her if her reputation were ever lost. Her grandfather would undoubtedly stand by her, but Kintyre would be well-excused for withdrawing his offer if her illicit adventure were to be discovered, and surely no man would ever offer for her again after that.

And yet, that direst of calamities for a female seemed less threatening than it should. Partly it was because she had little doubt that with luck her deception would work for so brief a time. Kintyre had no reason to be suspicious, and

Sir Giles was unlikely to be curious enough to investigate any unexpected indisposition in his granddaughter. It seemed it was woefully easy to stray from the path of virtue once one set one's mind to it.

And partly it was because it was impossible to deny the truth to herself any longer. However much the adventure appealed to her, she did not try to fool herself that she was risking her name and future merely for a stolen journey to Ireland. She clearly had developed a foolish infatuation—she dared not call it more—beyond reason or sense for a man who defied all the conventions and lived outside the law. It was farcical; in fact there were not words enough to describe the folly of it, and she could only wonder what had become of the sensible, practical woman she had always known herself to be.

At least she was still sane enough to realize there was no possible future in it. Even if she were willing to forget her upbringing and all her moral ethics to throw in her lot with a smuggler—and she would not acknowledge it had gone as far as that—she did not deceive herself that Rory would ever offer her the chance for more than this one stolen night. He might make flattering and half-mocking speeches to her, but she was doubtless no more than a pleasant diversion to him. Nor for all his protestations did she believe that her position as Kintyre's guest and potential wife did not have at least something to do with his unexpected attentions.

And yet none of it seemed to matter. Perhaps it was no more than one last fling at defying the conventions and limitations of her sex before she meekly bowed down to them. But she wanted her stolen night beyond anything she had ever wanted in her life before. And that alone should have warned her and made her stay safely at home. But it didn't.

It even proved ridiculously easy to get away for her illicit adventure. She had bribed her maid to say she was ill the next day, and on the appointed night let herself out of the house with surprisingly little difficulty. There had been a sticky moment when she had realized that though she and Sir Giles had retired to bed hours before, there was still a light under the study door. Kintyre was up late, perhaps working over his plans for the canal. She had already discovered that he often worked late into the night to be able to devote himself to her entertainment in the daytime.

That should have made her feel immensely guilty as she crept past the door on tiptoe, scarcely daring to breathe for fear some sound would betray her. He did not deserve such treatment from her. The only thing he had ever done to her was to make her a flattering offer of marriage, and show her nothing but kindness and consideration. More, he had no claim upon her, and was certainly not her jailor. It was absurd to feel as if she were an erring wife, creeping out to her lover behind her jealous husband's back. Nothing compelled her to accept Kintyre's offer; on the contrary every code of honor and decency demanded that she decline it if she could not promise him the fidelity and loyalty he deserved.

And yet she did not go back. To her great surprise, considering Kintyre's oft repeated references to the barbarity of the place, she found the great front door unbolted, so that it was easy to pull it open and slip through into the cool night beyond. It was only after she was outside, and her heart had begun to steady itself a little, that it occurred to her that some one of Kintyre's servants must have left the door deliberately open for her.

That at least succeeded in stopping her in her tracks, for however foolish she was behaving, and whatever hold Rory might have over Kintyre's servants, it was dangerous for any of them to know too much. Particularly were she to become mistress there, it could prove highly embarrassing in the future, and might conceivably lead to an unpleasant hold over her.

Then she caught herself up short, surprised that she could still be considering marrying Kintyre at all—particularly as she crept out in the dead of night like any straw-damsel to meet another man. It seemed she had no shame left.

But that was something she would not let herself think

about tonight. Not for a hundred servants and potential future difficulties was she going to behave like a coward tonight, and go meekly back upstairs again to her dull bed.

She defiantly gathered her cloak about her and went on, refusing to dwell on all that she left behind her in the sleeping house—and that she still had to sneak back in again before she would be safe.

Chapter 17

TO her relief, Lachlan appeared almost immediately, leading a horse. He looked her over, in her dark habit and cloak, and grunted, "So ye came, then?" His tone did not betray his thoughts on her wisdom or lack of it, but without another word he tossed her up into the saddle. A moment later he had remounted and they were away, leaving Kintyre House quickly behind.

The journey,which she had made twice before already, seemed unexpectedly short this time. Lachlan spoke scarcely a word except to warn her of an approaching obstacle, for it was a moonless night and she could see very little. Once, his *hsst!* startled her into immobility, and it was only a second later that she heard the unmistakable sounds of a late reveller walking unsteadily home in the darkness, singing to himself off-key.

But mostly she was grateful for her companion's silence. There was nothing to say after all, and she had no wish to be required to justify herself or make idle chitchat.

They reached the coast too soon as it was, and if she was of a sudden cold in the chill night, and all too conscious of the enormity of what she was doing, it was far too late for second thoughts. Besides, she scorned to appear so craven before Kilmartin, or even Lachlan, and so she stiffened her backbone and rode steadily forward toward the sea, shimmering pale and ghostlike before her.

Rory was there waiting for her, himself in a dark cloak and looking different in some indefinable way. Only much later did she realize that he had thrown off the mask of laziness he had heretofore shown to her, and looked alert and oddly formidable.

He greeted her matter-of-factly, and if she had expected some praise for her courage she was doomed to disappointment. "You're late. I'd almost given up on you. Did you waste hours lying in your bed trying to screw your courage to the sticking place, or is Kintyre a lighter sleeper than we expected?"

She lifted her chin and answered him in kind. "I would have more faith in my sanity if I were still home safe in bed. As for his lordship, however light a sleeper he may or may not be, he was still up working in his study when I left. I was lucky not to have run straight into him. I would have looked a fine fool then, trying to come up with some plausible excuse to explain my presence fully dressed at that hour and creeping guiltily with my shoes in my hand."

He grinned. "But then you had only to carry it off with a haughty air. A sudden desire for a walk in the moonlight. He might think you a touch eccentric, but he's no reason to suspect you, after all."

"I wonder," she said dryly. But then it was no doubt merely her own guilty conscience that day that had made it seem as if Kintyre was watching her, not with suspicion it was true, but a kind of grave question in his eyes. He was probably merely becoming impatient for her answer. "And far from thinking me eccentric, he would have every right to think I'd taken leave of my senses, if I tried to fob him off with so feeble an excuse as that I'd taken it into my head to go for a stroll in the middle of the night in unknown country. Which reminds me. For all his prudence, the bolts to the front door had somehow been left open. You wouldn't know anything about that, would you?"

"Kintyre should look to his servants. I fear they've grown sadly slack while he's off enjoying himself in England," Rory retorted audaciously. "But I must confess my interest in Kintyre's motives or possible actions is extremely limited at the best of times, and almost nonexistent at the moment. We'll miss the tide if we're not quick. Is that the best you could do for a cloak? You'll freeze before we've gotten halfway across. It's like a woman to allow her vanity to outweigh all else. Lachlan, fetch her a boatcloak, and hurry."

"It's not my vanity," she retorted, stung. "Somehow I came to Scotland ill-equipped for an excursion in a smuggling ship. I shall have to look more closely to my packing next time."

"Aye, it's a rare lass who is forward-thinking enough to foresee all possibilities," he agreed with a grin. "And is your maid reliable, d'you think?"

He sounded annoyingly unconcerned, but then it was not he who would suffer the consequences if she weren't. "Yes, she's reliable." It was scarcely a comforting thought. Now that Gillian was there her absurd bravado seemed to have completely left her, and she could only think she had been mad indeed to embark on such an excursion. It was not the thinness of her cloak that was causing her shivers.

As if to add to the perhaps inevitable cooling of her courage, a cold rain began to fall just then. The *Braw Lass* sat an anchor across the angry gray sea, and in that moment Gillian found it hard to believe she was not safely in her warm bed where she should be, and that this could all really be happening to her.

As if aware of it—and he had an uncanny habit of reading her thoughts that was increasingly unnerving—he said, "It's not too late, you know. We've no wish for a reluctant passenger. And it's going to be a rough crossing, so if you've any second thoughts, or are likely soon to regret your bargain, you'd best return to Kintyre at once. All hands will be busy once we're underway, with none to spare to coddle or dance attendance on you, and the run, though not particularly dangerous, is risky enough we've no use for a screech-ing or fainting female, getting under our feet and giving us away to the landguard. Well, which is it to be?"

Put like that, she bristled immediately. "I have no intention either of screeching or fainting. And if you are arrested for this night's piece of work, it will be none of my doing."

He grinned at that. "Aye, but you're like to find yourself

in something of an embarrassing fix if we are arrested. Have you thought of that?"

It was a stupid question, for she had thought of little else. "I had thought you at least competent smugglers, or I had indeed best stay at home," she countered sarcastically. "Do you anticipate being arrested?"

"One never anticipates being arrested. And if we cannot outwit the landguard hereabouts, I deserve to put my head in a noose. But nonetheless, I'll have your promise before we start. You'll do exactly as I say, or you'll not stir a foot. And whatever happens, we'll have done with pretense between us. If you come it will be of your own free will, and there will be no tears or accusations afterward, whatever happens. Is it agreed?"

She was surprised and hurt, as perhaps he meant her to be. But she said quietly, after a moment, "I am undoubtedly mad to trust you, but whatever happens, you will hear no tears or accusations from me. You've no need to fear."

"Aye, I know that," he said unexpectedly. Then as usual, before she could glow at his rare praise, he was suddenly all business. He seemed to find the promise he had extracted from her of little moment, but she was secretly a little appalled at it. The more because it was true, she suddenly realized. Wise or not, she did trust him, else she would not have come. And that was perhaps the most remarkable thing of all about this remarkable night.

Lachlan soon returned with a large boatcloak, which Rory insisted upon wrapping around her. Then, as before, he picked her up bodily and carried her to the boat, giving her no more opportunity to change her mind. There, Gillian looked back to the fast receding shore and indeed had to swallow a shiver of apprehension. She assured herself it was not cowardice, but merely a chill from the rain and an undoubtedly cold wind coming in off the bay. Besides, there was no going back now. With every yard of black sea widening between her and the shore, she had burnt her bridges, so to speak.

Once they reached the ship, Rory dispensed with gallantry and, to her indignant humiliation, threw her over his shoulder and climbed up the ladder as if she weighed no more than a child. At the top she was set on her feet, ruffled and annoyed, and had very little doubt there was amusement in the eyes of the sailors waiting there, ready to receive their captain's orders.

But at least if they resented her presence on board—as they might well have done given the nature of their night's business—none of them revealed it openly. Instead they regarded her with shy interest, and politely looked away if she happened to glance at one of them.

They were all large, amiable-looking young men, neat and respectful, and her visions of a pirate's crew, seedy and disreputable, underwent the same disillusion as her first glimpse of his ship had done. It seemed she knew little of modern-day smuggling. She could not resist smiling to herself at the thought, for it was one of the more patently ridiculous in a night of singularly foolish thoughts and actions.

Rory, consigning her to Lachlan's care, had little time to spare for her at the moment. He advised her to go below, for the rain had grown heavier; but instead she shook her head and removed herself to a safe spot on the deck while the bustle of upping anchor and casting off was attended to.

It was done with the efficiency of long practice, and Gillian had to admire the ease of the sailors' movements. She was grateful for the boatcloak, for on the water it was indeed cold; but to her surprise she found it more enjoyable than she would have expected to watch the shore gradually receding and feel the cold rain on her face.

They themselves carried no lights, understandably, and she soon found that away from the few lights on shore, the world devolved into shades of gray and luminescence. Their wake fell foaming behind them, and the mist and clouds became a lighter gray than the sea, while the sky, what glimpses she could catch of it through the fog and the rain, was a different color still.

She had no notion of how long she stood there, enthralled at being at sea, which she had never experienced before. The ship beneath her feet felt alive, and the noise of the sails and ropes, and the occasional shouted order, though for the most part they ran completely silently, filled the night, along with the wind and the sound of the water. She forgot to be cold, and even forgot her misgivings, for she could not deny that she was enjoying herself, and that to be safe home in bed would be immeasurably dull by comparison.

Then Rory was at her side, and said in amusement, "You're less trouble than I gave you credit for, lass. Well, and how are you enjoying your first taste of smuggling?"

"Very well," she said placidly. "Do you go the whole way without lights?"

"We've little need of them out in the open sea, for we can see clearly enough, and any approaching vessel will be showing lights itself, so that we can avoid it. And once we approach land, any lights are dangerous, as you might expect. A smuggling vessel needs an excellent pilot on board, for we usually must negotiate difficult shores in the dead of night."

"And suppose you encounter another smuggling vessel traveling without lights?" It was merely an idle question, for she did not feel particularly concerned.

He laughed. "Then we may be in trouble. But the odds are against it, and besides, we've the use of our ears, and sound carries amazingly far over water. Are you cold?"

"Not a bit. How long before we make Ireland?"

"Before dawn with any luck. There we'll hole up in a hidden cove I know of, and conduct our business, and then wait for dark to head back."

"And if any landsmen are lying in wait for you, either in Ireland or on your return?"

"We'll hope we have sufficient notice to avoid them," he said cheerfully. "Why? Are you worried?"

Somewhat to her surprise she discovered she wasn't. A part of her stood apart and looked with amazement on the fact that the sensible Gillian Thorncliff was standing on a smuggler's boat in the middle of the night, and might at any moment find herself faced with having to make totally unbelievable excuses as to what she was doing there. But a part of her was aware of a rising excitement that she was unfamiliar with, as if the danger merely added to the adventure.

He grinned at her, as if recognizing the truth of that statement. "Would you like to come steer her?" he asked. "You may as well be a proper sailor."

She came willingly, and stood like a child as he explained the course and the headings to her, his arms around her and his warm hands over hers as she found the wheel humiliatingly heavy to turn without help. And it was all part of the magic, the feel of his arms warm around her, the wind and rain in her face and the sails snapping overhead, the ship alive under her hands on the wheel. He had not needed to extract his promise from her, for tomorrow doubtless she would be returned to sanity again, and wonder at her lapse. But tomorrow would be time enough to remember that he was an admitted thief and a smuggler, and that she was weighing whether to become betrothed to another man. Tonight she had no wish to be reminded of such dismal facts of life.

They sailed thus for some hours, until the sky began to grow lighter, and she had no thoughts of anything so mundane as cold or fatigue. Once near to shore he took the wheel from her, while a lookout high in the topmast shouted directions below to him. The soft green of Ireland came up gradually before them as the dawn rose from behind, and she was entranced to watch the shore come faster and faster to meet them, and the skill with which Rory handled the wheel.

Once into the hidden cove he had spoken of, and at anchor, he turned back to her, faint amusement still in his face at her rapt interest. "You're a born sailor, lass," he said in his lazy voice, teasing her. "I'd never have expected the prim and virtuous Miss Thorncliff to possess so many hidden talents. But it's been a long night, and we've a longer one ahead of us. You'd best get some sleep while you can."

She wanted to go ashore with them, but he gave a flat veto to that. "Nay, lass. You'd only be in the way, and I confess the next part is the most dangerous of the enterprise." He grinned. "Besides, you're no' dressed for the part. I should have insisted you don breeks and boots for the adventure, except that doubtless your modesty would never stand such a thought."

"And doubtless your immodesty knows no bounds," she retorted. "But I'll gladly don anything you choose, if it means I may come along. I've no wish to be cooped up here for hours, while you're off having all the fun."

"Nay, lass," he said again, more gently, smiling disturbingly down at her. "You'll have adventure and enough, before we're done. Besides, you'd be no use to us, exhausted and beginning to whine and complain and long for your bed. You'll be safer here."

Red-cheeked with annoyance, she snapped, "I would not whine and complain! You've a typical male's arrogance and conceit where women are concerned."

"No, I know you would not," he surprised her by saying. "Else I would not have brought you along in the first place. Did you think I really made a habit of bringing women aboard the *Braw Lass*? My men would not stand for it, for one thing, and I've yet to meet a woman, till now, who I trusted aboard her. But still you'll stay behind, for all that, and get what sleep you can. Remember you promised to do exactly as I said, and I'm holding you to it."

Chapter 18

SHE found herself left without an answer and, indeed, somewhat bemused. She was somehow doubtful he could really have meant so great a compliment to her. He was far more likely to depress her pretensions than to praise her, so it was necessary to resist feeling absurdly gratified by his words.

He led her down to his cabin, the first time she had been below, and she found it more roomy and comfortable than she would have expected. Indeed, it was almost luxurious, with its panelling and comfortable bed and rich hangings, and she could only stare about her with astonishment.

Amused, he removed her wet cloak for her and tossed it on a chair. "Here's food and wine for you, and Lachlan will stay behind to see to whatever you require. Hell and damnation! You're soaked to the skin, you foolish girl! I should have sent you below long since. Have you no more sense than to wear such flimsy garments? Devil take all women and their foolish clothing. I'd have done best to put you in breeks and a warm coat after all. Though you've no right to look so fetching, with your damp curls rioting about your head and your face shiny and pinched with the cold. Here, you'd best have this again. And see that you get some sleep while I'm gone."

"This" proved to be the emerald dressing gown she had once before worn. He was gone on the words, and she was left alone, swallowing her resentment at being treated, however belatedly, like a tiresome woman. Though if she really looked as he described her, it was just as well he had gone. "Fetching," indeed. But she somehow did not care to examine herself in the mirror at that moment, and so hurried into the warm robe, wondering if Lachlan were equally blaming her for keeping him tied by the heels when he no doubt longed to be with his master.

Lachlan himself soon appeared to remove her breakfast—which she had surprised herself by doing full justice to—and did indeed seem to resent her presence, for he eyed her in the gaudy emerald robe with scant approval and vouchsafed few remarks to her. When asked when Rory was expected to return he shrugged and claimed no knowledge, and did not remain long. Gillian had to fight a sudden urge to ask him to stay, for it occurred to her that if he only would he could tell her much of the mysterious and annoying Rory Kilmartin.

But she was too proud to pump his servant, and so soon found herself alone again, in the captain's cabin of a smuggler's ship at anchor off Ireland. It was incredible enough to make her shake her head in astonishment and be half-convinced she could only be dreaming.

The bed proved amazingly comfortable and she was tired enough, in truth. She had unbound and dried her hair, and wrapped the warmth of the emerald velvet around her, and felt unexpectedly comfortable and content. It was hard to realize that back at Kintyre House the household would soon be stirring, and she found herself only mildly curious about whether her grandfather and Kintyre would be surprised by her sudden illness, and nurse the slightest suspicions.

She awoke much later, luxuriously rested and comfortable, to discover by the light that she had slept the day away. She stretched and yawned, still in that half-state between waking and dreaming. Indeed, her dreams would seem to have been uncommonly pleasant, though she could scarcely remember them.

Then a voice said in easy amusement, "You look like a cat, sensual and more than a little pleased with yourself, lass. Did you have a good rest?"

She sat up hurriedly, to discover Rory leaning against the edge of the table, watching her. It was the second time he had discovered her sleeping, and she should have been embarrassed and resentful of his presence. But it did not even occur to her. "Oh, thank God you're back!" she blurted. "Did it go safely, then?"

He grinned across at her. "Aye, and I've a surprise for you, later, for being such a good lass and doing as you're told. And I must admit you're a sight for a weary man to come back to. You almost tempt me to take you every time I go out."

Belatedly, she became aware that her hair was tumbled about her shoulders, and that the annoying velvet robe had slipped, leaving one shoulder bare. She flushed and tried to hitch it up, but he said lazily, "Nay, lass, leave it. I wish I were an artist so that I might paint you at this moment."

Her heart had begun to pound for some absurd reason, but she managed to find her voice. "And what would you call it?" she asked unsteadily. "*Portrait of a Foolish Woman*?"

He straightened and came toward her, laughter and something else in his face that she dared not try to analyze. "No. I would entitle it *Temptation*. You've no idea how tempting you are at this moment."

Folly was one thing, but she must put a stop to this at once. It had gone much further than she had intended, and if, she saw now with some shame, this had been in the back of her mind all along, she was even more of a fool than she had thought. "Temptation" was right, but flirting with danger was one thing, and leaping willingly to meet her ruin quite another.

"And was this part of your plan all along?" she inquired a little breathlessly. "Seduce the sensible English spinster as just one more part of your jest?"

He had reached the bed, but made no move to touch her. Instead, he cocked his head to one side and appeared to consider the question seriously. "Part of my plan? No. In fact I suspect you cannot guess, however sensible an English spinster you may be, how you are managing to upset all my plans. Lachlan thinks I have taken leave of my senses, and I begin to suspect he is right."

Her heart was pounding so loudly now that it seemed to shake her entire body. "And how many women have you said that to? I have no doubt that the circumstances are tempting enough—to my own shame and folly!—but d'you expect me to believe that any woman wouldn't do, in my place?"

He smiled down at her, the dangerous look in his eyes no longer mistakable. "Lass, lass," he chided her mockingly. "Have you no more vanity than that? Has no man yet convinced you of your beauty and desirability? I'd have expected Kintyre to possess more finesse. 'Tis little wonder you've not yet consented to wed him. He's a clumsy oaf and deserves no better."

It was as well he had introduced Kintyre's name into the conversation. "I don't need a man to convince me of my beauty or desirability," she managed to retort. "Especially a thief and a smuggler."

"Ah, I thought it'd not be long till we were back to that. And it's best you remember it. I'll make you no promises and tell you no lies. What there is between us goes beyond that."

"There is nothing between us." She had not known there would be so much desolation in her voice and was horrified to hear it.

He still had yet to touch her, but he half-smiled at that. "But then I warned you about lying to yourself," he said deeply. "Marry Kintyre if you must. But don't lie to yourself. Or to me."

"I . . ." She wanted to protest, but it was true. He saw more clearly than she did. And she had been more than a fool not to see that this moment had been inevitable as soon as she'd agreed to come with him tonight. It certainly had told him everything he had ever wanted to know about her.

She closed her eyes, unable to face the shaming knowledge in his face, and he once more sounded amused, though his voice was still curiously deep. "Open your eyes, lass. You're safe enough. I'll not do anything to force you. You must come to me of your own free will, or not at all."

She reluctantly opened her eyes at that, to discover he

had come even closer, and that her heart had unaccountably gone up into her throat and was threatening to choke her. His face was very close to her own, all planes and hard angles, and she could see the brown skin, and the little laugh lines about his eyes, and the faint frown of tiredness between his brows. It was suddenly as familiar to her as her own, and at the same time alien and mysterious, and she could not penetrate the gray depths of his eyes, or begin to guess what he was thinking.

And it could only be some unsuspected instinct for destruction, after his warning, that made her hand reach out, as of its own volition, and touch his lean brown cheek, as if the feel of his skin was somehow necessary to her in order to live.

His eyes darkened then, and became even more inscrutable. But still he made no move. He let her explore his face, the warmth and the strength of it, and then only slowly did he reach out his own brown hand, and run it through her tumbled hair, stroking it back from her brow.

She instantly began to tremble, though she knew she had no one to blame but herself. She had not been able to resist playing with fire, even knowing she would be burnt. He was no saint, and she had given him every invitation. And yet it did not occur to her to try to draw back. It was far too late for that.

His hand, infinitely gentle in her hair, reached her face and raised her chin so that she was forced to meet his eyes. The look she found there made her tremble even more, for there could no longer be any mistaking what was between them, or the inevitability of what was to come. Gone was all hint of laziness or amusement, and though she found herself suddenly shy before that look, and even possessed of a certain belated panic, she scorned to play the coward. So she met his eyes bravely, however difficult she found it to look upon the flame that was so shortly to consume her.

For a long moment neither of them moved or said a word, and afterward she was to wonder and fear what he must have read in her face. But it seemed she could not tear her gaze away, or disguise anything from him, however shameful it might be.

Still he did not move. If she were going to save herself it must be now. She knew that he would never force her, and that she had only to draw away, pull the velvet back over her shoulder and break the spell of the moment, and he would resume the easy banter that had come to be a habit between them, and the moment would go no further. She would in time be returned safe and whole from her smuggling adventure, and might get on with her life with only a few memories to remind her that she had ever given in to so wild an impulse.

And yet she found she could not take those simplest of steps if her life depended upon it—and perhaps it did. The golden evening sun gilded everything in the cabin, including his brown face and dark hair, and she was in thrall. All her sensible plans for choosing a husband lay in shatters about her, and there was no room for concern about tomorrow and the pieces she must somehow pick up and try to put back into the semblance of a life. At the moment she wanted one thing only, and that more than she had ever wanted anything in her life. Her whole being trembled and cried out for it.

At last he lowered his hand, and quite deliberately stroked down her bare shoulder, lowering the emerald velvet even more. "You take my breath away," he said, his voice low. "Whatever comes between us, I want to remember this moment always, with your hair afire and your face looking just like that."

Whatever comes. He clearly made her no promises, and though his words were incredibly sweet, no protestations of love. She did not need to be told that his feelings did not equal her own, and that doubtless he had shared similar moments with countless lasses, and would no doubt with countless more.

And yet, what had she expected? If she were honest with herself, she did not want him to demand she give up her plans and throw in her lot with him, for it would only place her in a dilemma for which there was no answer. Smuggling for one day was one thing, and yet for all her new-found love for danger, she did not fool herself into believing she could undertake it as a life's work. And whatever her feelings for the dark-haired mesmerist before her, she had no intentions of throwing everything away to have him.

Then she looked up and saw that he understood that, as he seemed to understand all else. As before, he was deliberately forcing her to face the truth, and giving her every opportunity to draw back before it was too late.

"Aye," he said deeply, reading the question in her eyes. "I've said I will not force you, and passion can be a greater bond than physical force. I'll not deny I want you right now—and that I've thought of little else from the moment I first looked into those bewitching green eyes of yours—but it is a tremendous step you are taking. I won't make it easier for you by sweeping you off your feet—as I flatter myself I could—or by giving you the right to convince yourself tomorrow that you were overpersuaded. There can be no shame between a man and a woman, but only if they come to each other with honesty between them, and not lies and deceit. And the most dangerous deceit we practice is usually upon ourselves, or hadn't you noticed?"

It was true. She had subconsciously wanted him to overwhelm her with passion, to take the decision out of her hands, so that she could afterward excuse herself for taking so dangerous a step. She had come knowing that this moment would happen, and yet preparing herself with a ready-made excuse when it did. And he was honest enough to see through her foolish guile and force her to face the truth, however unpalatable.

Still he waited. They both knew he had no more than to touch her again, and she would indeed go up in flames and be consumed. But he was clearly not going to make it easy for her. Or allow her to escape the consequences of her decision.

At last she lifted her head proudly. "Is your experience with women so negative?" she inquired cooly. "You obviously believe us foolish and craven creatures who must be forced to face the brutal truth, however much we might like to hide it from ourselves."

He smiled down at her in a way that made her heart turn over. "Not craven, no. But sometimes foolish and prone to regrets after it's too late, and the passion has cooled. And to be fair, you've far more to risk than men have, so perhaps it's only natural."

"Then you needn't worry," she said as calmly as she could manage. "I promise I won't come crying to you tomorrow that I was overpersuaded, or did not know my own mind, if that is what you fear."

"If I fear it, it is not for myself. I should not like to think myself the unwitting cause of so much unhappiness," he said truthfully.

She drew a deep breath, seeing that whether he knew it or not, the unhappiness he was talking about must inevitably come to her, no matter what she did. Were she to stop him now she would regret it the rest of her days. And were she to give in, though pride would prevent her from crying to him over the consequences, there would be unhappiness in store for her nonetheless. For however soon or late what was between them ended, she would have the rest of her life to endure without him. And that would, perhaps, be the hardest to bear of all.

He looked down at her, a little sternness suddenly about his mouth and eyes, as if he were sensing that even then she was uncertain. "So I will ask you once only. Are you sure this is what you want? You've a lamentable habit of playing with fire without any real intention of being burnt. And I'm vain enough to assure you that if we continue you will, this time, be a little singed about the edges, if not completely consumed, Miss Gillian Thorncliff."

He would force her to say it, then. But suddenly it came easily to her, for he was right that there could be no shame between a man and a woman if they came together honestly, without deceit and lies. She lifted her chin. "Yes, this is what I want. You were right. It is what I came for."

Chapter 19

F OR a long moment he still did not move. Then he gave an odd sigh, as if he were letting go of an unbearable tension she had not even guessed at. The next moment he was beside her and kissing her, and she belatedly discovered that for all her brave words, she had not known what the conflagration she had invited would be until she was consumed by it.

His passion soon threatened to overwhelm her, for there was no denying he had vastly more experience than she did. He managed to teach her in a short space of time exactly what there could be between a man and a woman, when both came willingly and acknowledged no shame. His hands threaded through her unbound hair, and everywhere his lips touched trailed fire. When he parted her robe, she felt only an exultant pride at the look in his eyes, one that seemed to be made up of equal parts passion and unexpectedly fierce possession. And when his lips followed his hands, she realized with a gasp that she still had a great deal to learn after all.

In that moment, she could not imagine why she had hesitated so long. There was no longer any room for fear, or concern for the future or the past. All there was were his lips and his demanding body. And then even the ability to think was lost, her thoughts splintering and spiralling away from her on a wave of passion.

Surprisingly, he was the one to pull back first. He held her tightly against him, stroking her hair, and murmuring in a breathless voice she had never heard from him before, but in which laughter trembled at the corners, "I had not imagined you so apt a pupil, lass. But unless we mean to run the risk of presenting Kintyre with a black-haired brat to search his conscience over, we'd best stop now, before it's too late."

It took a moment for his words even to sink in. And when they did it was like a douse of cold water. If she had known no shame in their lovemaking, she was suddenly stung with shame that he could control his own passion so easily, when she herself had no wish yet to be forced to face bitter reality. More, she was ineffably hurt that he would drag Kintyre's name in at such a moment.

But what had she expected? This must be no more than a brief interlude to him, one shared many times before, and not the mind-shattering experience she had found it. She had foolishly allowed passion momentarily to blind her to the all-too-unpalatable truth: he had made no pretense of offering her anything more than a few brief moments of pleasure. She should doubtless be grateful to him for having the control to stop what was indeed in danger of going much too far. And yet she knew that gratitude was not the most dominant emotion in her heart at the moment.

She sat up hurriedly, her back to him, and grateful for the growing darkness that prevented him from seeing her face. "Yes, it is indeed time we stopped, before a brief moment of pleasure can lead to a lifetime of regret."

His voice was suddenly cool in the growing darkness. "And if you can speak of it in those terms, it is past time we came to our senses. Though I'll confess you go to my head like wine, lass."

Hurriedly she pulled the shameful velvet back around her, wishing she could disappear and not have to face the next few moments. She wanted to be alone to weep and rail against fate, instead of forced to face him and try to salvage what little pride there was left to her. "What other terms should I speak of it in? Don't pretend it's not what you yourself were thinking. After all, you might find the black-haired bairn you spoke of a considerable risk to your high and mighty freedom, and that would never do." It was impossible to keep all of the bitterness out of her voice.

He too sat up with ease. "I confess that it would be somewhat of an inconvenience," he conceded in amusement.

"How fortunate it must be to be a man," she countered bitterly, "and have the luxury to regard such things in the light of no more than a minor inconvenience. But then you would not be paying the price of that black-haired bairn after all; I would."

"Aye," he said more gently. "And it is that, that I would protect you against. I will concede that in that respect life is harder on women."

"In *that* respect?" She almost laughed. "I begin to think it is true in all respects. And I should not forget that you've coaches to rob and goods to smuggle—all clearly far more important than tying yourself down due to such an untimely *inconvenience*."

"And I should have known it would not be long till we were back to normal. You'll soon be slapping my face for me if I don't watch out," he said lightly.

Every word he spoke seemed aimed at her heart, but she would be a fool indeed to let him guess as much—or that she was gallingly near to tears. "At least you are honest, and I should be grateful to you for that. You have made me no false promises, as I daresay most men would have done under the circumstances."

His voice deepened, and he at last put out a hand to stroke her tumbled hair away from her brow. "Aye, I may hurt you, however unintentionally, and you may have cause yet to regret knowing me."

"Yet?" She could not prevent herself from crying out at the willful blindness of that.

He once more took her chin in his hand and made her look at him. "Be honest with me," he said a little sternly. "What harm have you had from me? I make no pretense to being the most noble of men, but at least I have never lied to you. You knew from the beginning I had no promises to make you, and nothing more to offer but a few moments of sweet pleasure, which is at least more than most people get in their lifetime. Do you expect as much from the loveless marriage you are intent upon making?"

He'd said he would never intentionally hurt her, but that struck straight to the bone. If she were at all honest with herself as he demanded, she knew now that she could never go through with such a marriage. But she had no intention of admitting as much to him. So she said valiantly, "No. But I lack your freedom. It is the fortunate woman who may choose to wed for love."

He was fully recovered now, as frustratingly inscrutable as ever. "And yet I confess I see no other reason for marriage between a man and a lass."

She wondered if he were deliberately torturing her, but at least gave him credit for more kindness than that. Nevertheless she wished the conversation over, so that she could begin to put the pieces of her shattered self back together again. "At least Kintyre is honest and decent and kind," she said wearily. "Few women find as much, whether they wed for love or not."

"And yet I would have said even that was a poor enough bargain. Have you so little pride in yourself, Gillian Thorncliff?"

That stung unbearably. "It is easy enough for you to say. You have your freedom and can make your way in the world, and need not care a jot for your reputation or your future. Unfortunately marriage is the only career women have open to them. Or would you have me become one of those pitiful women forever dependent upon the kindness and charity of their relations, fated to be aunts to other people's children?"

His voice softened slightly. "Aye, life is indeed unfair to such women. I only hope you may find Kintyre the paragon you so obviously seem to think him."

There was the faintest of contempt in his voice, and something in her heart leaped at it. She wanted desperately to believe he might at least be jealous. "I am far from thinking him a paragon. But then I daresay it is few women who do not wake to find themselves wed to a stranger if it comes to that. But do you have any particular reason for believing that I might regret it? Or are you merely being a dog in the manger: unwilling to have me yourself, but resenting anyone else who may offer for me."

He openly laughed at that. "Nay, lass, I'll not make your decision for you. But I sometimes wonder if you know Kintyre at all, or merely see him in the light of the role you have cast him in."

She was exasperated and weary, and still having to fight back annoying tears, and so demanded unsteadily, "Cannot you answer a question straightly for once in you life? Do you not wish me to wed Kintyre?"

He shrugged. "If wishes were so easily converted into pounds Scot, we'd all be as rich as kings. You must do as you see fit, as we all must. He's a most eligible *parti*, respectable and rich, as you are so fond of pointing out to me, and will doubtless soon be even richer. But then you know all that or you would not have so carefully selected him. I know I once predicted you'd not wed him, but that was mere egotism on my part, I'll confess it now. I've nothing to offer you, as you so rightly point out, and no intention of throwing myself at your feet to be rejected, if that is what you hope for. I play fair, whatever else may be said of me. Remember that."

Yes, he played fair, if only according to his own lights. He had not spoken one word of love or made her any promises, to be kept or not. It was only she who had been changed, perhaps forever, by a few brief moments that plainly meant little or nothing to him.

She could only gather about her what remnants of her pride and dignity she had left. "Yes, you play fair. But you will forgive me if I confess, in turn, that I have had more of an adventure than I had bargained for. But no doubt you think I should be grateful for the valuable lessons you have taught me?"

"You should be," he said with irritating smugness. "Though knowing the fickleness of women, I somehow doubt you are. But if it will do your vanity any good, I will confess that for a sensible English spinster you have given me far too many sleepless nights, lass. I will even confess that I am jealous of Kintyre, or any man who weds you. I wish I might be the man to teach you exactly how beautiful and desirable you are. But I may perhaps be forgiven for re-membering you, looking just as you do in this moment, with your mouth swollen and soft from my kisses, long after you have forgotten your brief brush with a freebooter, and become the respectable Countess of Kintyre, with babes at your knee and a husband to satisfy."

And then he leaned forward and kissed her, one last time. Despite her words, despite all she knew of him, her eyes closed of their own volition, and she could not have denied him if she had wanted to.

But for all its bittersweetness, it was over far too soon. The next moment he had left her, and when she opened her eyes again he was gone. She was alone to come to terms with the supreme irony of the fact that he thought obviously to do her a kindness and protect her against her own weak-ness and folly, when all she wanted to do was throw herself in his arms and beg him to stay.

But as she drearily dressed again and put off the emerald velvet for surely the last time, she knew that however painful, he had indeed done her a favor. Given his reputa-tion, he might well have thought himself justified in taking what was so freely offered, and she might all too soon have found herself suffering the very regrets and consequences of her actions that he'd spoken of.

A part of her heart might leap at the possibility, but he was far wiser than she in that respect also. She would little relish finding herself having to explain so highly inconve-nient a fact of life to Kintyre or her grandfather.

And though he'd said he had no desire to see her wed Kintyre, he might have prevented it if he chose in the easi-est way possible. By drawing back when he had, he had seen to it that the choice was still hers. She might accept or reject Kintyre's offer as she chose.

It was true that she would not be the first woman, nor surely the last, forced to marry in haste and foist a black-haired brat, as he so crudely put it, onto an unsuspecting husband. But the necessity of it would have left her with very little pride, and no doubt he knew that as well.

Yes, she should indeed be grateful to him. She wondered why, in that case, she could have wept and railed against him for depriving her of a moment she might never know again.

She went up on deck again soon after, but the magic was clearly gone. They said little more to each other, for in truth it all seemed to have been said. The return voyage was no longer an enchanted adventure, but merely a crossing in foul weather where the crew had little enough time for leisure, and after a brief appearance for her pride's sake, she retired below to nurse her wounds. Rory did not again invite her to come and steer his ship, and she was too proud to push herself forward.

They docked in the misty dawn, having encountered no more danger than if they had been out for a pleasure sail. Rory saw her to shore, and said lightly, after a brief look at her face, "I had forgotten that I said I had a present for you. But perhaps it is not the time, after all. Lachlan will take you home, for I must see to the consignment."

When she said nothing he hesitated, then put her up in the saddle and looked up at her for a brief, intense moment, almost as if he were memorizing her face, though she knew wearily that it was pinched with cold and no doubt the rain was dripping off her nose.

Then, surprisingly, he put a hand on her cheek, and said, almost under his breath, "I doubt you know, lass, that a good part of your charm is that you little realize how damnably hard you make it for me to remember my resolution. Which is perhaps just as well, if I'm to protect us both from ourselves."

The next moment he had slapped her horse on the rump and turned away, back to his ship and its illegal consignment, and she was left to ride back with Lachlan, and struggle against the weary tears of loss and self-contempt.

She and Lachlan exchanged few enough words on the ride back, and she slipped into the house—the great front door again left conveniently open—with scant care given to whether she was discovered or not. It scarcely seemed to matter.

It was sheer luck that she met no one, and made it to her room safely. There she shut the door and leaned back against it, still having to fight back the foolish tears, for she feared if she once gave into them she would never be able to stop. And in truth she had little enough to weep about. Thanks to Rory her virtue had been preserved if only against her will—even the very word "virtue" had a sound of mockery to it. It was merely ironic that it seemed a remarkably hollow victory in light of all she had given up.

It took her a very long moment to realize that the room was not empty and that her grandfather sat before the fire, fully dressed, and regarding her with harsh condemnation.

Chapter 20

AT her entrance he rose to his full bony height. "So there you are!" he said grimly. "Where have you been, girl? Answer me!"

She jumped, having no doubt she looked the very picture of guilt, stealing in at dawn with her gown crumpled and her hair wet from the morning mist and only inadequately pinned up. Moreover, she very much feared her face must show all that she had gone through and that she was by no means the same woman who had crept out at dead of night only twenty-four hours ago.

When she remained silent, he repeated more sharply, "Well? Have you nothing to say for yourself? Are you wholly without shame? Claiming you are sick and withdrawing to your bed, while all the time you are gallivanting out God knows where."

She did not even bother to wonder how he had discovered it, or whether Kintyre knew as well. All she said was, "Have you sat up all night? You will make yourself ill if you're not careful."

He brought his hand down hard on the mantel, making the china ornaments on it rattle. "Don't trifle with me, my girl. I asked you where you had been. Have you gone to meet your lover? Eh? Is that it?"

The last was but a querulous fit of temper, for he was indeed an old man now, and she did not suppose he really believed it of her. He knew her very well—or thought he did. But she was too tired and too emotionally churned up herself to think of any excuse, and so said baldly after a moment, "Yes. If you must know, I have."

Then she was sorry, for of a sudden all the fight seemed to leave him, and he sat down heavily again. "Have you run mad, girl?" he demanded querulously. "And what of Kintyre? You dragged us all this way, only to shame us both and insult him? Or do you still intend to marry him despite everything?"

She took off her wet cloak and said dully, "No. I don't mean to wed Kintyre now."

"I suppose that is something. Although you may yet have cause to be grateful for so eligible an offer," he said bluntly.

"No. There will be no ... consequences. Grandfather, I love you dearly, but please just ... go. I feel as if I could sleep for a week."

She saw that her very lack of a defense defeated him. He looked suddenly older than she could ever remember him looking, and muttered, "Your grandmother should still be alive. She would have known how to handle you. I confess I do not."

But after he had gone, troubled and uneasy, and she had stripped off her damp garments and tumbled into bed, she knew that she would never sleep. She supposed she should be making plans to return home, and trying to find some way to explain her inexplicable behavior to her grandfather. But instead she found herself dwelling on every moment of that last scene in Rory's bedroom, and wondering how she could ever go about her life again and pretend that none of it had happened.

During the next week Gillian saw no more of Rory Kilmartin, which was undoubtedly just as well. She had decided against going home immediately, for the simple but ignominious reason that she had no wish to give him so easy a victory over her. And if her conscience sometimes troubled her for Kintyre's sake, she would be gone soon enough. Had he been deeply in love with her it might have been different, but she had come to see that he felt no more strongly for her than she felt for him. It would have been a marriage of convenience on both sides, and he would no doubt soon find another, more suitable candidate. His heart would not be broken.

Kintyre, luckily, seemed oblivious to anything different in her manner, and had asked no awkward questions about her mysterious illness. Nor had he yet pressed her for her answer, and she could only be grateful for his forbearance.

In some ways, however, he behaved as if he expected her to become his wife. She longed to disabuse his mind of that notion, but shrank from doing it. For one thing, it would mean she would have to leave, and she discovered that for some reason she was not yet ready to leave Scotland forever.

It was not that she hoped for any different solution to that last painful scene with Rory. There could be no different ending, and once she had gotten over her earlier hurt, she saw clearly that he had done her more of a favor than she perhaps deserved. And though she weakly longed to see him one last time, she knew that nothing would be served by it and it would only cause her more heartache. He had shown her plainly that she was no more than an amusing diversion for him. As for her, however hurt and unhappy she might feel at the moment, she could never forget her birth and principles sufficiently to throw in her lot with him—even if he had asked her. They were clearly at a stalemate, and at least they had parted without recriminations or guilt on either side. It was far better that way.

She roused from another round of the same dreary thoughts to realize Kintyre had spoken to her. They were at breakfast, and she realized guiltily that she had not heard a word he'd said. "What? I fear I was in a brown study."

He gave his warm smile. "Nothing. I merely asked if you would care to see the muniment room this morning. It is one of the few rooms you have not seen yet, and I think there are one or two things there you would find of interest."

It had commenced another period of raining every day, and they had consequently been tied by their heels indoors for some time. She put down her napkin and rose immediately, glad for anything to take her out of her unpleasant thoughts. "I would like to very much. The house itself shows few enough reminders of Scotland's rather violent past. I had begun to wonder if they were all merely tales developed for the entertainment of us lowlanders."

"Oh, we've a violent enough history, I can assure you," he said in amusement.

And she soon saw that he was right. If Kintyre House had proven far more civilized than she had expected, the muniment room held plenty reminders of the country's violent past. It was filled with portraits of rough Scots warriors, all painted in full battle regalia, and the walls were everywhere hung with targes, swords, maces, and daggers. All this war-like show made her shiver a little, inevitably reminding her that she had indeed found Scotland far more violent than the peaceful green country she had left behind. But it was fascinating nonetheless.

Kintyre showed her a portrait of his own father, who bore a discernible resemblance to him, and then one of his immediate predecessor. Gillian found herself particularly interested in the latter, for reasons she preferred not to delve into. It was not a good portrait, but showed a large bull-like figure in full Scots dress, brandishing a broadsword as his ancestors had done, and looking remarkably fierce.

Kintyre laughed over it. "A second-rate piece of work, I'm afraid, but his portrait pretty much tells the story. Like many a Scot, he was still fighting Culloden over and over again fifty years after the fact. He had an abiding hate for all things English—which is why he and my father fell out, no doubt. But he looks what he was, doesn't he? A stubborn, often violent man who ruled over his people like a minor despot and never came to terms with the modern century."

There could be no denying that. But there was something about the gruff, painted face that held her eyes, and even struck a faint chord. No doubt a family resemblance, though the portrait of Kintyre's father showed a far more civilized man, still bluff, but with none of the bristling defiance the seventh earl showed.

Kintyre bore a superficial resemblance to both, though he seemed far more kindly and good-natured than either of his relatives. In fact, it occurred to her, guiltily, that he had never shown her anything but kindness and generosity and concern. She did not like to think how she had repaid him.

She said, merely for something to break the silence, "You must have your portrait painted to add to the collection."

But he answered her seriously. "Yes. I have been too busy so far to attend to it. But perhaps I will do so when I am married."

He left a gentle question at the end of it. So he was getting impatient. She was thrown a little out of countenance, and so pretended to be absorbed in examining some miniatures in a case.

But it seemed he was not to be put off. He gently took her hand and said, "My dear, I have not wanted to seem to press you in any way. But we have gotten to know each other rather better, I think, and I will admit I am growing more and more eager for an answer. I flatter myself we have demonstrated a decided ease in one another's company that argues, I think, as much promise of future happiness together as one can sensibly hope for. And I am most happy to observe that you seem to have developed a tolerance, even a liking for the country that I must consider in some part my own. Dare I hope that I might look for an answer from you soon? I hope, I need hardly say, that you would make me the happiest of men by agreeing to become my wife."

But she was scarcely listening to his rather passionless declaration. Her eyes had fastened on one miniature in the case, and she demanded abruptly, "Who is this?"

He betrayed some faint irritation, as well he might at being so rudely interrupted in the middle of a proposal. But after a moment he managed to swallow it and obediently bent his head to examine the faded miniature she was pointing to. It showed the delicate watercolor portrait of a boy— a youth, really, perhaps eleven or twelve years old. The artist was again less than excellent, but he had somehow managed to catch, along with the dreaminess he had obviously meant to portray, as the medium and the fashion dictated, a certain spark of mischief in the youthful face, and a habit of looking out at the world with detached amusement from the long gray eyes.

"Who is—oh, that, I believe, is a portrait of my cousin. I confess I didn't know it was here." He showed no particular interest in it. "But my dear, happy as I am that you are showing so much interest in my background, I also confess I am little interested in family portraits at the moment. Do you think—"

But the words flowed over her, and she made sense of none of them. She felt suddenly hot and cold all over, and faintly sick, as if she had eaten something bad at breakfast. The portrait, though badly executed and made of a boy, was damning enough. In fast everything made dreadful, painful and humiliating sense at long last. She could not believe she could have been so blind.

She scarcely knew what she said to Kintyre, or how she managed to get away. No doubt she looked pale enough that he accepted her excuse that she was not feeling well and needed to lie down. He solicitously escorted her to the foot of the stairs and would have seen her to her bedroom door if she had permitted it. But she needed desperately to be alone, and so refused.

But when she reached her bedchamber at last, it was not to lie down, or even to think. In a fever she threw off her clothes and donned her habit, not bothering to ring for her maid. She knew she was incapable of appearing reasonable or calm at that moment.

She scarcely troubled to worry about anyone seeing her, but luckily no one did. She made it to the stables, and was relieved to see it was Ewan who came out at her appearance.

He looked startled at the sight of her, and doubtless she looked wild enough, for she had taken little pains with her dressing, and suspected her face was still white and strained. But she was beyond caring, and so merely ordered him to saddle a horse for her and quickly.

He frowned still more at her peremptory tone, but went to do as she bid. But after he gave her a leg up to the saddle, he hesitated as she gathered her reins, and said reluctantly, "Shall I escort ye, Mistress? Forgive me, but ye look—"

She wheeled her horse, having already almost forgotten him and beyond caring for either propriety or appearances. "No. I am in no danger this time," she said harshly. "Tell me, has he gone yet? Has he put out to sea?" She made no effort to explain whom she meant.

Nor did he pretend to misunderstand her. He said reluctantly, "No, Mistress, he's still here."

She waited for no more, but spurred violently out of the yard leaving the youthful groom to gape after her.

It was still drizzling, but once in the saddle, she set out with little attention paid to how wet she got. Indeed, she pushed her poor horse unmercifully, in a way that was unlike her, so that they arrived both of them soaked and liberally splashed with mud.

Despite the youth's words, she was relieved to see that there was indeed smoke coming lazily from the chimneys, for that was the one thing she could not have borne, that he should be gone before she could tell him exactly what she thought of him. She slid down and left her mount tiredly cropping grass and strode for the second time into Duntroon Castle, this time of her own free will.

Kilmartin was at ease in his hall, his feet propped on the hearth and a book in his hand, when she burst in upon him. He rose, lazy pleasure in his face, and put down his book, and it occurred to her with a renewed pang of self-loathing that even two hours ago, the expression would have had her melting inside. What a fool she had been!

But he was saying, indulgently, "It seems I seldom see you but you are wet and bedraggled, lass. Have you no more sense than to go out on such a day?"

When she said nothing he stopped, something in her white face perhaps at last getting through to him. His brows rose, and he said, gently for him, "Lass? What is it? Why have you come?"

"You—you—" Even now she could barely speak for the rage that choked her. "What an easy conquest you must have found me, scarcely even worthy of your considerable talents! Did you laugh it over, you and Lachlan between you?"

His own face altered subtly, but he still said mildly, "Perhaps you would tell me what the sweet hell you are talking about?"

"Don't pretend you don't know! 'I will never lie to you,' you said! You have done nothing but lie to me from the beginning. God, what a fool I have been, but no more."

Every sense was alert, but he had leaned against the huge mantel, as if wholly at his ease. "I am still waiting to hear what it is you think you have found out," he said patiently.

"Think? I know, do you hear me, I *know*! I accidentally ran across a miniature in the muniment room today. You didn't know it was there, did you? Kintyre was surprised to see it. Or did you imagine no one would guess from a twenty-year-old portrait?"

He had stiffened a little, but still he waited, no discernible alarm on his face.

And suddenly she was tired and wet and sorry she had come. What did it matter anyway? She turned away and said drearily, all life gone from her voice, "It all suddenly made sense, after all this time. Even if I had not recognized the portrait, the name was below it, for all the world to see. You had doubtless forgotten that as well. For the first time I saw the name of the disgraced and mysteriously dead heir. It is Alexander *Roderick Kilmartin* MacMillan. Rory Kilmartin never existed. You are the disinherited heir. It is no wonder you sought me out. How it must have amused you to get back at your cousin by making his future wife fall in love with you."

Chapter 21

AFTER a moment he spoke, but it was just to say merely, "You're cold and wet. Come in and dry off and we'll talk it over."

She was shivering, but it was not merely from the cold. "There is nothing to talk over. You used me. You set out from the first to seduce me as a way of getting back at the man you hate for taking your title away from you. It wouldn't have mattered who I was or what I looked like."

"You will allow me to point out a trifle in my behalf. I failed to seduce you, nor did you take any harm from me."

That at least roused some of her anger again. "Any harm? *Any harm?* At least I notice you don't even trouble to deny the other. How proud your father would undoubtedly be of you now. I understand he died of a broken heart over your misdeeds, but that should matter little to you. Hearts are also a trifle to you, I have no doubt."

"Are you quite finished?" There was still nothing but polite patience in his voice. "I have no intention of denying anything, or explaining myself. Except to say this. If there is any victim between us, it is me, not you."

She could only gasp at the extent of his cruelty. "*You?* That would be laughable if it weren't so deliberately evil. Are you mad? Or merely entirely lacking in conscience or feeling?"

But it seemed she could not touch him. "Yes, me." He still leaned against the mantel, and spoke as if her words little mattered to him—which was no doubt the truth. "You came on your own admission to contract a loveless marriage, and as an unexpected aside enjoyed flirting with danger for a little while. Can you deny it?"

She could have struck him in that moment. "How dare you!"

"But then, as the blackguard you have so accurately painted me, I dare a great deal. It is you who used me. You never had anything more in mind than a brief fling before you settled down to wed Kintyre or some other poor devil you didn't love. I must have seemed like manna from heaven to you, in fact. Available and conveniently susceptible, but completely ineligible, and thus unable to make a fuss later or make any claims upon you. And when you had tired of playing with fire, you could safely return to your ice castle, and again regard other people's foibles and emotions with a fine contempt, as you have always done. In fact, even for you to talk of heart is laughable."

She could only gape at him, for like Kintyre's before him, his words seemed incapable of making sense to her. How could he twist it so? But then he was doubtless a past master at duplicity, so she should scarcely be surprised.

When she remained silent he went on deliberately, "I will confess that for a few brief moments, on board my ship, you thawed most delightfully, and I really began to believe you might possess a heart yourself. It is fortunate I remembered the truth in time. Or did you think I would be content to play second fiddle to my cousin even in that? He to possess title—as in all things else—while I make do with crumbs?"

For the first time she saw the implacable hatred in his face and voice that he had kept so carefully hidden, and began to realize a little of what she had had to deal with—and risked. None of what he said made any sense to her, and she wondered if even he could believe it. She was indeed lucky to be well out of it.

But he was not finished with her yet. He came easily toward her, and though she flinched from him and refused to meet his eyes, he took her chin rather cruelly in his fingers and forced her head up. "And now you've discovered the truth—or your skewed version of it—and you can console yourself with a fine show of anger. If you are very lucky, you may even believe it for yourself, and why should I protest? After all, I am myself a past master at ignoring the unpalatable truth. But when you are safely my Lady of Kintyre, and lording it over the rest of us, don't ever forget that you are not nearly so remote and untouchable as you like to think yourself, for I know differently, don't I? And don't forget, either, that it was I who drew back, not you, else you might have found out sooner than you expected that my cousin is not the saint you think him. You see, you have every reason to be grateful to me. I have given you a harmless taste of experience and I think I deserve at least a slighting reward for it. Surely you're not so churlish as to refuse me."

And he held her chin in his hard grip and leaned down and kissed her, negligently, insultingly, then let her go.

She stood for a moment, breathing painfully and more hurt and angry than she had ever been in her life. She wanted to slap his face, lash out and hurt him as he had hurt her, but she knew that she lacked his skill, and that he was immune to her barbs, anyway. She could find only one weapon to use against him, and so said contemptuously, "You must be proud of yourself indeed. You threw away a title, and now amuse yourself by theft and smuggling. When they hang you—as they inevitably will—I hope you will be as proud then."

And she turned without another word and strode blindly for the door.

He made no attempt to follow or detain her. Once more it seemed they had said all there was to be said between them, past hope of recall.

Once returned to Kintyre House, she changed like an automaton out of her soaked habit and then went straight in search of Kintyre and accepted his offer of marriage. She had not consciously meant to do it, but once it was done she knew that it had been lying at the back of her mind all that wet, dreadful ride home. As revenge, it was but a weak and pitiful thing, in comparison to that Rory had exacted from her.

She had found Kintyre in the garden, for ironically the rain had disappeared in a fine, hot afternoon. And if she felt as if she were acting and moving in a fog, Kintyre seemed to notice nothing wrong. He made it plain he wished the marriage to take place almost immediately, and she did not care enough to object. But while discussing arrangements for the wedding and the bridal trip to follow, he had more than once to repeat a question, for she was scarcely attending.

In truth, she had little idea and less interest in what she was consenting to. She was content to let Kintyre arrange it as he wished.

She did at least rouse from her cloud of unhappiness long enough to suffer a brief pang at his obvious and sincere happiness at her answer. But to her shame, even that was not enough to make any difference.

As usual, he was assiduous in guarding her comfort, inquiring if she were too cold, and insisting upon drying off a bench with his handkerchief before allowing her to sit down. With a stab of regret, she tried not to remember a man who possessed much rougher manners, and had been known to dry her face for her in his careless fashion and send her off to change her wet clothes as if she had been a recalcitrant child.

Besides, Rory had, with his betrayal and subsequent contempt, revealed himself for what he was—a man without conscience or honor. She must forget him or she could not hope to get through the next weeks and months.

Again it was only belatedly she came to with a start, realizing Kintyre had said something. "I'm sorry. What did you say?"

"Nothing, really. I was only saying that we must find out which dates Argyll is available. I would not wish to offend him, and I must confess, both of our futures will soon be tied up in his patronage. Which reminds me. Your answer comes at a particularly opportune moment, for I received a letter today informing me that his grace is back in residence and inviting us to dine. I cannot think of a more appropriate place to announce our engagement, can you?"

She realized with a jolt that once it had been formally announced, it would be more difficult for her to back out. But then she did not mean to back out. She must marry someone, and it might as well be Kintyre as another.

The same fog of misery got her through the next few days, and enabled her to endure her grandfather's suspicion. He'd said nothing, but she was aware he was watching her closely, and for his benefit tried to act the happy bride at least in his presence. She feared it was scarcely a successful attempt, for he knew her far better than Kintyre did. But no doubt Sir Giles drew his own conclusions about the haste of the coming marriage, and she did not bother to correct them.

The day of the projected dinner party dawned clear and beautiful, though Gillian scarcely bothered to notice. Kintyre had suggested they might drive over early so that she might see Argyll Castle and the village while it was still light, and then they could dress for dinner and remain the night, to prevent them having to face the drive back again so late.

Sir Giles had unexpectedly declined to accompany them, so it was just the two of them who climbed into Kintyre's well-sprung coach. During the journey Kintyre seemed in an expansive mood, and discussed their host more openly than he had yet done in her presence.

"There is some stupid prejudice against the Campbell name still in the west," he said a little impatiently. "But to my mind they do far more for Scotland than those who moan over her lost glory and do little else. In fact, there will soon come a time when the Campbells will own most of the west of Scotland, save only what I carve out for myself. So you can see why I do not care to offend him. It was his grandfather, of course, who built the castle, but I think you'll be impressed with it. At the time he had the entire village torn down and rebuilt, so that I believe it to be the most modern in Scotland."

She made some inconsequential answer, scarcely attending to him. But when they came to the village, she found it little to her taste for some reason. It was admittedly neat and modern, unlike anything she had yet seen in Scotland. But she discovered she preferred the less-planned and far more charming version to be found everywhere else, however poor and humble.

As for Inverary Castle when they reached it, she thought it rather ridiculous, despite Kintyre's obvious admiration. It might have been built by Mr. Walpole himself, so ostentatiously neo-gothic it was, and so much did it resemble a larger version of Strawberry Hill, which she had seen once and laughed at. Particularly in a country where so many early castles still stood, she could not find the fake turrets and crenellations of so artificial a monstrosity anything but ludicrous. Nor could she help comparing it unfavorably with the much humbler and shabbier charms of Duntroon Castle, where Rory lived in careless and threadbare splendor.

His Grace, the Duke of Argyll, proved to be a thin, ascetic-looking man with only a faint hint of arrogance in his demeanor. He welcomed them kindly enough, but his wife, even thinner and with the small, unfleshed face of a cat, was languid and more obviously condescending. Gillian surprised herself by disliking them both on sight.

She called herself firmly to order, having reason to distrust her instinct and emotions at the moment. She had heard nothing but good about the Fifth Duke of Argyll, and for Kintyre's sake made herself deliberately suppress her feelings. After all, it was Argyll who was backing the canal scheme, and she reminded herself rather sharply that his patronage and good will meant a lot to the man who was shortly to become her husband. It was more than time she began facing the duties and responsibilities of the life she had chosen.

But during the protracted dinner that evening, she found her new role more trying than she had anticipated. The Duke had professed himself delighted by his protégé's coming nuptials, though there was little real warmth in his manner. His wife was less forthcoming, but then she seemed to possess a colorless and belittling personality that Gillian could not warm to.

The Duchess dressed expensively and richly in the latest fashion, but without much taste, and wore too many jewels about her person, as if merely to flaunt that she possessed them. She found constant fault with the servants, coldly correcting the maid who served them tea upon their arrival, and then complaining later of the service at dinner. But then Gillian was soon to discover that she had little good to say about anything—particularly that corner of Scotland. She was, as Gillian also discovered, herself a Scotswoman, but betrayed little but contempt for her native country.

The Duke was more forbearing, but Gillian found him cold and distant, despite Kintyre's obvious admiration for him. At dinner talk naturally turned to his plans for the district, and Gillian found Kintyre's almost exaggerated respect somewhat unpleasant.

Argyll seemed pleased to be gracious to him, rather in the nature of a great man dispensing favors, which also set Gillian's teeth on edge. They talked of the poverty of the district, and of Argyll's efforts to exploit the local fish and seaweed stocks to support the rising population. Kintyre was full of admiration, but it seemed to Gillian, listening without comment, that on the Duke's part, at least, he seemed far less concerned with the welfare of his tenants than he was with the potential profit to be made.

"If you ask me, it is all ridiculous," said the Duchess coldly. "The old clan system is dead, and in most of Scotland even in the Highlands, they have come to realize that the land cannot profitably support so many people. In many places the lord has forced them out, or forcibly removed the less productive, which I think is only fair. The Scots people cannot continue to live in the old feudal system, expecting to be taken care of from cradle to grave as they always have been."

"Yes, yes, but it will not come to that here, I hope," said the Duke a little impatiently. "With the building of the new canal, and the establishment of industry here, I have every hope the whole district will prosper."

"And yet the fools are still fighting you every step of the

way," she remarked disdainfully. "If you ask me, they are not worth all this consideration."

There was an awkward pause, and Gillian said tactfully, "It would seem you have done a great deal of good already. The model village you built is quite—er—remarkable."

The Duchess sniffed. "But, would you believe, there were some who fought Argyll's grandfather over even that? In the end they had to be burned out, for there was no other way to make them leave their filthy and vermin-infested hovels. It is little wonder Scotland has always been a poor cousin to England."

Gillian was chilled. "They were burned out?" she repeated incredulously.

Kintyre hurried into speech. "For their own good, of course. I fear Her Grace is right that too many Scots can scarcely see beyond next day's dinner. Even things that will ultimately prove to their benefit must often be forced upon them, as I have found to my cost. But then what can you expect? They are ignorant and uneducated and living at least a hundred years behind the times."

Gillian was still shaken. "Nevertheless, it . . . seems a rather drastic measure," she pointed out dryly.

"But then I fear you little understand the Scots mind, my dear," said the Duke. "To the logical English it seems quite mad that they can none of them see what is in their own best interests. But they seldom can. Clan loyalties and stiff-necked pride has so riddled the society that almost any progress is impossible without some violence or upheaval. They must be made to see what is good for them, and dragged, kicking and screaming if necessary, into the present century."

Gillian lifted her head, frowning. "I am perhaps not so logically English as you seem to believe. Surely they should have some choice in the matter?"

"Nonsense! If we left it up to them, we should still be at war with England," the Duchess pointed out acidly. "It is why we were delighted when your fiancé came into the title over the incumbent. The late earl was a backward fool of appalling vulgarity of manners, who used to take delight in thwarting our intentions for the mere joy of it. And his disreputable son promised to be as bad. It was a dispensation from heaven when he disgraced himself openly and then was killed in that vulgar way. Now we have every hope of seeing our most ambitious plans come to fruition. For I don't hesitate to say that while either of them held the title there was no chance for the canal to be built. I admit frankly that I am delighted they are both dead."

Chapter 22

GILLIAN felt almost as if she was emerging from a cloud, after having been groping and searching blindly in it for days. "The late earl resisted the building of the canal?" she repeated slowly.

"He was fifty years behind the times," said Kintyre a little impatiently. "He had a foolish and inexplicable prejudice against it, even though it would undoubtedly have made him a rich man. But then my father used to say that he was impossibly stubborn and proud."

"What 'foolish prejudice' did he have?" inquired Gillian carefully, trying to keep nothing from showing in her voice.

It was Argyll who answered. "I must say I certainly always found him a most blind and pig-headed man. Simply because some of his tenants would be displaced, and the local fisheries disrupted, he refused even to discuss it with me. He wholly ignored the fact that jobs would be supplied for many of them while the canal was being built, and that the whole area would benefit from the profits once it was finished. In fact, he insisted that his people should share in the profits, which was absurd. Because of his stubbornness, years were wasted and countless thousands of pounds lost."

Gillian thought her chest was about to burst. She was hot and cold, and there was a strange ringing in her ears. "And since the canal is on his land, his agreement and permission were required?" But she did not need the answer. She knew it already.

"Yes, unfortunately. I tried to buy the whole from him long ago, but he refused to sell. And at that point, since he had no notion what I intended to use it for, he had no other reason to refuse than that I am a Campbell, and my grandfather sided with the English during the Forty-five. It is precisely the sort of blind and willfully obstinate thinking that has limited this country's future so drastically this far."

"I am beginning to see," said Gillian, and she was. At long, long last. She could not believe how blind and stupid she had been. "You tried to buy the land from him without revealing your purpose for wanting it—even though whoever builds the canal will reap a fortune from it."

The Duke grew a trifle less pleasant. "There was nothing underhanded in it, I assure you. Merely a good business deal."

"As your grandfather before you no doubt thought it a 'good business deal' to side with the enemy?"

"Gillian!" Kintyre was flushed with annoyance. "You know nothing at all of the matter. Anyone with the slightest eye to reality could have forseen the Scots were doomed to lose. If my own ancestors had seen which way the wind was blowing, I might be in much better shape today. Besides, that is all in the past and has nothing to do with what we are talking about."

"Apparently it has more to do with things than I would have believed," said Gillian dryly. "I congratulate you, Your Grace. It must indeed have seemed a gift from heaven when the old earl died and his son disgraced himself. But I have always been a little confused as to what exactly happened. Was the young heir positively proved dead before —er—my fiancé inherited?" *Kintyre* stuck in her throat for some reason, and she could not give him the title any longer.

Kintyre was looking ruffled and furious, but though the Duke had stiffened, his faith in his own greatness seemed proof against her questions and he answered readily enough. "Affairs are seldom that neat and tidy, my dear. There was an unhappy period when the old earl was dead, and no one had the slightest idea where to find his hotheaded young son. A most unsatisfactory state of affairs, I must say. More, even if he could have been found, nothing but a gibbet awaited him. I am glad to say that the government agreed with me, and that I have some influence in high places. When I petitioned to have the title declared vacant, and awarded to the next of kin, it was done. Only later did we hear of the fortunate death of the incumbent. And if I may say so, you have every reason to be satisfied with the present state of affairs, my dear. Your future husband now holds the title and estates, and will be the richer for my friendship, and you need not ever fear having the scandal renewed by the reappearance of his predecessor."

She knew she had said too much already, but it was only with an effort of will that she forced herself to bite her tongue and not give voice to the wild accusations that tumbled feverishly in her brain. It would do little good anyway. The Duke of Argyll's vanity and conceit were clearly proof against any assault.

Still, she could not quite keep some of the irony from showing in her voice when she answered, "Yes, it was indeed convenient for all of us."

Kintyre hastily changed the subject, and she was left in no doubt that she had seriously displeased him. As he gave her her candle at bedtime, he seemed to be holding on to his temper with a tight rein. "My dear, whatever possessed you to go on as you did at dinner? I thought I had made it more than plain that I owe a great deal to Argyll and dare not risk offending him."

"Yes," she said dryly, taking her candle from him and starting up the stairs. "I had not realized quite how much you owe to him. I wonder if you do?"

She did not look back to see what reaction he had to that, if any.

She scarcely slept all night, and was up at an early hour, eager to be gone. Kintyre was still reserved at breakfast, and when the Duchess grudgingly suggested an outing of pleasure, made no objection when Gillian pleaded a headache.

In fact, he seemed to latch onto it gratefully as an excuse for her indiscretion of the night before. "If so, I am sorry for it. Of course we shall leave immediately. You should have informed me last night if you were not feeling well, instead of coming down to dinner. I am sure we would all have excused you."

Gillian did not trouble to dispute it. The Duchess made vague and obviously insincere offerings of regret and commiseration, and said they must do it again sometime. It had been thoroughly delightful.

Even Kintyre did not pretend to believe her. He closed his lips rather tightly, and went away to order the carriage.

On the drive back Gillian had reason to be grateful for her plea of a headache, for she was able to close her eyes and pretend to sleep, thus preventing Kintyre from airing his grievance. But the miles had never dragged so much, and long before they reached Kintyre House again her head was aching in earnest. The many sleepless nights and her misery had caught up with her, and even Kintyre, on seeing her pale cheeks and smudged eyes, made no further comment when they reached home, but urged her to go upstairs to bed at once.

"Shall I send for the doctor again?" he asked, obviously containing his impatience only with a strong effort. "I have no doubt it was your present indisposition that made you behave so unlike yourself last evening. I only wish you had said something earlier and not tried to hide it. I believe I have explained to you how much Argyll's support and good opinion mean to me. In future I will expect—" then he caught himself up, as if doing silent battle with himself. When he spoke again, his voice was kinder. "But I daresay it can't be helped, and if you write and make a graceful apology, no lasting damage will be done. Now you must go up and bathe your forehead. I shall send your maid up to you immediately."

Gillian had no intention of writing and making any kind of apology to Argyll and his harpy of a wife, but she wisely did not say so. She was in a fever to be away, and was thus cravenly willing to have Kintyre believe her rudeness last night sprang from nothing but ill health.

"Yes, you are very kind. It is nothing. If I could just lie down for an hour or so, I'm sure it will go away. Pray, pray don't fuss!"

She broke away from him and almost ran up the stairs, little caring any longer what he thought. But instead of lying down, as she had said, she once again hurried to put on her habit, and to make her way to the stables and demand that a horse be saddled for her.

Even the horse knew the way so well by then that she need scarcely have directed it. She reached Duntroon Castle at last, to find Rory, bare to the waist, engaged in the hard physical act of planing some wood with some of his lads.

He looked very brown and very male as he straightened unselfconsciously to watch her ride up. His eyes were narrowed against the sun, and his expression remained unreadable, but he put down his tool, wiped his face on a towel, and taking up his shirt, came slowly toward her.

She looked down at him from horseback, suddenly shy and self-conscious enough for them both. "I . . .can we talk?" she said abruptly.

His expression was at its most enigmatic. "I'm not sure what there is to say. I must felicitate you, by the way, on your betrothal. Kintyre is a lucky man."

She had almost forgotten that, as if it had happened in another life. "What? Oh, that. I didn't come to talk of that. Please—may we go somewhere so we can speak privately?"

He shrugged, and gestured toward the door. "If you must. Have you had lunch yet?"

She had forgotten what time it was or that she had had very little breakfast. "No, but I'm not—"

"But I am." Abruptly he reached up and lifted her down, and she watched the muscles ripple in his brown chest, and was suddenly breathless and in danger of forgetting why she had come, however important it was.

But he let her go all too quickly, and shrugged into his shirt as he led her inside and set up a shout. "Lachlan! Where the devil are you? My stomach is cleaved to my backbone and we've unexpected company. Bring something to eat for Miss Thorncliff and myself at once."

Lachlan appeared, incongruously wearing an apron and carrying a carving knife, and looked rather sourly on

Gillian, but made no comment. She blindly followed Rory to the study she had eaten in so long ago, and accepted the chair he held out for her.

"Well?" he inquired mockingly, taking up his habitual position before the now-empty grate. "I must confess this is a surprise. Or have you come to berate me further?"

Her cheeks were hot, and now that she was here she found it unexpectedly difficult to begin. "No. It would seem I've said enough already," she said quietly. "I've come to listen this time, as I should have before."

But she might have known he would give her no help. "What about? D'you expect me to give you protestations I am in no position to give? You were right. It's more than time our . . . friendship came to an end. I have no doubt you have chosen the better man."

"Don't pretend I had any choice in the matter," she responded rather bitterly. "You made it more than clear . . . but I haven't come to talk of that either. I have come to hear your side of the story. As I said, I'm ready to listen now."

But he seemed determined to thwart her. "And why this sudden reversal, may I ask? What has changed from a week ago?"

"I have spent a day or so in the Duke of Argyll's company," she said deliberately. "And I suspect I know the answers already. But I would like to hear you tell it. Must you always be so stubborn?"

He grinned at that. "It's a Scots trait," he acknowledged. "And you are moving in exalted circles these days, I see. What did you think of Inverary Castle, by the way? I hope you were properly impressed by the showplace of the district?"

"Exactly what I suspect you think of it," she retorted, feeling suddenly more at ease. "I found Duntroon more to my liking after all."

He grinned. "Then you've better taste than I gave you credit for, lass."

Lachlan came in then, and they had to wait until he had served them with cold beef, cheese, and wine, and stomped out again. Gillian wanted him to go, and scarcely glanced at the food. It seemed that she had not made Rory completely despise her as she had feared, and she was in a fever to be alone with him again. She had not realized just how much she had missed his mocking banter, and how oppressive Kintyre's good manners had become to her.

But when Lachlan had gone, the easier mood between them seemed to have evaporated. Rory addressed himself to his food, and remained silent. She should have known he would offer no excuses or explanations to her. If she were to get anywhere, she would clearly have to ask.

She said slowly, watching him eat hungrily, "Why did Mrs. MacDonald tell me all about Rory Kilmartin? She must have known who you were."

He glanced up indifferently. "It's clear you've little grasped the loyalty of the Scot, even yet. The title may no longer be mine, but I'm still MacMillan of Knap, and thus chief in these parts. Your fiancé may hold the earldom, but that's of little moment when all's said and done. I'm not boasting when I say most of the people around here would willingly die for me—as they would have for my father and his father before him. In the face of that a few lies were nothing. As to the name, I'd always been called Rory by my friends, and as you discovered, Kilmartin is one of my names. It seemed a natural enough choice when I needed a new name. I hadn't anticipated you poking around and nosing out the truth."

She ignored that, for it was an answer she had long since come to on her own. "Then most of the locals know who you are? And yet they kept the secret all this time?" she inquired incredulously.

"Good Lord, I could never hope to disguise myself. Nor had I any need. I knew none of them would ever give me away, and my so-called cousin had never set eyes on me. There was very little risk."

"But why did you come back? Surely this must have been the most painful place you could choose under the circumstances?"

"I told you, I'm still MacMillan of Knap," he said, at last

a little impatient. "I'd a responsibility, and besides, this is my home."

She looked at his strong brown face and saw that it was true. She had been a fool in far more ways than one. "Yes, I can see that," she said slowly. "Will you—will you tell me your side of what happened? It's . . . somehow more important than I think you can guess."

He shrugged, then told it matter-of-factly, as if it had happened to someone else. "If you are expecting some startling revelation from me, I've none to give you. I daresay the version you heard was accurate enough, as far as it went. I was a hotheaded young fool, and can scarce complain of my reputation. Even after university I preferred the debaucheries of Edinburgh, and even London, to playing the dutiful son. I've no one to blame but myself."

When he hesitated, she said meekly, "Please go on."

He studied her frowningly for a moment or two, then shrugged and did so, as if only because it was easier to comply than argue. "I've told you I was hardly a model son. My father and I quarrelled a good deal—which is part of the reason I stayed away—but I thought that underneath there was a genuine affection between us. And in my defense, I did no more than he had at my age. We've ever been a wild family, I'll confess. Then . . ."

He hesitated, and she supplied for him, "Then you got in with the wrong crowd. It's natural enough at that age to be idealistic and want to right the wrongs of the world. It's nothing to be ashamed of."

He was once more amused. "You're far too idealistic yourself, lass. But I must confess that has never been one of my failings. To put it bluntly, my excesses didn't tend toward the political. Oh, I'd flirted around with independence movements when I was in university, what Scots youth hasn't? And I've as much sentiment for the *auld glorie* as the next. But my solutions tend to be more practical than mooning over lost causes. No, I was in no movement, dangerous or otherwise."

She asked in bewilderment, "Then why . . .?"

He hesitated, then shrugged ruefully. "Why did I shoot

the soldier? It seems trite to say I didn't, but it's the truth, whether you choose to believe it or not. Most chose not to, including my father." He spoke lightly, but she could read the old bitterness in his face. "On the fatal night I was buttonholed by an acquaintance of mine and dragged off to some party, but even though I confess I was none too sober at the time, I'd have refused to go if I'd guessed it was nothing more than some fringe political meeting, with a lot of boring speakers. To be honest, I was after more interesting entertainment."

"And then what happened?" She was scarcely breathing.

He took a pull from the tankard of ale at his elbow and seemed to be looking into the past as at an unpleasant picture. "Once I realized what I'd let myself in for, I was annoyed. But before I could get away in search of better game, the meeting was broken up by the soldiers. I escaped easily enough—I'd had considerable experience at it, from one cause or another—and went home to nurse a hangover, thinking no more about it. It was only the next day I discovered one of the soldiers had been killed, and one of my pistols was found on the scene, and had been fired. I had also been seen and recognized, though I never knew by whom. And that, as they say, was that."

It was again no more than she had expected, but she had had to hear it from him. "In other words, you were set up," she managed, trying to sound as matter-of-fact as he did. "Someone meant you to take the blame. The only question is who."

Chapter 23

RORY looked faintly amused. "That seems to be the logical explanation. But proving it is another matter."

"Why didn't you stand your trial and try to prove your innocence?"

He shrugged. "I intended to. But the 'friend' who had dragged me to the meeting in the first place seemed to think the evidence was too strong against me. Besides, I wanted to see my father and tell him the truth before he learned it from some other source. So I slipped out of Edinburgh and came here."

Again he looked as if his memories were none too pleasant. "I was too late. The story was before me, and my father believed it. We had one last hell of a row and since my temper is, unfortunately, quite the equal of his, I stormed out, promising in the best romantic tradition to go straight to hell, and that he would never see me again. It would seem I was right on both counts," he ended with a shrug.

"And?" she prompted when he showed no signs of going on.

He came to the present with an almost visible shaking off of the past. "There's little more to tell. I jumped a boat to Ireland, which is all I could get on the spur of the moment, and then eventually made it to the Continent. I traveled around there for some while, and if it hadn't been for the cause of my exile, I have to admit I thoroughly enjoyed myself. Then in short order I learned that my father had died, and that the title and estates had been declared forfeit and gone to my cousin. Since there was very little else left to lose, and I could not even return home without risking arrest, I decided it was politic to stage my death and thus call off the manhunt. Not a very edifying story, I admit, but then you insisted upon hearing it. And it should at least serve as a cautionary tale, which gives it some value, I hope."

She ignored the deliberate mockery of his tone. "But you have not yet said why someone hated you so much he had you framed for a crime you didn't commit," she said softly. "Although I think I can guess."

"Then you are doing better than I did for a good while. The estate was not wealthy enough to be worth all that trouble, and my esteemed cousin seems to consider the possession of a Scots earldom of dubious honor at best. He certainly spends little enough of his time here."

"Yes, but there is one thing that makes your estates suddenly of considerable value. The canal," she said still more softly, watching him.

When he remained silent she went on, "I'll admit when I was first told of it I thought it sounded a good idea. After all, it should give ships access to Loch Fyne without having to use the hazardous passage 'round the Mull of Kintyre. I know nothing of shipping, and still less of this area, but surely that will increase shipping and trade and be of general good to the area?"

"No doubt," he said sardonically.

"And yet your father was against it, even though it would have made him very wealthy. Why?"

"For the same reason I am," he said indifferently. "If it were done for the local good, and not just to line the pockets of a few wealthy men, it might be of considerable value. Argyll had been trying to convince my father to support the scheme for years. But neither of us would go along with it unless provisions were made to ensure compensation for the homes that would be lost, not to mention the disruption to the fishing, and at least some of the profits were plowed back into a desperately poor area."

"*Argyll!*" Gillian breathed triumphantly. "His name does seem to crop up all the time. I think it was that that first made me suspicious. And the fact that the canal would undoubtedly give someone a motive for seeing you out of the way."

He was eyeing her in amusement again. "Aye, it's impossible to ignore Argyll around here. He's made his weight felt in most things."

"And yet, most of what I've heard is to his advantage," she countered. "He rebuilt Inverary village, is cultivating industry for the locals, and seems to be a most conscientious landlord."

"I can recognize the source. Kintyre has been truckling up to him since he arrived in the area." This time the satire was unmistakable.

"And you disagree?"

He was watching her lazily, as if she were a pupil he was measuring to see if she would come up to scratch. "I understand you've just been on a visit to His Grace, lass. A signal honor, by the way. I hope you were properly appreciative. But I'll leave it up to you. If you'd no taste for Inverary Castle, what did you think of Inverary village? I'm told people come from miles around to gaze upon what can be done with a little capital and forward thinking."

"In that case I fear I lack His Grace's forward thinking," she answered steadily. "I found it neat and modern and very much like a stage setting, not a village."

He grinned at her in approval. "Few would agree with you, I fear. Argyll is considered a great philanthropist—at least in other parts of Scotland. Here we have suffered from his philanthropies first hand, and so perhaps might be forgiven for suspecting that he rebuilt the village to please his own fastidious taste, and to improve the view from his bedroom window, rather than for the benefit of the villagers."

"The duchess said some who refused to leave had their cottages burnt down. I . . . had hoped she had exaggerated."

"Nay, lass. If you spend much time around Their Graces—as you surely will once you are wed to Kintyre— you will soon learn that they are by no means alone in their somewhat drastic solutions to Scots poverty. It is happening all over the country, and where the peasants resist being forced off their land so that cattle or sheep may graze there, or being relocated hundreds of miles from home to so-called 'model industries' that seldom get off the ground, such forward-thinking reformers are prepared to burn them out or forcibly remove them in any way necessary. And, perhaps only coincidentally, wherever such reforms take place, locals who had been freeholders find themselves tenants afterward—either of his grace the Duke of Argyll or some other modern laird. But then they told you, no doubt, that the clan system was dead and these people must learn to look out for themselves."

"Yes. They told me. They told me as well of Argyll's plans to develop local industry. I was obviously supposed to admire him for his great benevolence."

"And did you?" he asked interestedly.

She chose her words with care. "I found that . . .for some reason I could not warm to either of them. I must confess I disliked them both heartily."

He burst out laughing. "Such a reaction does credit to your natural good taste, lass. I confess I have always found them a pious, self-congratulating pair who look down their long noses at anything Scots, and pride themselves on being the new Briton—not Scots nor English, but something in between. If they are right, then God help Scotland."

"But is it so wrong to put aside old enmities? We are one country now surely?"

He shrugged. "I've no quarrel with England. But nor have we any love for Campbells around here, and a previous Argyll showed the clan's true colors by betraying his own country in Forty-five."

She was a little impatient with that. "But that is scarcely the present duke's fault," she pointed out fairly. "At least I agree with him that what happened so long ago little matters. And you have yet to tell me why his local schemes are so little appreciated."

"Which only proves that you are not a Scot, lass. It still matters, believe me. As for the other, if you must have it in words, by 'local industry' Argyll means that he has asserted his ownership over the kelp that the peasants used to claim

as their own, and need to fertilize their miserable plots.
Now he pays them a miserly wage to gather it for him, and
theft from the shore is punishable by eviction. He sells it to
industry as a source of alkali in the making of soap and
glass and makes a handsome profit, I've been told, while
local poverty increases and the pittance he pays does little
to stem the gap made by the failure of their crops."

"But that's . . . that's terrible."

"Oh, aye. And he's other such profitable schemes as
well. The new canal, if it is built, will deprive a number of
families of their land, and you can bet the profits will go
straight into Argyll's pockets, and Kintyre's as well, though
I suspect to a much lesser degree than he hopes. You must
know the canal is to be built on MacMillan land, so he
needed a complaisant partner, which neither my father nor I
would have been. I sometimes suspect Argyll won't rest
until he's stamped the hated Campbell name over the whole
area and most of Scotland as well. Even Campbelltown, to
the south of here, was called Kilkerran until the last century, when a Campbell had it renamed for himself."

This was clearly more of the feuds between clans, which
she little understood and had trouble sympathizing with.
Kintyre was at least right that such feuds kept the whole
country in turmoil and should long since have been abandoned. "But why is Campbell such a hated man?"

He must have heard the skepticism in her voice, for he
smiled mockingly. "It's obvious you have no' heard of the
massacre at Glencoe. That was typical Campbell treachery,
if you will, though I could name you a dozen other episodes
nearly as bad. The Argyll of that time took English money
to wipe out the MacDonalds of Glencoe, for they were considered a threat to English plans to subdue the country not
by war this time, but by union. The Campbells claimed
MacDonald hospitality, and when, in true Highland fashion, the MacDonalds welcomed them and gave them food
and shelter, they turned on them in the night and slaugh-
tered as many as they could, including women and babes in
arms. That was in 1692, but you'll discover we've a long
memory in Scotland, and no Campbell will ever erase the

shame of that. Not that they have not tried to better even that black deed. Argyll was one of the few supporters of the government hereabouts during the Forty-five, as I said, and did much to improve his finances from condemned rebels' confiscated property. 'Tis said he was not even above informing falsely on anyone whose property would make a handsome addition to his own lands—which grow almost daily, it seems."

She was indeed shocked, despite herself. "No, I hadn't heard," she conceded faintly. "It would seem his grandson is merely following in his footsteps, in that case. But why did you not tell me all this before?"

"Would you have believed it? Besides, it changes nothing."

"Doesn't it? It is more than obvious Argyll wanted a willing dupe for his schemes about the canal, and had you discredited. He knew that Kin—your c-cousin lacked your ties to the land or people. Surely you must have seen that long ago?"

"Aye, it's possible," he conceded. "But you've no need to stutter over your fiancé's name. He is at present legally the Earl of Kintyre, and likely to remain so."

She flushed and looked away, for some reason not wanting to see the mockery in his eyes at that moment. "I've no particular wish to see him dispossessed. But justice is all on your side. Surely you mean to fight for it? You can't just let Argyll have his way and ruin so many lives unchallenged."

"I am flattered by all this interest, lass, but while you may believe me, I promise you few others would. And I've no way to prove a word of it. Why else do you think I am content to remain here and be reduced to the life of an outlaw?"

"The smuggling!" she exclaimed abruptly. "I feel such a fool. You do that to help support your people, of course!"

He grinned. "Nay, don't run away with your altruism. It's enabled me to continue in something of my former style of living, and keeps me from being bored as well. Whenever I get too melancholy, a fast run to France or Ireland usually cures me of my self-pity."

She had no answer for that, for she could see it was true. And she had told the truth when she said she was torn. She longed to see the wrong put right and Argyll thwarted, but the man she had always known as Kintyre was as much Argyll's victim as Rory was. She would not believe him either a party to the fraud, or willing to take advantage of it once he knew the truth.

"But all this is surely beside the point," she said impulsively. "Why have you not told your cousin the truth? You little know him, I'm sure, and despite your assertions to the contrary, obviously blame him to a certain degree. But he is little more than Argyll's dupe in this, I promise you that. And I won't believe he would not wish to see so grievous a wrong put right."

"Aye, you've assured me before of his kindness and sympathy," he remarked politely. "I have endeavored to bear it in mind."

She could sense the mockery in his voice and said more sharply, "You clearly cannot be reasonable on the subject. But perhaps if you had explained to him from the beginning, instead of going through this ridiculous and elaborate charade—"

"And deliberately seducing his fiancée to get back at him," he put in. "Don't forget that."

She flushed again. "I was not his fiancée then. And—and when I said that, I confess I was in a temper and desperately wanted to hurt you. I absolve you of that crime at least. But not of being foolishly prejudiced against a man you don't know—and who is your own cousin to boot. I . . . I may have made a mess of everything, and immensely complicated matters, but I have at least learned that he is an honorable man, and tries always to do what's right. If you were to go to him and explain—"

"He would hand me back my property and my title on a silver platter? I have indeed wronged the man, if so."

This time she ignored the sarcasm. "Perhaps not that. Or at least not . . . immediately. But what are you proposing instead? To go on enjoying yourself playing at highwayman and smuggler, while Argyll puts through his plans to cheat your people? If so, you deserve to have lost the title."

He grinned a little ruefully at that. "You've occasionally a shrew's tongue, lass. But unfortunately it's no' so easy as you seem to think."

"No, it's far easier to idle the time away building boats and sailing off to the Continent when you get bored, instead of trying to right the wrongs that have been done. Perhaps Mrs. McDonald and all the others here who are so loyal to you have misjudged you all this time."

This time he looked merely amused, not upset by her words. "It's possible. I have said I'm no saint. But what of yourself? It would seem you have a stake in the outcome now as well. After all, you are Kintyre's fiancée. Would you have me do you out of the luxurious life you've envisioned for yourself?"

She flushed and said abruptly, "I don't come into it. Besides, you must know perfectly well that I am not going to marry Kintyre. I only said I would because I was hurt and angry with you."

"Oh? And may I ask what you are going to do, in that case?"

This was a question she had not bargained for, but it was like him to cut through all polite pretenses and thrust to the heart of the matter. Her cheeks flamed still more, and she became suddenly engrossed in studying the congealed beef on her plate. "I . . . I have no idea. It would seem I have dragged my grandfather all this way for nothing. And yet, I cannot be sorry I came, for I have developed a . . . a fondness for this part of Scotland. And I would like to help you regain what is rightfully yours."

"Nay, lass." His voice was unexpectedly gentle, but as usual it was impossible to guess what he was thinking. "I told you nothing has changed. And much as I am . . . touched and tempted by your offer, there is no place in my life right now even for a lass with mahogany hair and green eyes who has managed to bewitch me far more than she suspects, and whom I'll always remember."

She looked up suddenly, her heart seeming to stop in her

breast, and even her breath became suspended. This was cutting to the heart with a vengeance, and she realized she was still unprepared to hear it. "I . . . see," was all she could manage.

All humor had fled from his face by now, and she found it impossible to look away, much as she longed to. "I doubt you do. You clearly think it all no more than a game, easily won by a few words of truth. But it is no game, and you've still little understanding of exactly what is at stake. You can help me best by going home, for at least then I won't have you on my conscience."

Her eyes stung with sudden bitter tears, but she lifted her chin and would not let him see that he had once more managed to hurt her almost past bearing. It would seem she'd learn, soon or late, to protect herself where he was concerned. "Which is a polite fiction to disguise the fact that I'd only get in your way. I have not forgotten that you told me once there was no room for women at Duntroon, for fear they would soon grow less bonny and more of a scold. It's obvious you fear I would."

He smiled faintly. "I'm flattered you remembered such foolish words spoken long ago. But I believe I also told you once that women were sometimes apt to experience regrets after it's too late to undo what's been done. I would remind you that I've no guarantee of success. I would spare you that, if nothing else."

The tears were much closer, but still she held them back. "I see. You are still determined to protect me from myself. And if I am prepared to take the risk?"

"Nay, lass," he said again, and his gentleness was almost her undoing. "You chose to wed Kintyre because you recognized you were not prepared to abandon everything to throw in your lot with me. I have said that things are often much more difficult for a woman than a man, and I don't blame you. But it never does to hide from the truth."

"But that was only because you made it clear then, as well, that you'd no lasting place in your life for me!" she cried hotly, beyond pride any longer.

"Was it? Be honest with yourself, lass." He spoke a little sternly.

And meeting his gaze, she was suddenly filled with shame, for she knew he spoke the truth. She had not been prepared to risk everything, for it was true that a woman had far more to lose than a man. Nor was she yet sure, however much she loved him, that she was ready. He was right, he had no guarantee of success, after all. Was she truthfully willing to embrace a life of poverty and danger and ostracism? For she could expect little else if she threw in her lot with him and he were not successful. And if she waited to find out the outcome before she committed herself, he was more than justified in finding her offer too little too late and rejecting her out of hand. It seemed they were once more at checkmate.

He clearly recognized her answer in her silence, and smiled again, a little sadly. "Aye, lass," he said deeply. "It seems fate and the tides are against us. And now you'd best go back, before Kintyre misses you."

Chapter 24

GILLIAN scarcely remembered the ride back toward Kintyre House. She felt aching and empty, and certain of nothing any longer—least of all herself.

Or perhaps she was certain of one thing, though it was scarcely a comfort. She had realized from the moment she turned away that she loved Rory past caring for right or wrong any longer. But the checkmate was more complete than she had known. Were he not to succeed in clearing his name, she could not go and live openly with him, as she now realized she was perfectly willing to do, even assuming he wanted her. It would kill her grandfather, and she could not snatch her own happiness at such a price.

Even more ironically, were Rory to succeed in regaining his title and estates, she would be just as trapped. How could she jilt Kintyre so cruelly and go to the man who had dispossessed him? No one, particularly Kintyre, would ever believe the two were not related or the one caused by the other.

It was almost laughable, for she had made her bed and now she clearly must lie in it. Rory was right, anyway. She had been lying to herself from the first. She had come to Scotland looking for adventure, but she saw now that that had not included anything that might actually risk her safety or comfort. That was precisely why she had chosen Kintyre. He pretended to offer the lure of the unknown while in truth promising exactly the same. Marriage to him would be no different from marriage to any one of her suitors at home. The locale was the only thing that would change.

It was no wonder she must have seemed like the most foolish of hypocrites to one like Rory, who had seen his comfortable existence and even his identity snatched away from him and been forced to live precariously by his own wits. She had enjoyed flirting with danger in his company, but he must have known she had never intended it to be anything more than that. And if he had not known it, she had gone out of her way to prove it to him. When she had discovered the truth of who he was, her first instinctive reaction had been to go straight to Kintyre and accept his proposal.

She had thought at the time that she acted only out of anger and betrayal, but now she was no longer so sure. Perhaps it was far more basic than that, and had been a way of placing herself permanently out of the way of temptation. Once safely betrothed, her secure little world had been preserved, and she need not worry any longer. Rory must have known that as well.

Well, if so it had worked better than she had intended, for it was clear he no longer wanted her—if indeed he ever had. And it would merely be the ultimate of ironies if he should now succeed in regaining his inheritance, for then the joke would indeed be on her. In snatching for safety she had unwittingly thrown away the very thing she was grappling for.

Not that it mattered. Kintyre still had his estates in England, where she supposed they might live a pleasant enough life together. If it now seemed unutterably dreary to her, she supposed she must marry someone. And under the circumstances it would no doubt be best not to have to live where she was in constant danger of running into Rory.

Besides, no one would dispute that Kintyre would make a far better husband than Rory ever would. He was stable, even-tempered, reliable, sober—all the virtues a woman should look for in a mate. It was why she had chosen him, after all. If that was but another irony, she had no one but herself to blame.

By contrast, Rory would clearly make any woman a damnable husband, for he valued his independence and freedom too much. She could not see him content to devote himself to his estates and sit tamely at his own hearth. Even were he suddenly to regain his title, he would still be far too inclined to grow bored and want to sail off to France, or Ireland, or America, or China, even. He had lived too many years an outlaw to turn willingly to respectable domesticity now.

Yes, it was as well to be brutally honest. And if he didn't regain his inheritance, aside from all the other difficulties that would entail, she would never know when he left whether he was safe, or had been arrested or was lying dead in some ditch. No woman could be expected to live with such uncertainty. He was right to say there was no room in his life for women. There, too, he saw more clearly than she had done.

And yet. *And yet.* She was painfully aware that she was not the same woman who had come into the west of Scotland all those weeks ago. Thanks to Rory she had had a taste of freedom and adventure and romance, and it had been headier than perhaps she had acknowledged to herself. At least she understood, if only a little, why Rory lived as he did. What use were safety and comfort to him when he might sail the brilliant sea at night, and feel the rain-laden wind in his face? It was only cowards like herself who deliberately chose the secure and familiar, however narrow and constricting they might ultimately prove to be.

But it was best not to think of that. Best not to wonder if her heart had not been wiser than her head after all. There would have been arguments aplenty between them, for they were two strong-willed people, as her grandparents had been. From the beginning he had aroused strong emotions in her—by no means all of them positive. By contrast, she had known Kintyre on close daily terms for weeks now, and he had yet to instill in her any stronger emotion than a mild liking. She had once thought that the best foundation for a marriage. If she were honest, she now thought it a recipe for intolerable tedium.

But it was wisest indeed not to dwell on what marriage with Rory might have been like. Or the bleakness of the future she now faced without him. She had deserved his rejection, but that did not lessen the pain, nor would it make the next weeks and months and years any the more bearable.

But that was ridiculous, of course. Pain inevitably lessened with time. However unhappy and desperate one might be, one got on with one's life. No doubt she would look back on this time, five or ten or even forty years from now, and be glad that she had been so sensible, and had not thrown away her life on a mere whim.

And if she wished with all her heart at that moment that five years or ten, or even forty had passed, and that much-to-be-desired certainty was hers already, she would not be the first, or the last, to do so. Hearts did not really break, however much they might sometimes feel like it.

But she had hoped to have at least some space of time to lick her wounds in private, and it seemed even that was not to be granted her. She had gone no more than two-thirds of the way back when she discovered Kintyre, on horseback, calmly waiting for her.

He was in a small clearing, and her heart jumped absurdly at the sight of him, whether with guilt or mere surprise even she was not sure. She told herself it was merely because she had no desire just yet to be obliged to speak to anyone, but she was very conscious suddenly of the hour, and of her earlier excuses.

He seemed the same as usual, however, and unsuspicious. He smiled at her in his rather grave way, and said, "I am glad to see your headache is so much better."

She had to fight a betraying blush, and reminded herself sharply that he had no reason to suspect her. It was no more than polite concern on his part, and not an accusation. "Kintyre! How you startled me! What on earth are you doing here?"

"I went up to inquire if you were feeling better, and your maid informed me you had gone out for a ride. I was worried about you, and so I came out to meet you. Did you ride as far as the sea? Are you sure that was wise?"

"Oh! I felt restless, but I didn't go as far as that." She

feared her voice was scarcely normal, and wondered desperately how long he had been looking for her. She had no wish to make matters worse by lying, but equally, she had no desire for him to guess exactly where she had been.

"I see. But I can't help wondering if it would not have been better to remain quietly in your room. You have not been well lately. In fact, I am growing concerned about you. I begin to fear the air here does not agree with you."

The concern in his voice made her feel even more guilty. "Nonsense!" she said a little sharply, and then had to control her voice with an effort. "I had the headache a little, but it is quite gone now. Though I confess I went farther than I meant to. Shall we go back now? I am growing a little tired and Grandfather will be wondering what has become of me."

He regarded her gravely. "If so, I am glad to hear you're feeling better. Should you object if we dismounted for a while? Or are you indeed too tired?"

Her heart sank, for the last thing she wanted at the moment was a *tête-à-tête*. But short of an outright refusal, she could think of no excuse, and so she allowed herself to be lifted down, wondering what on earth he wanted to talk about.

Kintyre secured the reins of both horses to a convenient branch, and turned back to her with his grave courtesy. "Shall we walk a little? I have always found this a pleasant spot. But then you must have grown quite familiar with the countryside. I am delighted that for my sake you have taken such an interest in it."

That naturally made her feel even guiltier, and she looked at him quickly, again wondering if there was any underlying meaning to his words. But his expression remained the same, and after a moment she accepted his arm, and began to walk with him.

For some moments he said nothing further, and she had just begun to relax a little when at last he said quietly, "I have begun to wonder, just lately, if you had changed your mind in any material way about our marriage?"

She feared she jumped a foot. "Wh-Why do you ask?"

"Because you have seemed to be different just lately. In fact, I scarcely seem to know you of late. And this is not the first time you have sought to escape from me."

She felt suddenly as if she were on the edge of a precipice, fumbling in the dark, and that any false step would send her hurtling over the edge. "I . . . nonsense. I was not escaping from you." She feared her voice sounded unnaturally shrill.

"I wish I could believe that." He turned to regard her directly, as if he were considering something carefully, trying to make up his mind. At last he seemed to come to some decision, for he said even more quietly, "Perhaps it would make matters simpler if I told you that I know about your— activities since you have been here."

For some reason, now that the worst had happened she felt only numb, and even oddly relieved. She had no idea how he could know, but her first thought was absurdly that to be rejected by two men in the space of an hour must be some kind of a first. It was almost amusing.

At her continued silence he gave a faint smile. "I am not quite so blind—or so foolish—as you seem to think me. But I have no intention of berating you. I didn't tell you for that reason."

She did not believe him, and wondered why he didn't just put an end to it all at once, unless he wished some sort of revenge. And if so, perhaps he deserved it. "Didn't you?" she managed steadily.

"At least I see you don't trouble to deny it," he remarked in faint amusement. "I am grateful you at least have that much respect for my intelligence. But as I said, I didn't tell you to berate you, or to play the outraged victim. It is still very much my desire to make you my wife."

He had succeeded in shocking her at last. "Still—? Is this your idea of some sort of a jest? You can't still wish to marry me, knowing—or at least believing that I am in . . . in love with another man!"

"I confess I find *love* a word with little meaning. Were you contemplating a more . . . permanent arrangement, it would naturally be a different matter. But I do not believe that to be the case. After all, you must be more aware than I am of all the drawbacks in the . . . particular attachment you have developed. It need have nothing to do with our plans."

"Nothing to do with our plans?" she repeated incredulously. He was either taking tolerance to an outrageous degree, or else he did indeed mean to have some form of revenge. "And do you know exactly who it is I am supposed to have . . . developed an attachment with?" She had no idea how much he knew, but that he could be speaking so calmly about such a matter astonished and repelled her.

He shrugged. "He calls himself Rory Kilmartin, I believe. He is a thief and a rogue, but is considered something of a ladies' man, as I understand it. It was perhaps natural you should have fallen into his orbit. In fact I blame myself that you were so bored you were . . . er . . . driven to seek out his company."

She felt as if she had stumbled into a nightmare, for none of it made sense. But at least he didn't know the whole truth. "And you wish me to believe you are not in the least *jealous?*"

"Hardly, my dear. I do not expect my wife to be a saint—indeed I would not wish her to be. And I have every expectation that after we are wed, your honor and discretion are fully to be relied upon. You are scarcely the first woman, nor will you be the last, to be momentarily taken in by a plausible rogue."

His unparalleled tolerance should have reassured her, but in fact it did the opposite. No man could be expected to be that tolerant. She thought, in addition, that he little understood women if he so clearly underestimated the "temptation," as he called it, of so plausible a rogue.

But he was going on without waiting for her answer. "You need not fear I will throw it up to you after we are married. It was a brief intrigue, no more, and as such, should be easily forgotten—on both sides. As I said, I am quite prepared to overlook it. After all, it has nothing to do with our marriage."

He said nothing of love or desire on his own part—but

then he had already dismissed love as meaningless. She blurted out before she could prevent herself, "And am I expected to feel . . . *grateful* to you for such unexpected tolerance on your part?"

"Grateful? By no means. I have said I will not throw it up to you after we are wed. You will make me a beautiful and advantageous wife. Argyll approved of you—though let us say you were a touch indiscreet there? You must learn to guard your tongue better. But I think we have proved that we are compatible. What else should one look for in a successful marriage?"

Argyll approved of her? That was somehow laughable.

But he went on in his dispassionate way without waiting for her reply. "Perhaps I should make it clear that I am not condoning any continuation of the affair after our marriage. But then that would be unlikely in any case, for he is almost certain to be hanged for his crimes in the immediate future."

The deliberate words struck a chill through her, but then with every word he uttered, her decision was becoming simpler. What he offered seemed monstrous to her. He had said he would not hold it over her head, but no man was that forgiving. It could only be some skewed revenge he had in mind, but that he could still wish to marry her, knowing what he knew—or suspected he knew—and believing her to be in love with a common highwayman, was beyond indecency.

And she knew in that moment that even without that, and despite her earlier compunctions, she would rather be dead than endure such a bloodless marriage of convenience as he had been proposing.

She lifted her head, feeling better than she would have believed possible a bare hour before. If nothing else, he had succeeded in showing one thing to her. For the first time she recognized clearly that she had more options than she had ever realized. He seemed to think she must be pitifully grateful that he was still willing to marry her despite her supposed transgressions, and why not, when even she herself had accepted that marriage must be the natural ambition of any woman. But was even such a loveless marriage as he proposed to be considered preferable to spinsterhood?

She now knew that it was not, and couldn't understand why she had always seen her choices in only those terms. It was absurd to think she must either choose to throw in her lot with Rory, with all that entailed, or marry Kintyre. She was free and independently wealthy enough to need no man to support her. She had thought to control her destiny while accepting as a given the most basic of controls over her sex. But the truth was she needed no man to make her complete.

It was all much easier than she had realized, after all. "I must thank you for showing me the error of my ways," she said calmly. "But I fear I must decline your gracious offer, despite your unexpected condescension. I have no intention of marrying you on those or any other terms."

Chapter 25

HIS face darkened, and she reflected almost idly that it was the first time she had seen any strong emotion in him. "I see," he said after a moment. "You are more of a fool than I believed. And do you imagine you will inveigle him into marrying you? Or did you not know that he has the reputation of seducing every woman he meets?"

But his words had no power to hurt her. She was even glad that he had shown his true colors at last so that she need not feel guilty any longer. "No. I don't expect him to marry me. I may never marry. But I am discovering there are worse fates for a woman."

"A noble sentiment." He was openly sneering by now, and was as she had never seen him before. The polite, calm mask she had known had been wholly stripped away. "And perhaps more prophetic than you know. Especially if your behavior here were to get about."

She almost laughed at him. "Are you seriously attempting to threaten me?"

"Threaten? Not at all. But I doubt your grandfather, for instance, would be amused to discover his granddaughter had been carrying on an affair with a common thief under his very nose."

"And yet not so common a thief after all," she said quite softly. "Or is it possible you don't know quite as much as you believe you do?"

His eyes narrowed, and then he actually smiled. "Ah! I begin at last to see. I wondered how he had succeeded so quickly in seducing you."

She was no longer in the least inclined to laugh. "So you

do know then. I begin to wonder exactly how long you have known."

"My dear, you really must believe me a fool, along with my dear, unlamented cousin. Most of the locals are absurdly loyal to him, but he could scarcely hope to keep it a secret. I have known of his presence for some time now, of course, but it makes no real difference to me. He may play his absurd little games and stir my people up against me as much as he wishes. The title is still mine."

She lifted her head sharply. "*Your* people? They have never been your people. That was what at first puzzled and bothered me so much. On the surface you seemed the most admirable of landlords, and yet it was obvious none of them liked or trusted you. And do you know exactly how the title became yours? Oddly enough, even yet I don't want to believe you could actually have been a party to such fraud from the first."

He actually laughed. "I am interested in hearing what lies my cousin fed you to earn such passionate partisanship. Or perhaps it was not what he *said* at all," he added with surprising crudeness. "But it seems obvious he neglected to mention the soldier he murdered and that he will ultimately hang as surely under his own name as the one he has assumed?"

"He mentioned it. But then he didn't kill that soldier. Argyll planned the whole, because he knew you would be more amenable to his plans. He has been like a puppetmaster behind you all, pulling the strings to suit his own greed and vanity."

He laughed again. "Really, my dear, if I were you, I would not boast of your acumen in judging men. It was not Argyll who planned the whole. He has scarcely the brains to see beyond his own nose, and allows his pomposity to serve for shrewdness. I planned it, from first to last, and I must confess it was ludicrously easy. My uncle and my cousin played right into my hands, and I flatter myself they never realized how effectively I had pulled the strings, as you so aptly put it. It was I who saw the possibilities, and the fortune to be made here. It should all be mine by rights, for my esteemed relations never had the ambition or sense to see what could be done with it. And by the time I'm through, I shall have far more than a useless Scots title and a crumbling estate, which is all they would ever have had to show. With any luck, in the end I shall have Argyll's estates as well, and like the others, he won't even know what hit him."

She had thought by then she was beyond being shocked, but she had been mistaken. He was right. How could she have been so completely deceived? "*You* planned it? You planned it from the first?" she demanded faintly.

"Your astonishment is hardly flattering. But I must confess I made one slight miscalculation. You have managed to surprise me. I even resent that it has taken my cousin to show me how mistaken I was about you. But since I shall be the ultimate beneficiary of it, I suppose I must be grateful to him."

"You . . . surely you don't think I would marry you after *this*?"

He smiled again. "But why not? If I am annoyed that he was the first to discover this unexpected wanton streak in you, I have no real objection to my cousin's leavings. After all, I have stepped into his shoes in all else. And it will gall him past bearing that I possess you on top of everything else that should belong to him. It merely adds the final fillip to my victory over him."

It was unbelievably obscene to her, but she suddenly remembered that Rory had said something similar and she had dismissed it. Had he known or guessed the truth all the time, then? It seemed incredible, for she could still scarcely believe it herself—or that she could have been so completely wrong in every way.

"You hate him, don't you?" she whispered with the utmost conviction. "I once accused him of hating you, but I was wrong in that, as in all else. It is you who has always been jealous of him and never forgiven him for being what you were not."

"And why not?" He spoke as if it were the most reasonable thing in the world. "He had everything, while I had nothing. From the moment of his birth fortune smiled on him. He had the title, the estate, the looks, the charm. And yet he squandered everything he touched. He didn't even have the sense to see the fortune that was lying under his fingers. He and my uncle between them would have lived on here, content in their mindless dedication to the Scots tradition of wasting one's heritage in drinking and carousing and senseless feuds with neighbors. I, on the other hand, will civilize this corner of Scotland and bring it into the present century. And I shall end by gaining far more than a mere theadbare Scots title and a few boggy acres."

"Yes, but at what cost?"

But she might have spared her breath, for her sarcasm rolled right off him. "Really, my dear, you should know that progress is always painful. You will see how much improvement I will make here given a free rein and enough gold to fulfill my plans. And once the canal is built, I shall have that."

"Yes, it always comes back to the canal. And I can imagine what you will do, in the style of Argyll. It is no wonder he is so hated around here. But thankfully I will not be around to see your desecrations, if they should come to pass."

"Oh, yes you will," he said quite mildly. "We will be married exactly as planned. If nothing else, I have no desire to be made to look a fool before Argyll until my plans are completed. You will certainly marry me, my dear."

"You're mad!" she breathed, and realized it must be true. That was frightening enough, but somehow it made her feel slightly better, for at least it made some sense. She could not have been so completely wrong in her judgment. "What on earth makes you think I would wed you after all this?"

"Because," he still spoke quite calmly, which made his words all the more obscene, "after I am through with you, my dear, you will have reason to be grateful that I still offer you marriage. You will be unlikely to get any other offer, I promise you."

She stared at him, for the first time beginning to be afraid. Surely he would not do what he threatened? If nothing else she could not see what purpose he could have. It was more than clear that he did not love her. He saw her as nothing but a convenient tool to get what he wanted. Why then would he take such drastic steps to keep her?

And yet she saw with a sinking heart that she had perhaps answered her own question. He was indeed mad. And he clearly could not brook any intervention in his plans. Still she could not prevent herself from saying incredulously, "You would . . . do that . . . merely to prevent yourself from losing face before Argyll?"

"And because it amuses me to possess everything that my cousin wants," he answered indifferently.

She thought that was the true reason after all. He was clearly not sane on the subject of Rory, and it made her suddenly very afraid indeed. "Even knowing I would . . . hate you afterward?"

"I must confess that it is of little moment to me, my dear, but you overestimate your sex, I believe. You will soon enough learn to accept your fate, and once we are wed, you will naturally be as eager as I to hush up any scandal and prevent my cousin Rory from reclaiming his rightful place. The choice is yours. Either agree to wed me willingly now, or I shall have to take steps to insure your compliance, willing or no."

She thought he was indeed mad, for even yet she could not believe he could mean what he said. Nevertheless she backed again before him, saying scornfully, "And do you imagine you will find it so easy to do what you suggest? Or that I would keep silent afterward and meekly agree to marry you? If so, you are indeed mad."

Still he advanced toward her, looking uncannily calm and even normal, as if he could not have said all of the monstrous things he had. "You know little of true evil, my dear. I must confess it is one of your chief charms. But to answer your question, yes, I am convinced I can easily overpower you. And I am even more sure of your, shall we say, 'compliance' afterward? I know your sex, you see."

It was somehow worse that he still spoke and acted quite dispassionately. It would have been less frightening if he had ranted and screamed abuse. Nevertheless she would not give in to his bluff—and she was convinced it was a bluff. No one who looked as calm and normal as he did could possibly do what he threatened. "Then you know it less well than you imagine, for I will not marry you, no matter what happens." She made an effort to speak almost as calmly as he.

He smiled and, before she could even guess at his intention, quite deliberately struck her across the face with his open hand.

It was a brutal blow, but its effects were even worse than he had perhaps intended, for she had backed too far before him, and was standing too near a tree. As she gave a strangled cry and went down beneath his blow, her head struck the tree and she felt herself falling endlessly, the scene around her fading and dissolving. She clung desperately to consciousness, knowing she had believed herself in deadly danger of being raped once before, mistakenly as it turned out. It seemed she was incapable of recognizing real danger when it stared her in the eyes, for she did not doubt this time that he truly meant to rape her.

Her last image, before the blackness overtook her completely, was of his monstrously smiling face above her, and the hands that reached out toward her, tearing at her habit and the fine lawn of her shirt.

She swam back up toward consciousness only gradually, unable to remember where she was or what had happened. Her head ached badly and she seemed to be lying in a most uncomfortable position, and it was only slowly that she realized she was in a heap against a tree, feeling cold and extremely sick.

But unharmed. She was convinced of that. Her blouse had been ripped at the neck and her jacket torn open, but the rest of her clothes were intact. And though there was an incredibly painful bump on her head, and her face felt stiff and sore, she was almost swamped with relief that is was not worse.

At first she could not imagine what had saved her, for

she had no doubt he had meant everything he had threatened. Then only slowly did she realize that the clearing seemed suddenly full of people. She could see Kintyre, standing half a dozen paces away, looking rumpled and his face for once livid with fury. Even more incredibly, Rory stood with his back to her, facing him, and at the edge of the clearing she could see a wary Lachlan, holding the reins of their horses and regarding the two of them with his habitual scowl.

Then Rory shifted slightly, and she could see more of his face. She was astonished first at the superficial resemblance between them. It was a wonder she had not seen it long before she guessed the truth. But she was also surprised to see that his usual flippant, half-mocking expression had completely left him. He looked calm, and betrayed no particular anger or hatred. But he somehow looked incredibly dangerous to her, which surprised her, for it was not a word she had formerly associated with him.

She had no idea how long she had been dazed, though it could not have been long judging by their stances. She could only suppose Rory had happened upon them for some reason, and pulled Kintyre off her. She shuddered with relief at the thought, but for all his unexpected formidability she recognized that Rory was in more danger than he knew. She must warn him, for he did not realize that Kintyre was mad, and would clearly stop at nothing.

But only Lachlan glanced at her when she tried to make herself heard, though it was in all conscience a pitiable enough attempt. Kintyre and Rory wholly ignored her. Kintyre was saying hoarsely, his horrible calm at last having deserted him, "I'll see you hanged for this! If not for murdering that soldier, then for the common thief you are! That will make pretty telling. The former Earl of Kintyre become a common highwayman."

"About as pretty as that you deliberately cheated me out of my inheritance," retorted Rory easily. "You see, I heard enough just now to confirm what I have always guessed."

"But you have no proof, and no one is likely to believe a convicted thief and murderer! Besides, you were declared legally dead years ago." Kintyre had himself at least partly in hand again now. "Who is to say you are not just some cheap adventurer, claiming to be whom you're not."

"I am." Gillian had managed to get unsteadily to her feet with the help of the tree, and had achieved more than her earlier croak. "I will gladly testify that you openly admitted your guilt to me, and . . . what you tried to do to me."

Rory glanced quickly around toward her, and it was that that spelled his undoing. Gillian had not guessed that Kintyre was armed, but in that moment he acted with incredible speed. She saw the movement even as he made it, and tried to cry out a warning, but she seemed frozen in horror, and could only watch as he brought out a pistol from his pocket and fired quite deliberately at Rory from point-blank range.

At the sound Gillian instinctively closed her eyes and swayed, unable to watch. She scarcely registered that two shots rang out in the quiet clearing, one so close upon the other that it was almost impossible to tell them apart.

Then she was in strong arms, and Rory was saying, "Are you all right, lass? One way or another you've taken quite a beating this morning, and for that I apologize."

She clung to him, shuddering. It did not matter that she gave herself away, and that he had previously rejected her. All that mattered was that he was alive. "Oh, God. I thought he'd—"

"Nay, lass," he said more gently. "You're safe now. Though I fear you've a sore head and a split lip to add to my account. I'm sorry. It never occurred to me that he would take it out on you."

For some reason she was furious at him for his sudden obtuseness. It was not her own safety she had been worried about. "He almost killed you! I thought he had. What happened, anyway?"

Then she looked over his shoulder and saw Lachlan standing there, a pistol still in his hand and his face wiped clean of all emotion. "Oh, thank God!" she said again, and averted her eyes from the bundle on the ground between them.

"Aye, you're a blood-thirsty lass," said Rory in amusement. "But he'll never disturb you again. I must confess I had suspected he was behind my own troubles all along, but I never thought he would prove dangerous to you. I should never have sent you back to him, lass."

"He was mad," she said truthfully. "And you are not to blame. I . . . chose to come back to him. I am the one who was vain and shallow and willfully blind. I deserved all that I got."

"I should not go overboard in abusing yourself, lass." Rory again sounded amused. "You've more than enough courage for most. But are you sure you're all right? You've little enough experience with the harsher realities of life, I fear."

He made her turn her face up to him and inspected her cheek and lip and then gently explored with his fingers the rising knot on the side of her head. "I don't think anything is broken," he said in relief at last. "But you'll have a headache and a fine bruise by morning. It seems I've much to beg your forgiveness for."

It seemed they had come full circle, for he had tended her hurts as gently the first time she had met him. It was the one thing that she had never been able to forget, whatever else she thought of him at the moment. She lifted her head and straightened proudly. "Then it's lucky I've a hard head. And you've nothing to regret. You were right. I had chosen comfort and security over all other considerations. It was my own fault, not yours."

"Aye, but you've still little enough exposure to any other thinking, and so might be forgiven for the error," he said gravely, watching her.

She returned his gaze, the beginning of faint hope stirring. She had feared she had forfeited all her chances, and she wouldn't have blamed him. "Then I shall just have to mend my ways," she said, equally gravely. "Do you know of any one who might be willing to instruct me on the art of clear thinking?"

The amusement was back in his eyes. "It's just possible, but I should perhaps warn you that it will require close and extensive study. Though if you dedicate yourself to the art, I do not despair of your finding the way of it by the end."

She smiled openly at him, uncaring that her face was bruised and her habit torn, and that he could undoubtedly see everything to be read in her face. "Then I must be sure and make a proper application." Then abruptly she abandoned the jest. "And I care not whether you regain the title or remain a smuggler to the end of your days—so long, of course, as you allow me to become a smuggler with you."

"Aye," he said, laughing down openly at her now. "You make a rare smuggler, lass. I have scarcely had the heart to go out without knowing you are in my cabin waiting for me to return."

"And robbing coaches," she reminded him. "My education will clearly have to include donning a mask and firing a pistol. You've been sadly lacking in your tutelage so far."

"I'd give much to see you at it. But this is all but a fine fantasy, I fear." There was unexpected regret in his voice.

The light died out of her own face, and she was suddenly deathly afraid again—more afraid than she had been even when facing Kintyre. She did not know how to make him see that she had changed, and understood clearly now what she wanted, whatever it cost. "I . . . see," she said through a constricted throat. "You have . . . every reason to doubt me, of course. But in that case I can see only one alternative. I will clearly have to set up in competition to you. Even without lessons, I daresay I could learn how to hold up a coach. What do you think?"

He burst out laughing. "I think you'd scarcely have to use any force to make your victims hand over their valuables, lass. But perhaps I should confess I heard your fine declaration earlier to Kintyre. Did you mean it?"

She was suddenly more sure of herself again, and deliberately cast off the remainder of her doubts. "That I had no need of any husband? Yes, I did. You have at least taught me that much independent thinking, you see. And if you reject my offer again, I shall quite happily make a life for myself. It is just that I had quite set my heart on becoming a smuggler, you see. But then I beg your pardon. Freebooter was what I meant."

He laughed again. "Aye, that's better. We've little liking for the other term."

"And I've a sudden ambition for going on the high toby, as well. I believe that is the proper phrase for holding up coaches, isn't it?" Her heart was beginning to sing again.

"Aye, lass," he said comfortably, "but I'm sorry to disappoint you. Indeed, I fear I have been masquerading under false colors, and only hope you will not reject me when you learn the sad truth. Your's is the only coach I've ever held up in my life, and that was merely to get a look at the sort of woman who would marry Kintyre. And though I've admittedly engaged in a spot of freetrading now and then, I'm scarcely the hardened smuggler you think me. Are you disappointed?"

She could scarcely disguise her happiness any longer. "No," she said carefully. "I . . . imagine I can manage to get used to it. Though I am a trifle disappointed, of course."

"Aye, I can see you are. And do you think you can as easily adjust to becoming the Countess of Kintyre after all? It lacks a certain romance, I know, but that can't be helped."

"I think I could manage to adjust even to that. But Rory," she said with sudden urgency, "I want you to understand now that it doesn't matter to me. Whatever happens, I still love you. If you remain no more than a freebooter and live the rest of your life outside the law, I won't care. For your own people's sake I hope you will agree to step back into your rightful place. But I would be content to sail off with you tomorrow, with no idea of where we were going or if we were ever coming back. You rightly rejected me before because I wanted my comfort and security more than I wanted you. But that is no longer the case. You have indeed taught me how to think clearly at last."

"Nay, lass," he said deeply. "You taught yourself. And if I rejected you, it was only because I did not want you to wake up one day and hate me for the sacrifice you had made on my behalf. But I will leave it up to you. Freebooting or being the Countess of Kintyre. Which would you choose?"

She smiled suddenly, completely free at last. "Freebooting," she said immediately. "I had never dreamed I could enjoy being at sea so much. It is no wonder you love it so. And—I must confess—there are other things I liked still more about that voyage."

She was suddenly breathless and could not look away from the demand of his gaze. "Aye," he agreed in amusement. "There are certain portions of that particular voyage that I, too, look back on with unalloyed pleasure. Or should I say that my pleasure has only been limited by my lack of opportunity to repeat what happened between us that night? And I have hopes that I may soon resume your education, at least in that respect."

And then she was in his arms, and nothing mattered any longer. Not the unhappiness or horror she had gone through, or even what was to come in the future. The only thing that mattered was here and now and the obvious hunger of his kisses, for they proved to her, better than anything else could have, that she had not ruined all her chances with her folly and selfishness.

It was, surprisingly, Lachlan who brought them back to reality. "I beg yer pardon," he said, oddly formal for him but with detectable sarcasm underlying his tone. "But if your lord and ladyship can condescend to come down from the clouds for just a wee moment, we've still a fair amount of details to attend to. We've a number of years to make up for, after all, and a dead body to dispose of. And speaking just for myself, o' course, I've just the sma'est urgency to let everyone know that the true earl has been restored at last. At least then there'll be rejoicing enough to make the pair o' ye stand out less, for I never could abide a pair o' newlyweds."

Rory laughed, but did not release her. "Pay him no heed, lass," he said. "Lachlan is secretly as pleased as I am. But he's right, I'm afraid. We've much to do. I only hope you can reconcile yourself to being wed to an earl, not a freebooter, for however tempting your offer may sound, I've some years to make up for, as Lachlan points out."

"Yes," she said simply and happily. "The Earl of Kintyre has come home at long last. There will indeed be rejoicing."

⊘ SIGNET REGENCY ROMANCE

SPECIAL REGENCIES TO CHERISH
